AMBUSHED!

McCarter had his driver's door open before the Chevy had stopped moving. The rest of the Force were quickly behind him, weapons up and ready.

A rapid-fire SMG opened up from somewhere near the Dodge. A lash of 9 mm slugs whacked into the surface of the road, falling well short of Phoenix Force.

"Let's separate," Katz said curtly, and the Force followed his command without a word. They broke apart and sought cover as they returned the fire of the Dodge's passengers.

James and Encizo both chose the meager protection of a shallow ditch that paralleled the road. As they bellied down in the thick grass, a line of slugs marched along the lip of the ditch, kicking up dirt and pebbles.

"Somebody wants to attract our attention," Encizo noted.

"Let him chew on this," James snapped, and fired off a burst of 5.56 mm replies in the direction of the attacker.

PHOENIX FORCE

SEARCH AND DESTROY

GAR WILSON

A GOLD EAGLE BOOK FROM

WORLDWIDE ®

TORONTO • NEW YORK • LONDON • PARIS
AMSTERDAM • STOCKHOLM • HAMBURG
ATHENS • MILAN • TOKYO • SYDNEY

First edition March 1989

ISBN 0-373-62202-3

Special thanks and acknowledgment to
Michael Linaker for his contribution to this work.

Printed in U.S.A.

PROLOGUE

Manila, The Philippines

"Long live the revolution!"

The stocky black-haired Filipino at the head of the table had extended his wine goblet toward his three fellow conspirators. "A fitting toast, my dear friends," he said. The three men raised their glasses and repeated the battle cry, their brown faces reflecting strong emotion.

"Tonight, comrades," the speaker continued, "we have set in motion the means to rid this nation of the capitalist doctrine that has reigned for far too long, and to give birth to a new socialist order. The wealthy have corrupted and debased our society. The time has come for a new regime."

The men drank, smiled at each other, and, save one, sat down. Lowering his wine goblet, the man who remained standing eyed his brethren. A slim, cold-eyed man, he finally descended into his chair, inhaled once from the thin cigar he was smoking, and addressed the group.

"While we congratulate ourselves, let us not forget the coups that have failed, whose leaders are either dead or in hiding."

"Major Castillo has a valid point," said the stocky man who was the leader of the group. "We must be cautious as well as optimistic. Overconfidence can lead to carelessness. Everything *must* run according to our planned timetable. If we follow this, I'm certain we will succeed."

"What if things do not go well?" asked the man across from Castillo.

"We do have our sacrificial lambs," the leader said lightly.

"The Americans?"

"Yes. The Americans—those greedy imperialist Yankee killers who call themselves mercenaries, who will kill *anyone* for a price, even our beloved president herself."

"The assassination will be our signal," Castillo reminded them. Castillo was aware that he was dealing with nonmilitary minds that needed constant coaching about the details of the plan. "The moment we hear that the president is dead and that the Americans have hit the prime targets, we attack the key installations and put *our* people in position. If all goes well, we'll be in command by dawn."

"And if the assassination should fail?" asked the pessimist of the group.

Castillo smiled. "In that event, our American dogs will be abandoned to their fate."

The stocky leader now leaned forward, fiddling with his goblet. "Should the coup show signs of being defeated, we will withdraw. There will be other times, other days for us to strike. But not if we push ahead with a doomed cause. If we are caught, or if we die, the dream dies with us. I am as loyal as the next man to the party, but I see no glory in dying through blind faith. My ambition is to be alive to enjoy the takeover.

"The Americans will spearhead the coup. If they fail, then *they* will stand accused of attempted assassination and armed insurrection. All negotiations with them have been carried out by a third party who will be eliminated himself once his services are no longer required—the Americans do not even know us. There will be no link between ourselves and the mercenaries. Any stories they tell of an attempted coup will be denied, and as they will be unable to identify their accomplices, their accusations will be dismissed."

Castillo puffed on his cigar and resumed. "If the Yankees fail and the coup is aborted, we will use them to arouse great anti-American sentiment. There will be a trial with full media coverage. The publicity will greatly embarrass the U.S. administration, and may even help toward finally removing them from the region. We will demand their departure from Subic Bay Naval Base, Clark Field, and all other military bases on Philippine soil."

There was a brief silence. Then the pessimist, a balding, middle-aged man in a well-made suit, asked, "What has happened to the traitor Hernandez?"

"As you are aware, he has been removed from circulation," the leader said. "Once we had confirmation that he was a double agent, we made certain he would be unable to pass any information." He rose, gesturing to the others. "There is only one thing that remains to be done. Come, we should all see this."

He led them from the dining room, along a white-painted passage. A flight of stone steps led down to the basement of the large, sprawling house. Here, where the warm night failed to penetrate the thick stone walls, they entered a low-ceilinged, vaulted chamber. Dampness streaked the stonework.

In a lamplit alcove within the room, a man stood manacled to the wall. Shackles encircled his wrists, which had been chafed raw by the rough iron. Short lengths of heavy chain ran from the shackles to rings set in the stonework. The prisoner's once neat clothing hung in filthy tatters from his bruised and battered body. His face was swollen from a severe beating. His left eye was almost hidden in the raw swelling of discolored flesh around it. The left side of his face was torn and shredded, a sliver of cheekbone protruding.

"Good evening, Mano," the leader of the conspirators greeted his fellow countryman.

"It could only be a good evening if you were lying dead at my feet," the prisoner said defiantly.

"Such courage," the head Filipino remarked, with a smirk of superiority. "A pity you had to channel it in the wrong direction. Now you are in no position to threaten me, Mano."

"Traitor!" Hernandez shouted, and spat. He lunged forward until his chains restrained him. "Betrayer! Communist scum!"

"To think we accepted this pig as one of us," Castillo said in disgust. "This fawning lackey of our corrupt government."

The conspirators nodded, each hurling abuse at the shackled man.

Restraining his comrades with a signal, Major Castillo unholstered the SIG-Sauer P-226 pistol he wore beneath his neat, tailored jacket, and stepped forward. The action was so smooth and deliberate that it caught the others off guard.

Castillo thrust the pistol's muzzle into the soft flesh beneath the prisoner's jaw.

In that instant the eyes of Mano Hernandez met those of Castillo—and terror showed.

But only for an instant.

Castillo pulled the trigger of the SIG-Sauer, propelling a bullet into Hernandez's skull. The 9 mm missile plowed through bone, tissue and brains, and produced a mushroom cloud of bloody gore that splattered on the stone wall. The dying man's body went into a spasm. At first the twitching form remained upright, then it collapsed, slumping forward until restrained by the wrist chains. Mano Hernandez was beyond pain. His corpse swung gently to and fro on the end of the chains. Blood dribbled from the hole in the top of his skull and spread across the cold stone floor.

As the echo of the shot faded, leaving only the smell of burned powder, the stocky Filipino nodded to Castillo, then turned to his other companions. He was smiling.

"Now we are committed," he said. "The first shot has been fired, and we have disposed of one of our enemies. With the same dedication we will do likewise to any who stand in our way."

As Castillo put away his weapon, his eyes gleamed dully. "Long live the revolution!" he chanted, and hardly noticed the docile response of the two less vocal conspirators.

PART ONE

1

Jim Dexter parked the dusty Dodge pickup truck outside the diner. He switched off the engine and, still behind the wheel, lit a cigarette. Exhaling, he looked in the rearview mirror to see if he'd been followed from the ranch.

Dexter was neither paranoid, drunk, nor suffering from insecurity. His caution was totally justified, especially at this particular moment.

He was living on a knife-edge that could slip at any moment and destroy him. All it took was a false move on his part. A wrong word and he was dead.

Dexter was an undercover agent for the U.S. government. He was good at his job. The fact that he had been involved in undercover operations for nearly seven years proved it. Dexter was an exception to the rule that undercover operatives generally have short careers. He was extremely versatile, totally dedicated to his craft, and fully committed to law enforcement.

He believed in the old-fashioned values of law, order and justice. His father, and his father before him, had been career cops. Dexter had started out as a rookie walking a beat, had attained a detective's badge, and before long had become an undercover cop. The number of his successful collars had grown at an astonishing rate, and before long he had been recruited by the Justice Department in Washington. Dexter did not hesitate when offered a post as an undercover agent for the Justice Department. He underwent long months of intensive training, becoming proficient in numerous police skills. After his training period, he broke his first assignment in record time. After that it was full-time undercover work for Jim Dexter.

For his present assignment, he had infiltrated a mercenary group commanded by a man named Cam Remsberg. An ex-Marine, Remsberg had left the service after ten years with a wealth of combat skills and a lust for action. Remsberg was unable to satisfy this need by staying in the service, so he quit and formed his own fighting force, which he called Remsberg's Raiders. His troops were comprised of ex-fighting men who needed to go on fighting, and Cam Remsberg was soon supplying them with the sort of action they craved. He had a simple dictum: Don't worry about the right or wrong of a contract, just make sure the money's okay.

The U.S. government became interested in Remsberg's Raiders when it learned that the mercenary force had been involved in a number of contracts in Latin America, Africa and the Middle East. Far from being true mercenaries, Remsberg's Raiders seemed nothing more than hired killers. It was rumored they would go anywhere and do anything if the price was right—and it usually was. There were, unfortunately, those who needed the services of people like Remsberg and his thugs. Contract killers would always be in demand in a world that seemed unable to exist without wholesale slaughter, betrayal and intrigue. Cam Remsberg offered an unrivaled service to his clients. He and his men were ruthless, unfeeling killers. They had no scruples. No religion. No conscience.

They were, however, becoming an embarrassment to the U.S. administration. The government wanted the Raiders out of its hair, but it understood that it couldn't just walk in and accuse the group. There was no actual proof of any of the Raiders' exploits. It was all hearsay, and the Justice Department knew well enough that if it did try to come down on Remsberg, he would yell for his lawyer and be back out on the street before the dust had settled.

The only way to get rid of Remsberg's Raiders was by due process of law, which meant gathering evidence to lay before a court.

Which was why Jim Dexter was posing as an ex-combat veteran and a member of Remsberg's Raiders. He had been with them now for five and a half months and was still on probation. The group did not yet fully trust him. He had not taken part in any of the Raider's recent assignments. When a bunch of them had taken off for almost two weeks, Dexter had remained behind on the run-down ranch in Arizona that served as their base. The ranch was isolated and never received visitors. Situated in a desolate area of the San Andres Mountains, where the sun-bleached land melded with the tortured black outcropping of the badlands, the Raiders' base had thrived as a horse ranch for years. But it had been up for sale when Cam Remsberg was seeking a home base for his growing band of mercenaries. Money had been no object, and Remsberg simply negotiated a price and handed over a check.

Outwardly the place didn't change much after the sale. The inside told a different tale. Remsberg had fitted it with various modern conveniences and electronic gadgetry, all powered by the big generator he had in-stalled in a newly-built shed.

The base's isolation meant that Raiders in training could fire their weapons without arousing curiosity. That was handy because they did a lot of training and a lot of weapons handling.

Dexter—calling himself Arnie Ryker for his under-cover role—had discovered that Remsberg kept only a small arsenal at the base. He apparently stored the bulk of his weaponry in a number of safe houses scattered around the country. That was a good strategy. If the authorities discovered one of his weapon caches, he still had the others to fall back on. The man was a cold-blooded killer but also someone who lived on his in-stincts; caution dictated every move he made. A survi-vor, he was far from stupid.

It took Dexter a long time to get even remotely close to Remsberg. The man was something of a loner, pre-ferring to keep his own company. Even those members of the Raiders who had been with him longest said the same thing. So Dexter had to move slowly. He watched and listened as he tried to assess the man running the Raiders—because knowing your man was just as im-portant as learning about unknown terrain.

As the weeks passed, Dexter learned more and more about Cam Remsberg. The man stood apart from everyone around him. Oh sure, his Raiders said, he was a damn good soldier. A sound tactician. And he made lucrative deals for them. But he was a man alone. Re-mote. Cut off from any intimate camaraderie with his men. Even so, Dexter realized, those same men would have followed Remsberg to the very doors of hell if he'd asked them.

Because apart from anything else, Remsberg had that elusive quality called leadership—the ability to command loyalty and complete obedience. No matter what the situation, Remsberg could count on the full support of his men when the chips were down. The individuals in the group acted in unison, each depending fully on the others. It was their teamwork that made Remsberg's Raiders so successful—and so dangerous.

Dexter had become aware of this soon after joining the mercenaries. He had learned early on in his undercover work that a lot could be gained by standing back and listening. People would give you the information you were seeking if you just allowed them to talk. A newcomer to a group could easily fall under suspicion by asking probing questions. The art was in letting the other guy volunteer answers without being asked. Dexter had developed this fly-on-the-wall technique slowly and thoroughly. Now he could join a group, be accepted, and not appear too pushy while showing a natural interest in what was going on. He played whatever undercover role he had assumed with professional ease; his life depended on it.

In Jim Dexter's world you got one chance.

With Cam Remsberg, the undercover agent realized he was going to have to tread very carefully. Remsberg had a violent temper that was easily roused. Invoking Remsberg's wrath would not be wise, so Dexter took his time. He accepted the orders he was given, and executed them efficiently and quickly. He played the part of an ex-soldier and fighting man to the hilt, aware that he was being watched continuously during the first few weeks. As time advanced, Dexter observed that his probationary status seemed to be diminishing. Still, he wasn't allowed to take part in missions, nor asked to any preoperational briefings.

It was galling, because he wanted to learn where and when particular operations were going down. Part of his brief was to find out where and when the Raiders were going to strike, and pass this information to his department chief so that a strike force could be assembled and hopefully catch Remsberg's Raiders in the act.

It sounded great in theory. In practice, however, real life never followed the written word.

Time had passed and Dexter's frustration had increased, though he knew from past experience that there was no such thing as a time limit on his work. An undercover operation couldn't be scheduled for a week or ten days or even a couple of months. The affair could drag on and on, showing no sign of breaking, until one day—often unexpectedly—everything would fall into place.

Dexter's break finally came in the form of snatches of an overheard conversation. It was between two Raiders fairly high in the ranks. They were strolling past one of the parked pickups, unaware that Dexter was sitting on the ground, leaning against a wheel on the far side of the vehicle. He was simply there for a few minutes of peace and quiet after a busy day spent training in the rocky hills behind the ranch.

The fragments of conversation that reached his ears offered him a few interesting facts.

There was a mission in the offing.

It was going to be a big one.

The Philippines played a key role.

Somebody high up was going to be taken out.

This one would set them all up for life.

After the talkative pair moved on, Dexter remained seated while he reviewed the scant information he had received.

Instinct told him this could be the one to topple the Raiders—if he could pass the word to his department and if his department could act fast.

This upcoming mission, he realized, was something special, which made it doubly important for his people in Washington to move.

Considering his situation, however, it was not going to be very easy to get a message to them.

But no one ever said undercover work was easy.

2

Two days later, Jim Dexter was still trying to figure a way of tipping off his headquarters. Then he was given the opportunity by the very people he had infiltrated.

Dexter was working on the engine of one of the pickup trucks scattered around the ranch. All were battered and work-scarred, with heavy tires for traveling the rough trails and dusty tracks. Under the dirt and bleached paint, though, were powerful, fine-tuned engines.

Replacing a set of spark-plugs, Dexter became aware of someone watching him. He carried on with his task, and acknowledged the presence of his audience only when he turned away from the truck, wiping his hands on a rag.

"Hi, Peck," he said.

One of Remsberg's close associates, Milt Peck was a thick-necked giant of a man originally from Texas. Peck had a slow way about him that could fool a person into believing he was dim-witted and clumsy. It was far from the truth. Peck was an expert in unarmed combat of all kinds. He also possessed a sadistic streak that emerged when it came to such tasks as interrogations. He was not a pleasant individual, but his closeness to Remsberg meant his word carried great weight. It was not wise to go against Milt Peck.

"You got that set of wheels fixed?" Peck asked. He still drawled out words in his native Texan accent.

"Yeah," Dexter said. He slammed the hood and patted it. "She'll do."

"Get yourself cleaned up and truck on down to Logan," Peck instructed. "Cam wants you to pick up some mail at the post office."

"Okay," Dexter said. "Give me ten minutes to throw on some fresh gear and I'm gone."

Peck watched Dexter cross the dusty yard. Abruptly he broke into a shambling trot.

"Hey, Ryker!"

Dexter turned, fished a pack of cigarettes from his pocket and lit one as he waited for Peck to catch up.

"Don't fuck about in Logan," Peck growled. "Cam wants that stuff back here fast."

"No sweat," Dexter said.

No sweat. Dexter recalled his words as he sat in the Dodge's sweltering cab, his eyes searching for any sign that he was being watched. During the sixty mile drive to the small town of Logan, he wondered whether the trip was some kind of loyalty test. He was being sent to pick up some important mail. It was quite possible that it was nothing more than blank paper inside an envelope. Perhaps Remsberg wanted to see whether Arnie Ryker could be trusted. Would Ryker deliver the mail as ordered? Or would he open the envelope to examine its contents?

Cam Remsberg was suspicious by nature. His occupation made him that way. Remsberg lived in a world of shadows, never able to trust more than a select few. Always on the alert against deceit, betrayal. There was never a moment when he could walk free of the threats against his freedom. So he developed a mistrusting nature and used it as a shield to protect himself.

Testing a new man was a simple exercise that would ultimately determine the newcomer's ethics, though such a test was never foolproof. Dexter had been anticipating it. He might, of course, be wrong. There were a lot of variables. But at least he could play out the hand so that he came through clean.

He finished his preliminary surveillance and opened the door of the Dodge. As Dexter stepped out he felt the dry heat envelop him. A soft, gritty breeze drifted across the flat land. He could hear the gentle hiss of sand stroking the sides of the pickup.

The town of Logan, if you could call it that, lazed beneath the midday sun. It was nothing more than a few buildings on either side of the highway. Back in the days of the cattle boom the place had been created simply to provide supplies and recreation for the local ranchers. It had consisted of a trading post, a few saloons and a couple of brothels. Over the years Logan had grown. Respectable stores and businesses appeared. Eventually the local stagecoach line had built a swing station to supply fresh teams of horses for the passing stages. Logan had prospered, declined, and prospered again before settling into its present state. It was still just a stop on the way to somewhere else. It was the kind of place you were nearly always leaving but very seldom coming to. Logan's post office was located in the general store, which stood on the site of the original trading post, across the street from the diner outside which Dexter had parked.

He entered the diner, hearing the screen door creak shut behind him. It was marginally cooler inside, and less bright. Dexter crossed to the counter and settled on one of the tall stools.

"Coffee," he said to the slim brown-skinned girl behind the counter.

Dexter saw that he had the place to himself. He drank his coffee slowly but his mind was working fast. He had not forgotten Remsberg's business, but there was also his own to consider. He had to get a message to his department.

There was a pay phone in the diner, but making a call would be too obvious. It took time and it was impossible to do without being seen. An innocent witness could cause him a lot of trouble if someone came around asking questions later.

There was a large board attached to the wall behind the counter. On the board was painted the diner's menu. Around the board were pinned a selection of color postcards showing famous national landmarks. They were the kind of thing you sent home when you were on vacation.

Dexter was smiling to himself as he finished his coffee. He dropped the money on the counter.

"Have a nice day," the girl called from behind the counter as her one customer left. "It's gotta be better than mine."

Dexter strolled across and entered the general store. A modern Aladdin's cave, the place appeared to stock everything. Food, clothing, kitchen utensils, guns, magazines. The list went on endlessly. Dexter moved through the aisles of stacked goods until he located the section that dealt with the mail.

A gray-haired oldster with grizzled looks and hawklike eyes stared at the agent, a fierce expression on his lined brown face.

"Do for you?" he asked.

"Here to pick up some mail for the Remsberg spread."

The old man grunted. "Been here two days," he mumbled. "Now you want it in a hurry."

"Take your time," Dexter grinned. "Hey, you got any postcards?"

The old man disappeared behind some shelving. "Take a look behind you, boy," he snapped, "but don't 'spect me to lift the damn things out of the rack. You do that yourself."

Dexter found the wire rack. It held a sorry collection of color postcards. Most of them looked as if they had been around for as long as the historic landmarks they were illustrating. Dexter picked the least faded of the cards.

The old man returned with a thick brown envelope and thrust it at Dexter, who took it and stuffed it inside his shirt. He held up the card.

"I'll take this," he said, "and a stamp."

The old man grunted, searched under the counter, then found a box from which he took a stamp. He took Dexter's money and wandered away without another word.

Dexter returned to the pickup and took a pen from his pocket. He wrote quickly on the card, addressed it and stuck on the stamp. Then he drove through Logan until he spotted a mailbox. Drawing the Dodge alongside, he dropped the card in the box and returned to the Remsberg ranch.

JIM DEXTER'S BODY was found eight weeks later, buried several hundred yards from the main buildings of the Remsberg ranch. He had been savagely tortured, then killed by a single bullet to the brain.

But the agent could not be denied his final and most crucial wish: the postcard from Logan eventually reached a man who would initiate the action ultimately leading to the discovery of Dexter's body.

Before that discovery, however, more men would die. All because of a few words on a faded postcard mailed from an insignificant town in New Mexico.

The man who held the card carried a heavy burden on his shoulders.

A man named Hal Brognola.

3

"What do you know about the Philippines?" Brognola asked, glancing around the Stony Man War Room.

"They have a cute lady President," Rafael Encizo said.

"Who is having problems at the moment," added Yakov Katzenelenbogen, the Phoenix Force commander.

"The whole country is having problems," said Calvin James. "There have been a few attempted coups since Aquino took over. She's been having a lot of resistance. And a lot of criticism."

"About not dealing hard enough with the Communist rebels," David McCarter said. "Among other things."

"Yeah," James agreed. "The lady can't seem to please anyone."

"She has quite a job running that country," McCarter said. "I reckon she's doing the best she can."

"Sounds like she has a fan here," Gary Manning chipped in.

"Too bloody true, chum," McCarter said.

"From what I know about the Philippines," Katz said, "they still have a long way to go before they sort out the political scene. They may have dumped Marcos and opted for a more democratic style of government, but there are a lot of old customs to weed out. Graft and corruption are still there. And a lot of older Filipinos still cling to the traditional values of their ancestors. It's a balance of the old and the new—and like oil and water, they don't always mix.''

Brognola nodded. "Katz is right. And while all this is going on it leaves the country vulnerable to attempted coups and further infiltration by the Communists. There are something like twenty-three thousand Communist rebels lurking in the shadows. All they need is someone to start the ball rolling and Aquino could find herself with a war on her hands.''

"And?'' Encizo prompted, knowing that Brognola had more to say.

The Fed couldn't help smiling. "And now I'll tell you why I sent for you all.''

"It wouldn't have to do with the Philippines, would it?'' McCarter asked dryly. "Oh, wow, don't tell me I've spilled the beans.''

Brognola chose to ignore McCarter, as usual, because he knew that the Briton was being impertinent deliberately. McCarter's sense of humor was notorious—notoriously bad. Everyone knew it. McCarter knew it, and that was why he inflicted it on others at every opportunity.

"This could take some time,'' Brognola said, "so if anyone wants to grab a coffee or Coke, go ahead.''

As several members of Phoenix Force took drinks, Brognola sorted papers in the folder in front of him.

"Okay,'' the Fed said as the Force settled back around the table. "I'll go through a number of reports that may seem unrelated at first, but I think you'll soon spot the connection.''

"Great," McCarter interrupted, "it's a quiz. What's the prize for the winner?"

Katz turned to give the ex-SAS man a stern look. "Do you really want me to tell you?" he asked.

McCarter lit a Player's. "I pass," he said lightly.

Katz faced Brognola again. "Go ahead," he said in a firm voice. Only the Fed saw the twinkle in the Israeli's eyes.

"Report one," Brognola said, "concerns intelligence gathered by our people in the Philippines. Rumors concerning possible coups against the government come out of the islands every week. We have to treat each one on its own merits until it has been proved positive or negative. Things seem to have cooled off since the last big antigovernment coup was deflected. The fact that democratic elections have taken place in the Philippines seems to have taken the edge off some of the hotheads.

"However, a recent intelligence report seems to indicate a serious coup attempt is in the works. Mainly because one of the Filipino agents who helped file the report was found dead a few days ago. He'd been following a lead on one of the Communist cells in Manila—the group is connected to this possible coup. At the same time the dead man was found, his partner disappeared. This man had infiltrated the Communist group as a sympathizer to the cause. His name is Mano Hernandez. Right now we don't know if he's alive or dead. If these agents were getting too close to something, Hernandez may have been snatched. Which would suggest there may be substance to this particular rumor. The report suggested that the coup was hatched by members of the government who are not democratically inclined, and military people who would prefer a Marxist administration running the Philippines.''

"Any names?'' Katz asked.

Brognola shook his head. "All the report said was that these individuals were keeping a very low profile. The agents hadn't been able to finger any of them. And it looks like they won't get an opportunity to file another report.''

Picking up a second folder, Brognola opened it and flipped through a sheaf of papers.

"There's a so-called mercenary group operating out of the United States that's been building a reputation. Unfortunately, it's not the sort of reputation the President wants for any of our people. The operations these guys have been running are mean and dirty.''

"Ramsberg's Raiders?'' McCarter asked.

Brognola threw him a challenging look. "How did you know?''

"Hell, they aren't that much of a secret,'' Calvin James said.

"Word's been going around for some time in the business,'' McCarter said. "A rotten apple soon stinks so bad that everybody notices the smell.''

"Very poetic.'' Manning grinned.

"Also very accurate,'' Brognola said. "Remsberg's Raiders are only interested in a mission if it pays their rate. Nothing else matters to those lowlifes. We've had reports from South America, Europe, the Middle East and the Far East. The Raiders will go anywhere, do anything, for the right money. Politics, religion, humanity—none of those mean a damn thing to this bunch. Women, kids, old or young, if the contract says take them out, Remsberg's Raiders will do it.

"The Justice Department planted an undercover agent in the group months back. His assignment was to get enough hard evidence on the Raiders so that Uncle Sam could haul them off to court and make it stick.

"A few days ago his department received a message from him on a postcard from New Mexico. Obviously the agent couldn't use any other type of communication. He was almost certainly under surveillance and this would have been the only way to send out the information he felt needed passing along—a card through the mail was the simplest and safest method.

"Anyway, the message was basically that the Raiders have been offered a contract. The strike is to take place in the Philippines. And it's going to be a big one. There was also mention of someone high up being taken out."

"Aquino?" suggested Encizo.

Brognola's look affirmed the possibility. He pulled a fresh cigar from his pocket, unwrapped it and stuck it in his mouth unlit.

"So we have a possible coup being planned and a team of hired assassins contracted for a job," Katz summed up. "The common factor is the Philippines."

"Coincidence?" James offered.

"Not impossible," Katz agreed.

"The two are bound to be part of the same deal," McCarter stated with his usual modesty. "No questions about it."

"How does the man do it?" James asked dryly.

"Wit. Charm. Intelligence, old chum," McCarter said with a grin. "Plus a total lack of affectation."

"I'm not so sure about his character profile," Katz said, "but I'm inclined to agree with David's feelings about the connection. I believe they are part of a bigger plan."

"To bring the Philippine government down?" James said.

"I don't think it'll be for the Coca-Cola franchise," McCarter remarked.

"Hal, do we have any other information?" Katz asked.

"Only a maybe," the Stony Man Fed replied. "We had a report that said Major Leoni Testarov was sighted in Manila about a week ago."

"Testarov?" Manning repeated. "I feel I should know something about that name."

"Yeah," James agreed, "I know what you mean. I've seen it on file somewhere."

"Leoni Testarov is a major in the KGB," Brognola told them.

"Morkrie Dela!" McCarter said.

"That's him," Brognola acknowledged. "He heads one of the KGB killer squads."

"And he's been spotted in the Philippines?" Katz mused. "Add that to all the other facts and that is stretching coincidence too far."

"How are we involved?" Encizo asked.

"A number of ways," Brognola said. "First, we certainly don't want anything to happen to the president of the Philippines. The maintenance of a democratic regime is important enough in itself—we can't allow the life of someone like Cory Aquino to be jeopardized.

"The involvement of American mercenaries, and especially the likes of Remsberg's Raiders, cannot be tolerated. If it got out the publicity would do a lot of harm to U.S. credibility."

"That may be why they've been involved," James suggested.

"That possibility hasn't been overlooked," Brognola said. "Remsberg may believe his group has been hired for its fighting skill. But if the Soviets are involved—and Testarov's presence indicates they may be—it could turn out that the Raiders are going to be used in more ways than they realize."

"Let's face it," Manning pointed out. "The Russians would like the U.S. out of the Philippines."

"That hasn't been overlooked, either," Brognola said. "The Soviets are making a point of staying away from the Philippines politically. But they'd gain a hell of a lot if we were pushed out."

"And *we* would lose a lot," Katz said. "Having bases in that part of the Pacific gives the U.S. the opportunity to place its forces in forward positions strategically. If trouble breaks out and we have to be involved, there are people and machines already in the vicinity."

"Our naval base in Subic Bay would be hard to duplicate anywhere else," Brognola said. "It has everything the Navy needs. A good harbor. Plenty of local labor—which is another point. If we had to pull out of the Philippines, it would hit the economy hard.

"The point is, we need a U.S. naval presence in the area. It shows we're ready to back talk with muscle. And it counteracts the Soviet presence at Cam Ranh Bay. That base of theirs in Vietnam is damn big. The same goes for the Air Force at Clark Field, and all the other military installations. Moscow would rub its hands with glee if we pulled out of the islands. It would leave the Soviets a clear field. They could move in by default, without having to commit men and arms to do it for them. And once they got a foothold, that would be it.''

"So they encourage a local coup in the hope of the democratic government being toppled," James said. "The Morkrie Dela team stands by to lend a discrete hand if it's needed. A cute trick."

"And not the first time it's been used," Encizo remarked. "The Soviets have got this down to a fine art."

"You guys ship out to Manila tomorrow," Brognola said. "The U.S. embassy has been informed that a team of specialists is coming in to assess the situation and handle it. Apart from your contact at the embassy, your presence in the Philippines is known only to the Man in Washington and the Lady over there. It has to be that way because we don't know who else we can trust."

"What's our brief?" Katz asked.

"Find out if Remsberg's bunch is involved. If they are, handle it." Brognola's instructions left little to the imagination, and for good reason. The rogue mercenaries had possibly put themselves into a situation liable to explode in their faces and create a lot of fire—fire that might be felt all the way over in Washington, where it could burn a lot of good people. Remsberg had placed himself and his men outside the law; he was therefore a fair target for instant justice.

"Could be kind of tricky out there," James said. "American mercenaries. Maybe Russian assassins. And local antigovernment agitators. Going to be hard sorting out who is who."

"Oh, come on, Calvin," McCarter said breezily. "There are ways and means of handling these situations."

"I know your methods, David," Brognola said. "Just try to curb your enthusiasm until you actually arrive. What I mean is, don't start anything while you're still on the airplane."

McCarter grinned. "The trouble with you, Hal, is that you believe all the rubbish this lot says about me."

"You mean it's all lies?" Brognola asked.

McCarter's grin widened. "Bloody hell, no." He chuckled. "They don't tell you half of it. All you get is the censored version."

Brognola shook his head as he glanced at Katz. "I should have known better than to ask. Katz, let's get this briefing over with so you fellows can get on your way—and I can get back to normal."

4

Manila International Airport's main terminal was packed wall-to-wall with a noisy mass of humanity, and it was unbearably hot. The airport was living up to its reputation as one of the world's busiest.

The members of Phoenix Force had disembarked from their flight some thirty minutes earlier and had passed through customs without difficulty. As usual, they were traveling on passports supplied by Stony Man, giving them all aliases.

Although Phoenix Force's involvement was being kept secret, the Stony Man warriors knew from past experience that there was no such thing as total secrecy. And though they were ostensibly entering the country as mere tourists, it was possible that their arrival was known to parties who were less than hospitable.

As they collected their belongings and drifted toward the terminal exit, each of the Phoenix pros scanned the busy throng filling the building.

The U.S. embassy had hired a car for them, and Manning had picked up the keys and paperwork for the vehicle at the rental agency's desk in the terminal.

They were each aware how vulnerable they were in such a situation. None of the Force was armed, nor would they be until the transport was picked up. Any one of the innocent-looking people in the terminal could be carrying a weapon, ready to use it on the Phoenix warriors.

They approached the exit.

Katz and Manning were in the lead, with James close behind. Encizo walked casually a few yards farther back. He seemed unaware of his surroundings, but nothing could have been further from the truth. Encizo was scanning the whole terminal area, his keen eyes probing and searching, ever vigilant.

Even farther back David McCarter strolled along with what appeared to be total nonchalance. The cockney's bag was slung over one broad shoulder while he sipped from a can of Coca-Cola. The Brit was dressed in lightweight clothing and wore dark glasses.

Behind the glasses the Phoenix action man was following the progress of a skinny man dressed in crumpled cotton pants and a gaudy shirt. McCarter noticed the guy as Phoenix Force had moved through customs. The stranger had displayed more than just a passing interest. As soon as he spotted the five men, the skinny guy had suddenly seemed to become agitated. He had lingered as the Force had cleared customs, then had followed them toward the exit. Intermittently, he would stop to look back, unable to resist that extra glance.

As Phoenix Force moved ever closer to the exit, McCarter saw the skinny guy make contact with a tough-looking man in a pale blue suit. This one had no nerves at all. He listened to the skinny guy, nodded, then turned and hurried from the terminal.

Catching up with Katz and Manning, the Brit caught their eye.

"We've been tagged," McCarter said casually.

"Are you sure?" Katz asked.

"Would I lie, guv?" McCarter whined in his best East End accent.

"Cut out the cockney impressions," Katz snapped. "How many are there?"

"Two so far," McCarter said. "See the skinny bloke near the door? The one in the fancy shirt? He was the spotter. He spoke to a tough-looking guy who left in a hurry."

"Maybe someone's arranging a welcoming committee," James suggested.

"Well, don't expect flowers," McCarter said.

Phoenix Force left the terminal building and went to the rental agency's parking area. A red Chevrolet Blazer 4x4 was waiting for them. The vehicle was fitted with heavy-duty tires and crash guards at front and rear.

"Whoever hired this must have heard about our reputation," McCarter grinned as he dumped his bag in the back.

"For that remark," Katz said, "you can drive."

The Israeli climbed in beside McCarter, while Manning, James and Encizo piled into the rear.

McCarter started the motor, then glanced at Katz.

"Something we've forgotten," he said, holding up his right hand with his first finger extended like the barrel of a gun.

Katz nodded. "Gary, break out some hardware. If we've been spotted, our ride to town might be interrupted."

"Might be?" McCarter muttered. "I'm going to be disappointed if it bloody well isn't."

"Oh boy." James sighed. "He's getting homicidal again. Did someone forget to give him his tablet this morning?"

Gary Manning located the aluminum case in the rear of the Blazer and handed out the weapons stored inside. He nodded in agreement at James's remarks.

McCarter grinned widely as he took his Browning Hi-Power and Ingram MAC-10 from Manning.

The Force spent a few minutes checking weapons. They slipped into their shoulder rigs and replaced their jackets. They stowed their submachine guns on the floor at their feet.

"Now can we go?" Katz asked.

"I've been ready for ages," McCarter said. "Don't know what you blokes have been up to."

Smiling, the Briton pulled the Chevy out of the parking lot and rolled toward the airport exit road. He coasted along at a steady speed, his eyes constantly checking the rearview mirror. As they headed in the direction of the South Expressway, which would take them into Manila, McCarter saw that the black Dodge that had followed them out of the parking lot was still behind them. Of course, it was entirely possible that the Dodge was simply going in the same direction—but McCarter didn't believe that for one second. Intuition told him that the Dodge was trailing them.

When he reached the expressway, McCarter took a right, heading away from the city, out toward open country.

"Manila is the other way," James pointed out.

"I know that," McCarter said.

"Is it that Dodge that's worrying you?" Katz asked.

McCarter smiled. There was no fooling Katz, he realized. The Israeli didn't miss a damn thing.

"I think we may have a problem," he said.

"Let's see how serious he is," Katz suggested. To the others he said, "Be ready."

Traffic was thin, the highway ahead clear. McCarter decided there was no reason the black Dodge should stay behind them. He increased his speed and saw through the rearview mirror that the Dodge had also accelerated.

Katz checked the mirror, too, watching the car for a few moments. "It's carrying a big load," he remarked. "Only way they could get any more inside would be to put them in the trunk."

"What do we do?" Manning asked. "Try to lose them?"

But there was no time for further discussion.

The Dodge suddenly accelerated, sweeping up behind the Chevy, then came alongside. The Dodge's windows were already lowered. The gleaming shapes of gun barrels poked through.

"Hang on!" McCarter yelled, stomping on the brake. The Chevy's nose dipped as the tires dug into the road, smoke rising from hot rubber.

The Dodge's driver was caught unprepared. Before he could react the Dodge had shot ahead of the Chevy.

McCarter gave a wild whoop of excitement. He swung the wheel and brought the Chevy up on the Dodge's tail.

"Now try this for size." The Brit grinned.

He pushed down hard on the gas pedal, sending the Chevy forward. The 4x4's crash guard slammed up against the Dodge's trunk, sending the vehicle fishtailing across the highway.

"David, let's get off the highway," Katz said. "There could be innocent bystanders involved if we get caught up in a firefight."

McCarter nodded. He accelerated, passing the Dodge, and exited at the first intersection he saw. He kept his foot down on the pedal as he steered the 4x4 around a few bends and onto a deserted back road.

"They're still with us," Encizo said. "And coming on fast now."

McCarter, watching the Dodge in his mirror, saw that Encizo was right. The other driver was pushing the vehicle to its limit, disregarding any safety precautions.

"Let's see if he falls for the same trick twice in one day," the cockney rebel said.

He selected a section of straight roadway that appeared to have a good surface. Then he waited until the Dodge was closer before he repeated the trick he had used on the highway.

McCarter shouted a warning to his buddies, then stood on the Chevy's brake and brought it to a screeching halt.

The Dodge's driver, though initially unprepared, reacted a great deal faster this time. He was already braking as his car shot by the Chevy. The heavy sedan swung from side to side, then broadsided across the road, tires howling in protest. It traveled a good forty feet before coming to a rocking, groaning halt, surrounded by swirling dust.

McCarter had opened his door before the Chevy stopped. The rest of the Force were quickly behind him, weapons up and ready.

A rapid-fire SMG opened up from somewhere near the Dodge. A lash of 9 mm slugs whacked into the road, falling well short of Phoenix Force.

As the dust drifted away from the sedan, the members of Phoenix Force were able to see that the passengers had all left the other vehicle. Three men had occupied the Dodge's front seat, while four had been crammed into the rear. Now they were all on their feet, all bringing SMGs into action.

A stream of slugs lanced through the air, whined off the roadway and clanged against the body of the Chevy.

"Let's separate," Katz said.

The Force followed his command silently. They broke apart and sought cover, returning the fire of the Dodge's passengers.

James and Encizo climbed into a shallow ditch beside the road. Luckily for them it was dry. As they bellied down in the thick grass, a line of slugs marched along the lip of the ditch, kicking up dirt and stones.

"Somebody wants to attract our attention," Encizo said.

"Let him chew on this," James snapped, and fired off a burst of 5.56 mm replies toward the attacker.

The black Phoenix warrior's slugs caught the guy in the throat, ending his life in a blinding burst of pain as he fell back across the hood of the black sedan.

Two of the ambushers ran from behind the Dodge, evidently hoping to catch Phoenix Force in a cross fire. But they had failed to observe where each of the members of the Force had gone when they separated. They found out very quickly.

The tall figure of David McCarter suddenly confronted them.

"Going somewhere, chaps?" the Briton asked, then grinned and added, "Only to hell!"

He ripped off a burst from his MAC-10, the stream of sizzling slugs chewing into the attackers' flesh. The closest of the two felt red-hot spears drive deep into his chest. He stumbled, dropped his Uzi SMG, and sprawled on the ground, kicking in protest against the pain even as he died. The second guy took half a dozen slugs through his stomach, the impact spinning him around and slamming him to the ground.

Katz, bracing his Uzi across the prosthesis attached to his right arm, traded shots with the man in the blue suit, who fired an H&K MP-5 in short controlled bursts. However, his target refused to remain still, and the attacker had to keep adjusting his aim. Concealed by the front of the 4x4, Katz calmly waited until the enemy paused, then took quick aim with his Uzi and fired. The burst of 9 mm slugs cored into the man's skull. He stumbled blindly, his MP-5 emptying its magazine at the sky, then collapsed in an untidy sprawl.

Gary Manning, the team's sharpshooter, spotted one of the attackers creeping away from the Dodge, evidently intending to circle the firefight area and come up behind Phoenix Force. The guy had slipped into the bushes by the side of the road, where he must have figured he was well concealed. Manning lifted his weapon. He had chosen the Enfield SA80, which he found easy to use in confined spaces. This had proved handy when dealing with combat situations inside buildings. Manning also liked the SA80's sight system. Known as SUSAT, the system provided a telescopic sight with a pointer the shooter could superimpose over his target. This pointer, dark in daylight and illuminated at night, gave the SA80 shooter a great advantage. Firing a 5.56 mm round from a thirty-shot magazine, the SA80 was proving to be a good combat weapon.

Utilizing the SUSAT technology, Manning located his target and tracked the guy through the bushes for a few yards, until he was sure he was locked on. Manning's finger stroked the Enfield's trigger. He felt the slight bump of the weapon's recoil and heard the crack of the shot. Watching through the telescopic sight, Manning saw the target jerk to one side, a dark stream of blood spurting from the hole in his skull.

Not intending to be left out of the action, Calvin James moved to the front of the Chevy on the opposite side from where Katz was crouched. Ignoring the shots coming his way, the ex-cop snugged his M-16 to his shoulder and snared one of the attackers in his sights. The Chicago tough guy stroked the trigger and released a burst that kicked the enemy off his feet. As the attacker went down he slammed his head against the rear fender of the Dodge, fracturing his skull. This, combined with the bullets James had planted deep in his chest, ensured that the guy didn't get back up again— ever.

At that moment, Rafael Encizo touched the trigger of his MP-5 and blew the life out of the remaining attacker. The force of Encizo's burst lifted the guy off his feet and rolled him across the hood of the Dodge, leaving behind a smear of blood.

The sound of gunfire drifted away through the dusty air.

Phoenix Force regrouped, moving to check out the opposition. None of the attackers had lived through the exchange. Whoever had advised them to move against the Force obviously had little knowledge of the team's combat skills. Phoenix Force had a brilliant success rate on their previous missions. They had suffered only one fatality; Keio Ohara, an original member of the Force, had been killed during one of the early missions against the Black Alchemists. Since then, though the super-commandos had suffered various wounds, they had all survived. Often against overwhelming odds and under conditions of great discomfort. But they had survived.

And for as long as they were able, the Phoenix warriors would continue the fight.

Aware that the local police might arrive at any moment, the Force quickly checked the dead attackers, looking for clues that might reveal the identities of the dead men.

"Take anything with a name or address," McCarter said. "We might be in the dark, but maybe Mahmud can tell who these jokers were."

Mahmud was an old friend of McCarter's. He had helped them during a previous mission that had taken Phoenix Force to the Philippines. Mahmud was a Bajau, a sea gypsy, but now he drove a jeepney, a hybrid vehicle based on the U.S. Army jeep, with oversize body parts, decorated with chrome accessories and gaudy paint. These customized vehicles could be found all over Manila and were exclusive to the Philippines. As well as being a taxi driver, Mahmud was also a mine of information. If there was anything to be deciphered from the effects taken off the dead attackers, Mahmud would decipher it.

"Let's get away from here," Katz said. "The last thing we need is to get involved with the local law."

"Especially if they remember us from the last time we dropped in for a visit," Manning remarked.

The Force climbed back into the Chevy. McCarter turned the vehicle around, drove back to the main highway and headed toward Manila.

5

The Manila Hotel, situated in Rizal Park, was not known as one of Asia's finest establishments for nothing. Originally opened in 1912 and overlooking Manila Harbor, the hotel had a long and rich history. Before the Second World War, General Douglas MacArthur lived in the penthouse. In the final days of the conflict, room-to-room combat was needed to flush out the occupying Japanese troops. In peacetime the Manila Hotel played host to many important social events. Reconstruction and renovation helped to maintain the hotel's high standards without detracting from the original facade.

Phoenix Force's cover for the Philippines mission was a group of businessmen on vacation. According to this scenario, the five had come to the islands to indulge in sight-seeing, scuba diving and maybe a little sea cruising.

McCarter—using the cover name of Brian Rawlinson—had halted the Blazer outside the hotel, jumping out almost before the vehicle had stopped rolling. The rest of the Force followed. McCarter handed the keys to the parking attendant.

"Look after her, chum," the cockney said cheerfully.

"But park it where we can get at it easily," Daniel Baum, alias Yakov Katzenelenbogen, told the parking attendant.

Slinging their bags over their shoulders, the Force entered the hotel lobby, a richly decorated area that showed off the skill of Filipino craftsmanship.

"Man, I don't feel comfortable in here," Calvin James—alias Louis Jackson—remarked.

"Well, just pretend you're sophisticated," McCarter hissed through the corner of his mouth as they approached the reception desk.

The beautiful Filipino girl behind the desk smiled at the tall Briton.

"*Magandang umaga,* gentlemen," she greeted in Pilipino, the national language. "Welcome to the Manila Hotel. I hope your stay with us will be a pleasant one."

"So do we," McCarter replied with a grin.

The girl glanced discreetly at the group.

"You are the party booked by Potomac Travel?" she inquired.

Potomac Travel was the name used by Stony Man when it wanted to prebook any of its operatives with undercover names. As far as the outside world was concerned, Potomac Travel was a company based in Washington. As long as that cover remained intact, Stony Man operatives could be lodged in hotels around the world without any connection being made to any security department.

"That's right," McCarter said.

"Would you please register?" the girl asked as she passed across several cards for the men to fill in.

The Phoenix pros filled in the cards with their cover details. On this trip Encizo was Marco Leopold, while Roy Callender was Gary Manning's cover name.

When the registration had been completed the Filipino girl passed over three room keys.

"The single room was booked for Mr. Baum," she informed the men, and handed Katz one of the keys. "The other rooms are double."

"Salamat," McCarter said politely.

The girl smiled, showing even, white teeth. *"Walang anuman,"* she acknowledged.

In the elevator, Manning nudged McCarter.

"How long have you been able to speak the local lingo?"

The Briton only smiled, which served to annoy Manning.

On their floor the Force separated and went to their respective rooms. Encizo and Manning were together, leaving James to share with McCarter.

The room James entered was spacious and tastefully decorated. The furnishings were solid and comfortable. The Phoenix pro turned to the bellboy who had brought up his luggage and handed him a generous tip.

McCarter unpacked his travel bag and hung up his clothes in one of the wardrobes.

Picking up the telephone, James asked for room service. He ordered a pot of coffee for himself and some iced Coke for McCarter.

After he had finished unpacking, McCarter also used the phone. He dialed a number that would connect him with his old friend Mahmud. He listened for a minute to the distant phone ringing, then replaced the receiver.

"Have to try him later," he murmured.

"What did you make of the welcoming committee?" James asked. He was seated on the edge of his bed, staring out the window.

"Bloody rum if you ask me," McCarter stated bluntly.

"Yeah," James agreed. "We were supposed to be coming in unannounced."

"*Somebody* knew."

"It had to have come from the embassy," James said. "They were the only ones who were told the particulars of our arrival. Not even the Philippines government knew when we were coming."

"Nobody knew where we'd be staying," McCarter added. "With a bit of luck we'll be safe here—for the time being."

"Let's hope so," James said. "Last time we were here practically everybody knew where we were. Remember?"

"Am I ever likely to forget?"

James walked to the window. "One day I'd like to take the time to look around Manila, get to know the city properly."

"I don't think that's possible," McCarter said.

"What do you mean?"

"There are so many faces to Manila, it's nearly impossible to know which is the real one."

"From what I've read on the country, it's pretty well all like that. There isn't one area that typifies the Philippines. It's so complex, no one has ever tied it down."

The Spaniards who came to the Philippines in 1521 found a nation comprised of separate tribal groups and kingdoms. There was no central government or anything remotely resembling a unifying power. This made the task of colonization comparatively easy.

Nonetheless, although Filipino acceptance of the Spanish sword-and-cross mentality is broadly acknowledged, regional customs and realities have been maintained. The members of the Filipino nation collectively have always been capable of absorbing that part of foreign influence they find attractive, while rejecting the nonessentials. Whether Chinese, Spanish, English or American, visitors to the Philippines have all left behind some of their national characteristics. Over the centuries these influences have been thrown into the melting pot, blending easily with the other facets of the Filipino makeup.

Mainly of Malayo-Polynesian origin, the Filipino has been exposed to many cultures, many life-styles. Language, attitude, views on life and death, have all contributed to the Filipino of the present day. He is, within the same person, carefree, volatile, a man of charm and wit, and capable of extreme dedication when it comes to perpetuating a vendetta of honor. There is no single description that will do justice to the Filipino. He is a man of extremes. A creature of changing moods. A good and loyal friend, he can also be a deadly enemy.

This theme of extremes can also be applied to the city of Manila. Already an important trading community due to its magnificent harbor and a natural waterway in the form of the Pasig River, the city of Maynilad—as it was originally named—played host to merchants from Arabia, Siam, India, China and Japan as far back as the twelfth and thirteenth centuries. Cargoes of silks, porcelain and musk were brought to Manila and traded for beeswax, pearls, jute and gold.

The sixteenth century saw Muslims of royal blood installed in Manila. By this time it had been turned into a palisaded city of some two thousand inhabitants, ruled by the warrior raja, called Sulayman.

The arrival in 1571 of Miguel Lopez de Legazpi was the signal for two epic battles that brought about the defeat of Sulayman. Within the year Legazpi began the construction of Spanish Manila. It was to become a durable reminder of Castilian conquest. Defended by moats and turreted walls, the city fortress was named Intramuros—*within the walls.*

Only the Spanish hierarchy lived within this closed city. The upper-class Castilians—soldiers, friars and government administrators—were the inhabitants. Everyone else stayed outside, populating the suburbs that were springing up to contain the trading and the businesses needed to help Manila survive.

In 1762 the English gained control of Intramuros. They held it for two years until the Spanish returned from the north—where the English had driven them— and recaptured the city. Spain resisted the Dutch, the Portuguese, and again the English, and controlled the city for another hundred years.

Toward the end of the eighteenth century the Spanish themselves realized that their isolationist attitude toward trade was no longer paying dividends, and they opened up to the outside world. Foreign companies began to establish themselves in Manila. The export trade boomed, with Manila shipping out great quantities of sugar, rice and hemp.

As trade expanded, and outside influences began to make their mark, the Spanish saw Manila take on a new character. Cultural contact with the influx of English and American traders added greatly to the city's cosmopolitan air. New political ideas came, too, and with this awareness came unrest; the Filipino population experienced a rebirth of national pride and a longing to regain control of their own destiny. Initially with reluctance, but eventually bowing to the inevitable, the

Spanish watched their Castilian influence being eroded. They knew that their time was running out.

The Spanish had named Manila *El Insigne y Siempre Leal Ciudad*—The Noble and Ever Loyal City. In retrospect they realized that, to the Filipino, loyalty meant embracing what is good in your conqueror without deserting what has always been your own.

The colonization of the Philippines had always been considered easy by the Spanish. In the end, however, they must have realized that they had been seduced. The Filipinos had simply demonstrated a beguiling acceptance of what had to be. They seemed to walk hand in hand with the invader, smiling and cooperating, but they had always retained their individuality—which was and is the way of the Philippines.

The coffee and Coke arrived, and McCarter and James had time to refresh themselves. A few minutes later, the telephone rang and Katz asked them to join him in his room.

6

Leoni Testarov's annoyance grew as he listened to the report of the near-cringing Filipino.

He was irritated that the local Communist cell had acted without permission, carrying out an armed attack in broad daylight, thereby risking a great deal of attention when it had been decided to maintain an extremely low profile.

But what had angered the KGB man more than anything was that the attack had failed. In fact, it had been a total disaster—the entire group had been wiped out.

Testarov didn't care about the individual members of the attack group. They had proved their inadequacy by getting themselves killed, so there was no point in wasting sympathy on such trash. Moreover, the KGB man was not completely surprised at the result of the exchange, and he did not approve of these untrained idiots rushing around trying to prove themselves, anyway. Professionals did not need to keep exhibiting their skills. It was only the amateurs, the rabid fanatics, who insisted on shouting and posturing, who went about blowing up people and property simply to advertise their existence.

They set back the cause of socialism with every atrocity they perpetrated. It never entered their tiny minds that they were achieving very little. All their efforts and expense could have been put to better use. But there was no telling them.

If only they would allow the *real* warriors to fight the battles, Testarov thought wearily.

He dragged his attention back to the babbling figure standing before him. He peered at the Filipino through half-closed eyes.

"Enough!" Testarov snapped. He was sick of listening to the half-baked excuses of this simpering moron. "Just shut up."

The Filipino closed his mouth with a snap. Sweat beaded the mahogany tan of his moon-shaped face.

He knew Testarov well enough to realize that the Russian was very angry. The unauthorized attack by Lopez and his bunch of trigger-happy goons had violated the KGB man's direct orders.

It meant bad trouble for Velasquez, the area head of the Manila cell.

Testarov had made himself quite clear at the last meeting.

Because of the complexity of the overall plan, there could be no provocative action or involvement liable to draw the attention of the authorities. There were not to be any exceptions, Testarov had emphasized. Too much was at stake.

They had everything to gain if the plan went well.

If not, then it wouldn't matter one way or another.

But until the plan went into effect, they had to exercise restraint.

Which they did—until Velasquez had received information about a team of specialists coming to investigate rumors of a coup.

Olivado Velasquez had always been something of a hothead. He allowed his instincts to overrule his good sense. He seldom took time to consider the implications of his rash acts. Velasquez believed he was invincible. An untouchable. He really believed he could get away with anything—simply by going right ahead and doing it. Velasquez *never* considered the consequences. It had brought him aggravation all his life, and he was constantly in some kind of trouble.

But this time Velasquez had bitten off more trouble for himself than he could ever have dreamed of.

Major Leoni Testarov leaned back in his seat. His agile mind was alive with thoughts. He extracted one and translated it via his mouth.

"I want all your people to drop out of sight," he said. "They are to stay inactive for the time being. We must let this disastrous episode fade from everyone's mind, give ourselves some breathing space."

The plump moon-faced Filipino nodded. "I will pass the word."

"Be certain they *all* hear it," Testarov said. "I hold you responsible for making sure the word is clearly understood."

"You can trust me, Major," the Filipino said placatingly.

"Trust is not a word I like," Testarov remarked. "It is used too easily and discarded just as quickly."

The Filipino swallowed uncomfortably. He was aware how vulnerable he was now that the Russian had given him the responsibility of informing the local cells to lay low. He would find his own neck on the chopping block if further mishaps occurred.

"Major Testarov..." he ventured.

The KGB man's cold eyes fixed on him. "What now?"

"I . . . er . . . Velasquez?"

"Forget him," Testarov said evenly. "Wipe him from your memory. From this moment he ceases to exist." The Soviet terror monger stared hard at the Filipino. "Understand?"

"I understand."

"Good. Now get out of here."

After the Filipino had left, Testarov remained seated for a while. Then, his decision made, he stood and crossed the room. Opening a connecting door he stepped into the adjoining room.

It was a lounge, well furnished and cool. In one corner stood a large television set, with a video machine housed beneath it. There was a tape in the machine, throwing its image onto the large screen.

In full color the video showed three naked people cavorting on a large bed. Two young women were engaged in graphic sexual play with a man. The scene changed regularly to huge close-ups of the trio's sexual organs, then to their faces. The whole episode was accompanied by dubbed-in groans and moans.

A few feet from the television was a comfortable armchair, in which a large muscular man was slouched. Testarov could hear him chuckling softly to himself as he watched the pornographic video.

"Ivan!" Testarov said.

Almost at once the chuckling stopped. The massive figure rose, turned away from the television, snapped to attention.

"Major Testarov," the man acknowledged. "Excuse me, I did not hear you enter."

Testarov held up a hand to dismiss the apology.

"I have an assignment for you, Ivan," he said.

Ivan Gorovitch craned his massive head forward, his small eyes fixed intently on Testarov.

"Yes, Major," he said eagerly.

"You are aware of the killings that took place earlier today?"

Gorovitch nodded.

"We have to live with that now," Testarov said. "I just hope it does not attract too much attention to the local cells. I have given explicit orders for all our sympathizers to stay out of sight until told otherwise. I expect them to obey this time. However, it might help them to understand if they are made aware of the consequences of further unsolicited incidents."

Gorovitch's broad peasant face smiled. "You want them to take notice, Major?"

"Precisely. It's unfortunate, but we have to do something to make these people realize they have to obey orders. When I received the information about the American specialists being called in, I naturally thought that it would be good policy to acquaint the Filipinos with this news. I would not have said a damn word if I had imagined that someone would initiate an attack in such a manner. These Filipinos have this character trait that forces them to go around proving how manly they are. It may be good for *their* image, but it isn't helping our cause very much."

"I believe the name of the local idiot is Velasquez?"

Testarov nodded. "Actually, Ivan, he is—from this moment—the *late* Velasquez."

Gorovitch chuckled. "Of course, Major," he said. "I think I should pay him a visit and let *him* know, too."

"Excellent idea, Ivan," Testarov said. "Be thorough—swift but thorough."

7

"We have a lot of bases to cover," Katz said. "The only way we can do it efficiently is to split into teams. David, you and Calvin work together. I want you to track down your friend, Mahmud. Use him to get as much local information as you can. See if there's anything we can learn from the people who attacked us. Also see if any of his contacts have picked up any street talk about anything unusual going on."

"Got it," James said.

McCarter nodded. "We'll get on it straight away."

"One thing," Katz warned. "Keep in touch by public telephone. We've been spotted already, so we have to treat everyone with suspicion until we trace the leak. My first job will be to let Hal know what's happened, then meet up with our embassy contact."

"Even that could be risky," Encizo pointed out. "How do you know the embassy isn't bugged?"

"I don't," the Phoenix commander said. "That's why I'll be meeting the man outside the embassy. He won't know about it until I make myself known."

McCarter grinned. "Real 007 stuff."

"What do you want us to do?" Gary Manning asked for himself and Encizo.

"See if you can get a line on Remsberg's Raiders," Katz told them. "As you recall, Hal's briefing stated that the Raiders number around twenty men. Moving that many men from the States to the Philippines requires an organized trip. They would want to enter the country as unobtrusively as possible, so we're looking at a party of conventioneers. Maybe a field trip by a World War Two historical society. Use your imagination. Trace them back to the U.S. See if you can pick them up there."

Manning nodded. To Encizo he said, "Let's go find a public phone. Bound to be one downstairs."

"Who are we calling?" the Cuban warrior asked.

"The Bear," Manning told him. "Who else?"

Confined to a wheelchair after a bullet in the spine had paralyzed his legs, Aaron Kurtzman, affectionately known as the Bear, was one of the survivors of the assault on Stony Man Farm that had almost destroyed the whole covert operation. Although his ability to walk had been lost, Kurtzman's brain had not been affected, and the Stony Man computer wizard soon returned to duty.

Prior to his incapacity, Kurtzman had been relentlessly devoted to his occupation. Now that devotion had become an obsession. The Bear spent every waking hour at his beloved computer banks, poring over the mass of information his machines pulled in.

The Stony Man communications/information-gathering section was second to none. Satellite links, which the Stony Man operatives could call in using special codes, were fed through state-of-the-art scramblers. They ensured fast contact with their base. Likewise, Kurtzman could access computer systems that were denied the average user. If a system put up barriers, the Bear would find some way of overriding or bypassing them.

There were occasions when information was needed immediately. If official sanction was liable to take time, or even be denied, then Kurtzman would simply reach out and take the information he required. As far as the Bear was concerned, there was no point in waiting indefinitely for vital information—especially if it might save a life.

Kurtzman's wizardry with computers was legendary. He literally made them talk, made them dig and probe and spit out data that no one even thought existed. He could take a jumbled mass of figures and make them read like poetry.

The Stony Man combat teams owed a lot to Kurtzman. He had provided them with detailed information that on many occasions had pointed them in the right direction. As far as the Phoenix and Able Team warriors were concerned, Kurtzman was the best.

Gary Manning was banking on some Kurtzman magic as he dialed the current code number into the telephone in the hotel lobby.

He listened as the number was fed to the orbiting communications satellite. Soft hums and clicks echoed down the line, gently irritating Manning's ear. As the connection was made, the automatic scramblers took over, securing the line.

Manning recognized the gentle tones of Kurtzman's assistant, Barbara Price, despite the slight metallic shading added by the scramblers. He identified himself and asked for Kurtzman. Moments later he heard the Bear's deep voice all the way from Stony Man.

Manning explained what he wanted. The Bear listened, and Manning could almost see the man's free hand keying instructions into his computer banks while still digesting the request for information.

"May take a little time," Kurtzman said. "I'll get back to you. How are the islands?"

"Hot," Manning said, and he wasn't referring to the temperature.

"Stay safe," the Bear rumbled and cut off.

Manning left the telephone kiosk and rejoined Encizo, who was seated in a deep armchair in the lounge. The Cuban glanced up from the magazine he was holding.

"Did you know the Philippines consists of some seven thousand separate islands?" Encizo asked, showing Manning the article he was reading.

"Great," the Canadian said. "Let's just hope we don't have to search each one personally."

8

Yakov Katzenelenbogen stood on Roxas Boulevard, watching the United States Embassy. It was almost five o'clock, the hour that Jack Milligan, the embassy security officer—and Phoenix Force's contact—was due to leave the building.

Katz decided to contact the man only after he had left the embassy. Until they pinpointed the source of the leak, Katz was unwilling to divulge information on the premises. A direct confrontation, out in the open where they were less likely to be overheard, seemed the ideal way to meet Milligan.

It may have seemed somewhat drastic to an outsider, maybe even paranoid. Far from it; Katz was simply making the best of a bad situation. Sometimes the simple approach was the best.

During the briefing back at Stony Man, Brognola had shown Katz a photograph of Milligan and had given him a brief bio of the official. As far as Washington was concerned, Jack Milligan was clean. But such information did not guarantee a man's trustworthiness, or prevent him from becoming a double agent. Katz was aware of such possibilities. Until he had reason to doubt Milligan's loyalty, however, he would have to trust the man.

There was no escaping that there had been a leak. *Someone* had passed information about Phoenix Force. There was no other way the reception party at the airport could have known of their arrival. And the only people who had been told were the U.S. Ambassador and his security officer—Jack Milligan.

One fact about Milligan stuck in Katz's mind. Although the security man had an embassy car at his disposal, he always walked to his apartment, which was ten minutes away. Milligan, a former Navy man, was a fitness enthusiast. He used his car only when official duty decreed so. Once off duty he walked, jogged or exercised.

Five o'clock came and embassy employees began to drift from the building. The majority drove from the grounds. Numerous women left in groups of two or three. At three minutes past the hour a tall, lean figure emerged from the building and strode toward the gate, pausing to have a word with the Marine on duty. Even at a distance Katz recognized Milligan from the photograph.

The Israeli allowed Milligan to get well clear of the embassy before he followed. The sidewalk was fairly crowded, but Katz had no trouble keeping the tall American in sight.

Milligan didn't appear to be in a hurry. He turned off Roxas and strolled along until he reached M.H. del Pilar Street, then cut left and headed up toward the Ermita district.

Here was a strip known for its nightlife, both high and low. Catering to the tourist trade and those looking for cheap pleasure, this area of the city came alive as darkness fell. There was something for everyone. Cafés and jazz clubs jostled for business along with go-

go bars where girls in tiny bikinis danced. Here, too, the young bohemian clique hung out. Aspiring writers, artists and musicians spent their days and nights in earnest toil or lofty conversation.

Jack Milligan had a small apartment over a café on Mabini Street. Shortly before he reached it, Katz fell in step alongside him.

"Pleasant evening, Mr. Milligan," the Phoenix commander said in a friendly tone.

The American glanced at him, deciding that the graying slightly paunchy man with a prosthesis instead of a right arm did not constitute a threat. He studied Katz for a long moment.

"You got the better of me," he said. "Should I know you?"

Katz smiled as he held up his Stony Man-prepared passport. "Only as Daniel Baum," he said.

Milligan's gray eyes clouded for an instant as he gazed at the passport and Katz's image on the photograph pasted inside.

"Anyone can fake a passport," the security man said.

"Not like my Uncle Sam," Katz replied, giving the correct response to Milligan's challenge; the Israeli often felt foolish having to play these word games, but they *were* sometimes necessary.

"Okay," Milligan said. "But why all this meeting in the goddamn street? You got a phobia about offices?"

"Only when they appear to have sprung a leak," Katz stated.

Milligan stopped dead in the middle of the sidewalk. He rounded on Katz, anger in his eyes. "Now look here, pal..."

"No reflection on you, Milligan, take my word for that. Unfortunately, though, there was a leak about our arrival."

Something dawned on Milligan. He took a deep breath.

"That news report earlier about a firefight down the highway from the airport. Anything to do with you?"

"Regretfully, yes," Katz admitted. "Those men tailed us from the airport and tried to wipe us out. They didn't make it. The point is that they were waiting for us. *Waiting*."

Milligan sighed. He ran a big brown hand through his short sun-bleached hair.

"I'll be damned," he muttered. "Okay, let's go. We got to talk."

A few minutes later Katz was facing Milligan across a table in a small café. The security man had chosen a corner booth next to the window. Neither man spoke until the coffee arrived.

"You mind if I smoke?" Katz asked.

"No, go ahead," Milligan said.

He watched in open admiration as Katz took out a pack of cigarettes and lit one. He realized that his earlier estimation of Katz's abilities had been wrong. Now he understood that the one-armed man could be a threat if the need arose.

"Did the news report indicate whether the police had any leads on the shooting incident?" Katz asked as an opener.

"Apparently not," Milligan said. "It was stated that the authorities felt it was the outcome of some local gangland feud."

"How did that sound to you?"

Milligan grinned. "That's usually what they say when they don't have a clue."

"Think they'll follow up on it?"

"Depends whether they feel the dead men warrant it. If they establish they were just local gangsters, they'll probably write it off after a routine investigation."

Katz nodded. "On the other hand, they might stick with it."

"That could be," Milligan agreed.

"If they identify the rental vehicle, it could prove difficult for me and my team," Katz pointed out.

"I rented the Blazer under a false name and address," Milligan said. "Paid cash in advance. If there is any trouble, we'll have to use our diplomatic clout to clear you."

"Let's just hope that doesn't become necessary," Katz said. "We wanted to keep our presence here as unobtrusive as possible. That hope seems to be fading fast."

"And that brings us to the main event," Milligan said, his voice taking on a hard edge.

"Like it or not, Milligan, you do have a leak," Katz said once again.

Milligan drained his coffee cup and reached for the pot to refill it.

"Yeah, yeah, I know," he growled. "It isn't you I'm mad at. I'm supposed to be the damn security man. A lot of good something like this is going to do my reputation."

Katz smiled. "I think you'll survive it, Jack," he said.

"I guess so. Hey, what do I call you? Mr. Baum? Or Daniel?"

"Dan will do."

"Looks like I'm set for a late night," Milligan said. "One way or another we have a rat to catch."

"Any immediate thoughts?"

"The communications from Washington came through on the ambassador's direct line. He passed the relevant information to me verbally. We have nothing down on paper or tape."

"Could there be a bug in the ambassador's office?" Katz asked.

"I do a sweep every few days just to be sure. Haven't found anything in the two years I've been here." Milligan shook his head. "I could have missed something. Hell, even machines aren't perfect."

"What about staff?"

"Mainly American. We do have a number of local Filipinos. They're employed for domestic duties. Cleaners. Maintenance."

"Our information suggests that the planned coup is being backed by the Soviets," Katz said. "Although they're keeping in the background, it seems logical to assume that local Communists are involved. Perhaps you have one on your Filipino work force. Planted to keep ears and eyes open—for the kind of information that has been leaked about our arrival. If the truth came out it would probably show that the people who attacked us were local Communist sympathizers."

"Makes sense," Milligan agreed. "If these people are in as deep as you suggest, they won't want any kind of interference."

"Exactly. And with the high stakes they're aiming for, a few isolated deaths won't matter to them. If they feel we're a possible threat, they'll do their best to take us out."

"From now on we'd best talk face-to-face off the premises," Milligan said. "Until I can flush out our comrade rat, we won't give him any more information."

"Unless it's the information we want him to hear," Katz suggested.

"A setup." Milligan grinned. "I'd like to work that on the son of a bitch."

"All right," Katz said. "Let's see what we can think up."

9

On his way back to the hotel, Katz realized he was being followed.

He didn't need to stop and look around. The feeling was there. A physical awareness that in the crowd milling along the sidewalk someone was walking in his shadow. Following the very same path he was treading.

The questions that popped into Katz's mind asked *who?* and *why?*

The Israeli didn't expend too much mental energy on debating the questions. If the scenario was played out to its logical conclusion, he would get both questions answered.

Nevertheless, his curiosity was aroused by this new element to the game. Katz had been involved in espionage of one kind or another for most of his life, yet despite all the years, he still maintained an open-mindedness toward his profession. He had never become soured or blasé about it—which was probably why he had survived for so long.

He left the main strip, wandering along dimly lit, narrow streets that took him into the more dubious parts of the area. Here the night spots took on a shabby, tawdry look, as did the girls who fronted them. The pimps standing outside the various seedy establishments, trying to attract the passersby, were carbon copies of their counterparts in any other country. They could have been in London's Soho or on Sunset Strip in Hollywood. They were all tinged with a hint of desperation, as though even they themselves were not convinced of the wares they were trying to sell.

Katz ignored the cajoling, the pleas, the near begging that reached him from all sides. He walked steadily, his sixth sense attuned to the footsteps behind him.

They were, he noticed, getting closer.

Someone was preparing to make his play.

Beneath his lightweight jacket, Katz was carrying his SIG-Sauer P-226. The 9 mm automatic nestled in a shoulder rig on his right side. Katz did not want to use the weapon unless absolutely necessary. But he was glad he was carrying it. Whether or not he put the SIG into action would depend very much on the way things went in the next few minutes.

Rounding a corner, Katz found himself in a small, dismal square. He cut across it, brushing aside the clutching hand of the pimp who tried to entice him into a dark and inhospitable strip joint. The nearest exit from the square was an alley. Katz dodged into it and made his way along its crooked course.

He heard the rap of hard-soled shoes on the sidewalk. There were two people following him now.

And then he came to a dead stop. The alley was blocked off. A high wooden fence had been constructed across it. The fence looked as if it had been there for a long time. At its base were piles of trash.

Katz turned on his heel, his left hand going in under his jacket, fingers curling around the grip of the SIG-Sauer.

Even as he turned, he sensed—before he heard—the sudden rush of movement.

The dark bulk of a solidly built man in a dark suit filled the Israeli's vision. He tried to pull back in order to give himself some combat room, but the other man was too close.

A hard fist clouted Katz across the side of the face. The blow was heavy and solid, and it knocked the Israeli across the alley. Katz smashed against the rough wall. The impact, coupled with the effects of the blow to his face, left the Stony Man warrior dazed. His fingers lost contact with the holstered gun.

The world was fading from Katz's consciousness—the sensation lasted for only a few seconds, but it was enough of a delay so that Katz was unable to defend himself against what was to come. He felt someone grasp his jacket, then he was violently swung around and released. The momentum threw Katz to the other side of the alley, where he slammed up against the wall, scraping the side of his face against rough bricks. The sudden stab of pain cleared Katz's head. As the mist left his eyes Katz saw one of his attackers lunge toward him again.

This time Katz made it harder for the guy. As the dark-suited heavy closed on him, huge hands outstretched, Katz drove his right leg up and out, the tip of his shoe connecting with the attacker's testicles.

The heavy let out an agonized yell. He stumbled away from Katz, clutching his crushed parts, his thick body bent. Katz seized his slight advantage and took the fight to the man. He smashed his clenched fist into the heavy's throat, drawing a startled grunt.

At that instant Katz remembered the second set of footsteps, and cursed himself for his momentary lapse of memory. He spun round, his left hand reaching again for the holstered SIG.

There was a muttered curse, and a blurred shape moved in the periphery of his vision. Katz, with the SIG-Sauer half-drawn, arched his body around in the direction of this new menace.

The wide-shouldered figure was already swinging in toward him. There was something in one of the guy's hands. It glittered darkly.

At the last moment Katz realized it was a reversed gun. It slashed down at him, striking his skull with a hard blow. Katz was knocked back against the wall. Seemingly out of nowhere, another fist brutally struck the side of Katz's face. He lost his balance and slithered down the wall until he hit the ground and lay still.

10

"This really is a marvelous surprise, David," said McCarter's Bajau friend, Mahmud. "If only I had known you were coming, I could have met you at the airport."

McCarter shook his head. "Couldn't be done, chum. We had to come in without a fanfare. As it was, things didn't go according to plan."

"You had trouble?" Mahmud asked, concern showing on his brown face.

"You could call it that," Calvin James said.

"Thank goodness you are all right. Are your other friends with you?"

"Yes," McCarter said. "But right now they're all busy. In fact, we all are, and we need your help."

"Of course, you shall have it. First, though, let's go inside. Have you been waiting long?"

"A couple of hours," McCarter said. "I called you a few times on the phone but got no answer."

Mahmud grinned. "My business is doing very well at the moment," he said. "So I don't spend too much time at home."

McCarter and James followed Mahmud across the busy street where he had parked his garish jeepney, and up the stairs that led to his second-floor apartment.

Mahmud unlocked the door and ushered them inside. The apartment was small, consisting of a combined living area and kitchen, with a bathroom and a single bedroom leading off it. The place was neat and tidy, with everything assigned to a particular place. The tidiness was a legacy of Mahmud's early life as a Bajau boat dweller, where space was at a premium and being tidy was as natural as breathing.

"Sit down, please," Mahmud said. He went to the refrigerator and opened it. "David, you'll have a Coke. How about you, Calvin?"

"Beer if you have one," James said.

Mahmud produced the chilled drinks, and a beer for himself, and sat down on a chair facing the Phoenix warriors.

"Now what can I do to help?" he asked.

McCarter pulled out the stuff they had taken from the dead strike team and dropped it on the low table in front of Mahmud.

"Take a look at that lot," he said. "See if you can tell us what it means to you."

Mahmud sifted through the effects. "I take it that the previous owners no longer need this stuff?"

McCarter shook his head. He went to the fridge and took another can of Coke, having drained the first one.

"Okay?" he asked Mahmud, indicating the can.

"You know you don't have to ask, David," the Bajau said.

McCarter's friendship with Mahmud had started in Hong Kong. The Briton had been working undercover on an operation to smash Communist subversives in the Crown Colony. McCarter had been investigating a drug-smuggling ring. During the long and exhaustive case it had come to light that an adoption agency was in the business of buying babies from poor families, then flying the infants to Thailand, where they were killed and their bodies emptied of all organs. The pitiful bodies were finally filled with bags of heroin and carried over the border into Malaysia as sleeping babies in the arms of mothers.

Due to family problems, Mahmud's sister had sold her baby to the agency. But Mahmud had tried to get the child back. When his private investigations drew a blank, he went to the police. They couldn't do a thing for him, and nothing seemed to be happening until the Bajau happened to mention the name of the adoption agency.

Mahmud and McCarter were brought together by the tragedy of the missing baby, and all the others who had been spirited away by the drug traffickers. Although the ring was eventually broken thanks to McCarter's relentless investigation, it was too late to save Mahmud's sister's baby. The truth was never fully revealed to his sister, with Mahmud keeping the terrible secret to himself.

McCarter was recalled to London after the investigation, but he and Mahmud had struck up a friendship that was continued through letters. Then Phoenix Force went to the Philippines on a mission that was to bring them face-to-face with the Oriental syndicate known as TRIO. Reunited with his Bajau friend, McCarter was able to use Mahmud's knowledge of Manila in tracking down suspects. Mahmud had even helped them through many a firefight.

Now McCarter was hoping his friend could help them again. He was keeping his fingers crossed that Mahmud might be able to gain some information from the personal items the Force had removed from the strike team they had clashed with after leaving the airport.

Calvin James stood at the window of Mahmud's small apartment, watching the lights springing up across the city as darkness fell. Manila, like all sprawling conurbations, changed appearances at night. The darkness erupted with a melange of multicolored illuminations. Along with the lights came the sounds of the night. Traffic noise. The surge of the crowds. Music issuing from a dozen different sources.

"It's one hell of a busy town," the Chicago hardcase said.

"You think *that* is busy?" Mahmud remarked without looking up from his investigations. "Wait until things really warm up."

Popping the tab on his second can of cold Coke, McCarter asked, "Any luck?"

Mahmud sat up, smiling. "Have I ever let you down, David?"

"Come to think of it, no."

"Most of this stuff is just what you would expect to find in a man's pocket. Not much use." Mahmud picked up one of the wallets. "But this one did it for me."

The Bajau opened the dog-eared wallet and pulled out a number of items. "Driver's license made out to one Miguel Roces. He even has a photograph of himself, which I recognize. Roces is—or should I say was— a hired gun with Communist leanings. He always hung around with the fringe crowd and I heard rumors he was a member of the NPA. Now I'm certain he was."

"Why now?" James asked, moving from the window.

Mahmud held up the photograph he had extracted from the wallet.

"See the man on Roces's right? The lean, dark man? That is Olivado Velasquez, local Communist-cell leader. A very slippery character. Should have been in jail years ago, but he has so many friends and contacts in high places, it seems he can get away with anything."

The British Phoenix commando took the photograph and studied it. As well as Roces and Velasquez, there was a pretty dark-haired Filipino girl. The three looked as if they were enjoying themselves at some party or celebration.

"Could be the chap to talk to," McCarter suggested. He glanced at James. "What do you think, partner?"

"We have to start somewhere," James agreed.

"You wouldn't have any idea where this bloke might be found, would you?" McCarter asked Mahmud.

The Bajau grinned. "Funny you should ask that. I have a friend who owns a small grocery store on the north side of the city. He told me only the other day that Velasquez has been living in a house nearby for the past two weeks."

"What are we waiting for, then?" McCarter asked, pushing up out of his chair. "Let's go and pay the blighter a visit."

11

Mahmud switched off the jeepney's lights and engine, pointing across the road to a single-story house standing in a tangle of trees and wildly overgrown bushes.

"That is where Velasquez lives," he said.

"He obviously doesn't pay his gardener enough," McCarter remarked as he cast an eye over the unkempt frontage. "He live alone?"

"As far as I know," Mahmud replied.

James tapped the Briton's arm. "He might have a visitor at the moment," he said.

Some yards beyond the rutted drive to the house, a dark saloon car was parked tightly in beneath low-hanging branches, its lights turned off.

"Come on," McCarter said. "Let's go and see."

"I suppose you want me to stay here?" Mahmud said.

"You bet, chum." McCarter grinned. "No point in you getting hurt if things get hot."

"All right," Mahmud said.

"Just keep the motor running and the brake off," McCarter said.

"Just make sure the damn meter isn't ticking over," James remarked.

With McCarter in the lead, the Phoenix duo crossed the street. There were no streetlights close to the Velasquez house, so they had only the light of the moon to guide them as they moved through the dense foliage surrounding the building. The unkempt garden provided good cover, and as they reached the house they heard a muffled cry from inside.

James shot a concerned glance in McCarter's direction.

"What do you think?"

The cockney shrugged. "If he has got company, somebody is pissed off about something."

Another exchange of angry words reached them, followed by the sound of something smashing.

"You want the back or the front?" McCarter asked.

"Back," James said.

McCarter nodded. "No time for waiting. Just hit the door and go in."

The Stony Man warriors parted company, James sprinting toward the rear of the house.

McCarter headed for the front door. He reached the roofed veranda in a half-dozen strides, and kept on moving. His left shoulder struck the thin door, tearing it from the frame as the cockney hardman went through. McCarter bulldozed into the house and found himself in the main living room.

Olivado Velasquez, recognizable from his photo, was trying desperately to fend off the relentless attack of a massive, heavyset man. The Filipino was wielding a broken bottle in his right hand, obviously the only weapon he had been able to lay his hands on. Velasquez's face was already badly gashed, blood pouring down from his forehead across his sweating features.

As McCarter turned toward the combatants, Ivan Gorovitch—following Testarov's orders to seek out and terminate Velasquez—threw up his left arm to deflect the Filipino's lethal bottle. The Russian's right fist drove at Velasquez's face. It connected with the Filipino's jaw on the left side. The sound of the blow was hard and meaty, and Velasquez's head snapped back at an unnatural angle, blood spraying from his slack mouth. Velasquez was thrown back by the sheer brute force of the blow, his arms waving helplessly. There was a curious limpness to his movements as he collided with a low table, sprawling across it and pitching to the floor with a jarring crash.

Gorovitch swung around to meet McCarter's attack, moving with more speed than would have seemed possible for someone of his size. The Russian's square face was expressionless, his cold eyes fixed rigidly on McCarter.

At the last moment McCarter altered his approach, turning sideways and launching a powerful kick with his left foot. It caught Gorovitch high on the thigh, drawing a grunt of pain from the Soviet. Following through, McCarter hammered his right fist into Gorovitch's face, crushing his nose. Blood poured from the broken nose. McCarter swung his left hand, edge forward, at the Russian's throat.

The blow never landed.

Gorovitch caught McCarter's hand with his own, closing powerful fingers around it. McCarter gritted his teeth against the pain that engulfed his fist. He tried to strike at Gorovitch with his free hand, but the angle made it impossible.

Gorovitch slammed his thick forearm into McCarter's side, badly bruising him over the ribs, then swiftly reached up and grabbed the Brit's throat. The Russian's fingers were like steel bands digging into McCarter's flesh. His air was being shut off. McCarter inhaled as much air into his lungs as he could before Gorovitch's stranglehold became complete.

Behind Gorovitch, entering through the kitchen door, Calvin James instantaneously took in the scene before him. Realizing that a shot from his handgun might endanger McCarter, the black Phoenix pro reached down and lifted his pant leg. He drew the G-96 knife that nestled in a thin sheath strapped to his calf. Without a moment's hesitation, James stepped up behind Gorovitch and laid the keen edge of the knife across the back of the Russian's exposed neck, just below the base of the skull. James applied heavy pressure as he drew the blade across the taut flesh. The cold steel sank in deeply, slicing through flesh and muscle, severing the spinal cord. A great shudder rippled through Gorovitch's body as his system reacted to the severe injury. His grip on McCarter relaxed, allowing the Briton to stumble away. The Soviet reached behind him to clamp fingers over the gaping, bloody wound in his neck, but before he could even register what he was doing, his body—devoid of support—collapsed. Ivan Gorovitch lay on the floor, twitching as he slowly bled to death.

"I owe you one there, pal," McCarter croaked, rubbing his aching throat.

"Glad to be of assistance."

The Phoenix pair crossed the room to Velasquez. It didn't take them very long to establish that the man was dead. The final blow from Gorovitch's huge fist had broken the Filipino's neck.

"A great start," McCarter growled as he straightened up from Velasquez's body. Rubbing his sore throat, the British warrior glanced at the still form of Gorovitch. "And who the hell is he?"

"No friend of Velasquez, that's for sure," James said. He knelt beside the dead Russian and searched his pockets. "He's clean. Absolutely clean." James stood. "What does that suggest to you?"

"A pro," McCarter said. "No ID. Nothing to indicate who he is or where he's from. Real pro."

"I'll tell you what I think," James offered. "He's KGB. One of our Morkrie Dela team."

"Velasquez must have done something pretty bad to upset them," McCarter said.

Before James could reply, a soft, low groan reached the ears of the Phoenix pair. They moved across the room in search of the source.

"Here," McCarter said.

He was standing beside a long couch that had been pushed partly against the wall. On the floor behind the couch lay a dark-haired young woman dressed in dark blue pants and a long tuniclike blouse.

McCarter and James dragged away the couch, then pulled the woman upright and put her on the couch. She stirred restlessly as they moved her, and seemed to become aware of her surroundings as they sat her down. As she came around she touched the left side of her face, where a large bruise was forming. Her soft brown eyes flicked back and forth between the Phoenix pair.

"Hey," McCarter whispered to his partner. "Recognize her?"

James nodded. "The girl from the photograph."

It was the attractive Filipino girl who had been sharing the fun along with Velasquez and Roces.

"How do you feel?" McCarter asked.

The girl winced against the pain in her face.

"Who wants to know?" she asked.

Calvin James held up his hands in mock surrender.

"Friends," he said.

"That's easy to say," the girl retorted. She sat upright, alarm showing in her eyes. "Where's Oli?"

"He's dead," James told her. "The big guy got to him before we could do anything."

The girl's shoulders slumped and she closed her eyes for a few moments.

"I told him he'd end up getting hurt messing around with those people," she said softly.

"What people?" McCarter asked.

"People like that one," the Filipino girl said, bitterness in her soft voice. "And the others."

"You know who they are?" James asked.

The girl shook her head. Her thick black hair swirled about her shoulders.

"Oli never talked much about them. I just know that he was spending a lot of time with them lately. He got very secretive. Whenever he and Miguel Roces got together he would make me go out. Many times over the last two weeks that one—" she pointed to the dead Russian "—would come and pick them up in a car and they'd go off for hours."

"Any idea where?" McCarter asked.

The girl stared at him suddenly, her eyes suspicious.

"Hey, you want to know a lot, mister. And I don't even know you. Maybe we should call the police."

"We don't want to do that now, do we?" James suggested.

"We're not going to hurt you," McCarter said. "All we need is a little help. Your friend Velasquez was into something pretty deep. So deep it got him killed. We're trying to find out *what* he was involved in."

"Just who are you guys?" asked the girl. "You're not Filipino. So where are you from?"

"We can't tell you too much," James answered. "Let's just say we work for Uncle Sam and leave it at that."

"What are you? CIA or something?"

"Something," McCarter said. "But not CIA. We're here to stop a deal going down—not start one."

"And you say Oli was involved? With what? Who are these people?"

"The big feller there is a Russian," James said. "Velasquez was tied in with them somehow."

"Russians? You mean Communists?"

"They sure aren't Democrats," the black warrior said.

The girl shook her head. "This is crazy," she said.

"Surely you knew Velasquez was a member of the Communist Party," McCarter said.

"I knew he played around with politics," the girl replied. "I didn't have much to do with that side of his life."

"It was more than playing around," McCarter informed her. "Your pal Oli was the boss of the local Communist cell. He was their organizer. Earlier today some of his chums tried to cancel our tickets the minute we flew in."

"Are you saying he tried to have you killed?"

"Bloody right," McCarter grumbled.

"Obviously," Calvin James said, "you weren't aware of Velasquez's business. But you're associated with him. That could mean you're as much a target as he was. Something he'd done had upset his Russian buddies, so they decided to take him out. I dare say that if the big guy hadn't been interrupted, he would have killed you after he'd dealt with Velasquez."

The girl touched her bruised face. "He almost did. When he attacked Oli and I tried to stop him, he just hit me. I was so scared I just crawled behind the couch. Pretty dumb thing to do."

James caught McCarter's eye. "Let's get out of here," he said. "In case we get any more visitors."

"Not a bad idea," the cockney said. To the girl he said, "You'd better come with us, love. We'll find you a quiet place to lay low for a while."

"You are serious about me being in danger, aren't you?" she said.

"I may joke about a lot of things," McCarter said. "But not about this."

They left the house by the shattered front door, pausing while McCarter checked that the coast was clear. The dark street was empty and silent. As soon as the Briton had given the signal, Calvin James escorted the girl from the house. They crossed the unkempt front lot and went along the street to where Mahmud sat patiently waiting in his jeepney, with the motor running.

Without a word, James helped the girl into the back of the vehicle and got in beside her. McCarter settled into the passenger seat beside Mahmud.

"Well, don't sit there like a stuffed dummy," McCarter said to his Bajau friend. "Let's go. Home, James, and make it bloody quick!"

12

At forty-three years of age Leoni Testarov was on the way up. He had a string of successful clandestine assignments to his credit and was considered one of the KGB's most innovative operatives. He was a dedicated party member, following the policies of the Politburo to the letter. His reputation as a loyal communist, with the interests of the party uppermost in his thoughts, had drawn the attention of the Soviet hierarchy and had ultimately led to him being given the task of overseeing the Philippines operation.

Testarov was a self-made man who had overcome early deprivations to rise above the norm. He had studied and learned, always pushing, striving. Always reaching for something more. He had learned early to close his ears to those who warned against trying too hard. He had left them behind years ago. Most of his contemporaries were either dead, or aged beyond their years as they struggled to eke out a living. While they had constantly whined and grumbled about their wretched lives, Testarov had devoted himself to succeeding in a society not geared toward self-achievement.

He had joined the army the moment he felt his education had reached a sufficient level. During his service he had exhibited his talent for undercover work, and before too long was recruited for the KGB.

Testarov had, without being aware of it, come under the close scrutiny of the man who was to be his mentor. The man who was to help guide and mold the younger KGB fledgling. That man was to become Leoni Testarov's hero.

Greb Strakhov was his name.

Even though Strakhov was now dead, his image burned bright in Testarov's memory.

Strakhov had been the ideal, the perfect KGB operative, a clever, wily, dedicated man. Totally ruthless in his dealings with enemies of the state, Strakhov had possessed a devious mind, yet one that was also capable of concise, clear, logical thought. There had been a relentless purity in Strakhov's actions. He never wasted thought on trivial matters. His mind was always turned toward the glory and the good of the state.

It had been a black day for Leoni Testarov when he learned of Strakhov's death—caused by a renegade American named Mack Bolan. Testarov had made a personal vow that if the opportunity ever arose, he would kill the man named Bolan himself. As yet that opportunity hadn't come to pass, but Testarov would always maintain hope.

Since the death of Greb Strakhov, Leoni Testarov had immersed himself in his KGB work, denying all other pursuits and personal interests. His utter devotion, plus his track record, meant that he had become a highly respected KGB operative. Not that Testarov laid claim to any of the kudos coming his way. He was single-minded in his approach to life and to his service to the Soviet Union. The state was everything. Nothing else mattered except maintaining its security and destroying its enemies.

Testarov desired little else. He was a man of simple tastes and pleasures. Even when tempted by the consumer society of the West, Testarov never allowed himself to be seduced. He was aware that other KGB agents working long-term in the West became addicted to the capitalist life-style. Some even allowed their addictions to reach disturbing levels. They dressed in Western clothing and affected Western habits. It was logical to assume, Testarov had decided, that an erosion of belief in the ways of socialism would follow. The next stage was defection to the West, or at worst for the operative to become a double agent—not only denying his birthright, but betraying it.

Testarov would never allow that to happen to himself. He believed implicitly in the Soviet way, and was convinced that eventually communism would envelop the world. It would take time. Maybe he would never see it. But a global Communist state *would* come to pass. An all-out war with the West was not the way, because what with modern weaponry, a full-scale conflict might destroy them all and leave the world to rot in a nuclear cesspool. No, the way was through revolution. Country by country. State by state. A slow but definite erosion. And helped along by individual actions of terrorism and sabotage and assassination. Anything to upset the balance of power.

To intimidate.

To terrify.

To destroy.

Which is just what they were planning for the Philippines. A wave of terror timed to coincide with the ultimate outrage—the assassination of the Philippines president. Once that had taken place the new regime would step in and seize control. The Communist rebels would team up with the military personnel already committed, and the momentum of the action would overcome any resistance.

Testarov had drawn up a detailed plan of action in cooperation with Major Diego Castillo.

Castillo was a professional soldier and a lifelong socialist. He had been operating as a double agent for the KGB for eight years, covertly assisting them in Soviet-inspired operations designed to upset the Philippine economy and national stability—in fact, anything that might disrupt the nation's existence.

It had been Castillo who had contacted Moscow with the initial information about the proposed coup. A number of pro-Communist members of the government were secretly plotting to take over the Filipino administration. Since the ousting of President Marcos, the country's new leader, Corazon Aquino, had resisted not only actual physical attempts to topple her, but also had to put up with a great deal of criticism of her handling of practically every aspect of political life. Although she had survived all attempts to remove her and to discredit her, the Filipino president was aware of her precarious position, and was forced to perform a difficult juggling act in order to keep everything on an even keel. It left her open to attack from many angles.

The group that had contacted Diego Castillo comprised three members of the current government. The men were highly respected public figures. They had also concealed their true allegiances. Each one of them was a Communist to the very bone. Their dream was to make the Philippines into a socialist state—to establish the nation as a Soviet satellite that would dominate the Pacific area.

Their planned coup had been thoughtfully set out even before Castillo was asked to join them. He was their key to pulling in the military. Castillo was a popular figure, a man with grass-roots appeal to the lower ranks, as well as to the officer class. Castillo was youthful and handsome, and commanded respect from all who came into contact with him. His superior qualities convinced the conspirators that they had chosen well.

Castillo had examined the plan of the coup and had suggested an addition.

He had advised that an outside force be employed to initiate the coup. An American mercenary force could carry out the proposed assassination of the president. Its act could be the signal for the main part of the coup to commence.

Castillo's brilliant master stroke was carefully considered and accepted. If the Americans failed and were captured, they would be abandoned to whatever fate had in store for them. Because Castillo cleverly sought to contact and employ them through a third party, the mercenaries had no idea who was behind the coup. So even if they came face-to-face with the members of the coup, they would not recognize them. The irony of the whole affair was that one of the conspirators was a member of the judiciary, and it was likely that if the Americans did end up on trial, this conspirator would be one of the men sitting in judgment on them.

The complexity of bringing together all the factions involved in the coup had meant that strict control had been placed on everyone. That control had slipped with the ill-conceived attack on the American specialists who had flown into Manila airport. The local communist cell, on the orders of their so-called leader, had staged a daylight ambush on the Americans. The attack had failed, leaving the local fanatics dead. Testarov had made it clear that he wanted no more of these unplanned attacks. And to that end he had dispatched Ivan Gorovitch to deal with the local hardman as an example.

Testarov knew that the fact that the Americans were in the Philippines was worrying. However, after sitting back and considering the matter coolly, he realized that the specialists were operating without much information. Somewhere along the line, word had reached the U.S. administration that some kind of plot was in the offing. Which was not unusual for the Philippines. The leak had obviously been extremely vague. If there had been definite information, including names, there would have been some kind of response from the Filipino government. As it was, the conspirators involved in the planned coup had heard nothing. Life went on as before. So, Testarov thought, it was not unwise to go ahead with their arrangements. There was no point in getting cold feet and abandoning all they had worked for at such an important part of the game.

The KGB man was not so naive as to ignore the possibility that perhaps the Americans knew more than they were admitting. Their apparent ignorance could be a ploy, a way of lulling the opposition into a state of complacency in which they might do something foolish and expose themselves. Testarov filed that possibility away at the back of his mind.

After speaking to his inside man from the American embassy, who had informed him about the arrival of the American team, Testarov had sent a part of his Morkrie Dela team along to keep an eye on Jack Milligan, the embassy security officer. There was no way of knowing how or where the American specialists might contact Milligan. So Testarov had decided to play it safe and have the man followed.

When one of the American team members had contacted Milligan there was an added bonus. The one-armed man had turned out to be a member of the mysterious commando force that had been causing problems for the KGB over the past couple of years. Apart from the fact that there were five members, little was known about this team. They were superb combat specialists and extremely dangerous. On more than one occasion they had clashed with Soviet specialists, and had always defeated them. Superior odds made no difference to these men. They fought like devils and at times seemed to be immortal. A number of KGB operations had been destroyed by these men. The body count of Soviet personnel did not bear recall.

When Testarov's agents had recognized this American commando, they waited until he had parted company with Milligan, and then followed him. In a lonely back alley they confronted him and after a brief struggle overpowered him.

Now the man was recovering consciousness in a room on the floor above Testarov's office. The KGB agent was about to go and question him. He needed to find out what the man knew about the Philippine conspiracy—before shipping him to Moscow. Staff at the KGB headquarters would barely be able to believe their luck when this American specialist was delivered into their hands.

Courtesy of Leoni Testarov.

The capture of such an enemy of the state could do him nothing but good in the eyes of his masters, Testarov realized.

He left his office and made his way upstairs, feeling extremely pleased with himself and with life in general.

13

"Anything?" Gary Manning asked when Encizo returned to the room.

The Cuban shook his head. He didn't voice it but he was starting to get worried. It was not like Katz to fail to call in. The Israeli had been gone for over three hours.

"Are we jumping too soon?" Encizo asked.

Manning poured himself a cup of coffee from the pot that room service had sent up at his request. He stirred the drink absentmindedly.

"I don't think we are," he said. "Let's face it, Rafael, there are too many dark corners to this operation. We haven't a clue who we can or can't trust. For all we know, Katz may have walked straight into a trap."

"How do we handle it? Go and find this Milligan guy ourselves?"

"It might come to that."

The telephone rang. Manning snatched it up.

"Yes? Where are you? Come right up."

"David and Cal?" asked Encizo.

Manning nodded. "Plus friends, apparently."

A few minutes later there was a knock on the door. Encizo unlocked it and stood back while McCarter and James entered. Between the Phoenix warriors was a beautiful brown-eyed Filipino girl. Close behind came McCarter's friend Mahmud.

Mahmud grinned when he saw Manning and Encizo. The Bajau greeted them warmly, using the cover names McCarter had given him for the Force.

"Any luck?" Manning asked.

McCarter related the evening's events, finally turning and introducing the girl.

"This is Linda Torres. She was at the Velasquez place when he got killed. The way things are, she could be in danger. And she might be able to give us some information."

Manning nodded. "Help yourself to some coffee, Miss Torres."

"Please call me Linda," the girl said nervously. "And thank you for getting me away from that house."

Manning drew the cockney to one side. "We could have a problem of our own," he said, and told McCarter his fears about Katz.

"It isn't like him not to call in," McCarter agreed. "The trouble is, who the bloody hell do we go to?"

"Our only contact is this Jack Milligan, the security guy at the embassy."

"Should we call him?" McCarter asked.

"We don't have much choice," Manning pointed out.

McCarter picked up the telephone and he dialed the number Manning showed him.

The phone on the other end rang for what seemed an eternity before the receiver was lifted.

"Jack Milligan?" McCarter asked.

"Yeah. Who is this? You realize the time?"

"The name is Rawlinson. I'm worried about Daniel Baum. He didn't return home after his meeting with you this evening."

Milligan was silent for a moment. "Is Rawlinson on your passport?" he asked finally.

Here we bloody well go, McCarter thought wearily.

"Yes," he replied, knowing what would come next.

"Anyone can fake a passport," Milligan challenged.

"Not like my Uncle Sam," McCarter responded. "Now can we get down to business?"

Milligan chuckled softly. "Baum said you ran on a short fuse."

"He was right," McCarter snapped. "What time did he leave you?"

"Just after eight," Milligan said. "Told me he was going straight back to your hotel to check with the rest of you. I take it you haven't seen or heard a thing from him?"

"Not a peep," McCarter acknowledged.

"I wish I could tell you more," the security man said. "We discussed our mutual problem and worked out a plan to flush the son of a bitch out. Baum was supposed to call me in the morning when I got to the office."

"There must have been a tail on him," McCarter said. "They probably waited until you parted company and then jumped him."

"Any thoughts on who it might be?" Milligan asked.

"Unfortunately, yes," McCarter replied. "But I'm keeping that to myself for the time being."

"All right," Milligan said. "It's your game. My orders are to give any assistance you require without getting too nosy."

This time it was McCarter who laughed. "I'll bet you think we're a pain in the bloody ass."

"I'll survive."

"By the way, thanks for the transport and getting our equipment through."

"That was easy," Milligan said. "It arrived at Clark Field as diplomatic luggage. All I did was pick it up and stash it in the Blazer."

"Much appreciated, chum," McCarter said.

"Is there anything I can do about Baum?"

"Hell, there isn't even anything *we* can do at the moment. No telling where he might be. But if you think of anything, let me know when I call you in the morning. Now tell me what to say when I do call. Let's see if we can make this rat you've got at the embassy bite."

14

Earlier that evening, Milt Peck had crossed the open compound and mounted the steps that led to the roofed veranda outside Cam Remsberg's command post.

Peck had to admit grudging respect for whoever had chosen the deserted island that was serving as a base for the Raiders. Not only was it totally uninhabited, the island had once been the site of a military training base. Abandoned by the Filipino government due to lack of funds, the army base had been left standing because it was cheaper than razing it to the ground. Although the buildings had been stripped of everything useful, they were still in sound condition. It was all the Raiders needed. Compared to some of the places they'd had to adapt to, this seemed like paradise.

Accommodations apart, there was even an assault course and firing range on the far side of the island where the Raiders could exercise and check their weapons.

The Raiders had landed on the island ten days before the planned strike. In that time they had to lay out their plan of action, assign specific duties and study in detail the maps and floor plans of their objective.

Cam Remsberg, as usual, handled the strategy himself. He had spent the last two days shut away in virtual isolation, finalizing the assault. It was the way he always operated.

As second-in-command, one of Peck's responsibilities was weapons acquisition. On this particular contract that responsibility had been eased, since their unknown employer had a large cache of weapons already in store for them. These weapons, held somewhere in the Manila dock area, were due to be shipped to the island within the next forty-eight hours. Peck had insisted on early delivery because he wanted time for his men to familiarize themselves with the arms and also to have the opportunity of trying them out for adjustment. There was no way he was going to allow the Raiders to embark on a hit-and-run strike without first having fully checked their weapons.

Peck knew of too many operations that had been terminated through improper planning. Faulty weapons were just one of the reasons a strike could fail. Peck would never allow that to be the reason for a defeat for the Raiders.

The Texan had insisted that he personally visit the arms cache so that he might select the weapons needed by the Raiders for the planned strike. A helicopter was arriving at dawn the next day to fly him to Manila.

Pushing open the door, Peck stepped inside the single-story concrete building. His heavy combat boots rapped loudly on the plank floor. He was in a large empty room that had once housed desks and filing cabinets. Discarded telephone cables snaked across the dusty floor, terminating in exposed wires where the instruments had been disconnected. The plaster walls had previously been covered with maps, charts and bulletin boards. Now they were bare, with only discolored patches to show where the paraphernalia had been.

The other buildings on the base were in a similar condition. The barracks block where the Raiders were housed had been completely stripped. However, the men had sleeping bags. A good supply of canned food had been shipped in, along with large plastic drums of fresh water. They had even brought fuel for the generator that was still on the premises.

Cam Remsberg used a large office at the rear of the building. It had most probably been the former base commander's office, as it was the only one with a smaller outer office, and it was the only office to still have an item of furniture in place. There was a huge desk that was angled across the far corner of the room, facing the door. Its sheer size, plus the fact that it was bolted to the floor, probably had something to do with it being left behind.

Remsberg had made good use of the desk. It was covered with his paperwork—maps, plans, street layouts. There was also a file supplied by their employer, giving close detailed information on the overall schedule of the operation: times, dates and locations.

This apparent jumble of papers had now been pared down to Cam Remsberg's strike plan. He had taken all the isolated, separate scraps of information and molded them into *his* design. Now all that tangle of data had been fused into a tight, workable, cohesive pattern.

It was Cam Remsberg's blueprint for terror, designed as the catalyst that would fuse a chain reaction of revolution.

A revolution that was intended to alter the Philippine nation's destiny. To forcibly tear it from the path of democracy and hurl it, with brutal finality, onto the shackled treadmill of the Marxist grinding wheel.

Cam Remsberg didn't give a damn about the politics, or ethics, of his current employer. As far as he was concerned, this was just another contract in the eternal struggle between global ideologies. What mattered to Remsberg was the paycheck at the end of the day. He was simply providing a service. His profession was presently in high demand. There was always someone—somewhere—needing the skills of combat-hardened soldiers.

The whole damn world seemed intent on kicking the shit out of its neighbors, for an infinite variety of reasons—or excuses—and if a particular party didn't possess its own army to do the job, then the services of a fighting force could always be purchased in the international marketplace.

Every man who applied to join the Raiders was put through a deep and selective screening process. Remsberg turned down more men than he accepted, but finally he had the force he had envisioned at the start.

His Raiders were true professional soldiers to the core. Hard, experienced men who between them had combat experience that stretched to every corner of the globe—Southeast Asia, North Africa, Latin America—both in regular service and in clandestine operations.

Remsberg's group contained penetration specialists and demolition experts, men who were totally skilled in weapons handling and martial arts. Jungle warfare specialists were balanced by men skilled in desert and mountain combat.

During the time the Raiders had existed, Remsberg had never made a mistake with any of the men he had chosen.

Except one.

And that had been a bad mistake—fortunately rectified now. It had been a bad moment for Cam Remsberg when the man he knew as Arnie Ryker turned out to be an imposter, a man who had wormed his way into the Raiders by deceit. Ryker had turned out to be a government agent, and though the spy refused to talk—despite being put through terrible agony by Milt Peck—Remsberg assumed that he had been placed in the Raiders to gather information that could be used against the team. Remsberg admired the man for his refusal to talk. He had courage, and even at the end, when he had been reduced to a raw, barely living *thing*, he had still refused to divulge any information.

Remsberg himself had put the bullet through his head, ending the man's suffering.

Even with the agent dead, the doubt still remained. Had Ryker passed any information to his superiors that was liable to put the Raiders at risk? Ryker had left the ranch only once during his entire time with the group. Remsberg had sent him to Logan to pick up some mail. It was possible he had attempted to contact his people during that visit. If, of course, he had anything to report. Ryker had never been invited to sit in on any briefings. Nor had he been told any of the Raiders' business. But part of an agent's job was to obtain information by any means he could. He could beg, steal or borrow. The method didn't matter, only the prize at the end.

Cam Remsberg had wrestled with that concern for a couple of days after the death of the infiltrator, while the Raiders were preparing to leave the ranch for the Philippines. Plane reservations had already been made, and other arrangements were underway. Three groups would travel to different locations to pick up their

flights, arriving at Manila Airport over a three-day period. It would have been difficult to alter the arrangements then, anyway. Not that Remsberg even wanted to
consider such a move. There was too much at stake. The
Philippine deal was a big one, and would make the
Raiders very rich. The risks were high, but that was part
of the game—and Remsberg and his men were in the
business as much for the risk as for the money.

Remsberg had built a reputation as a man of his
word, someone who honored a contract once it had
been signed. He was well aware that the future of the
Raiders depended on their record. It was not looked on
favorably in the business if a merc leader dishonored a
contract. The word would quickly spread that his force
could not be trusted; and once that had been passed
around, they would find many doors closing firmly
against them.

So, doubts or no doubts, Remsberg decided to carry
on with the mission. And up to the present moment
there had not been any indication that problems might
arise.

The timetable was strictly adhered to once the Raiders had reached their island refuge. As the days slipped
by and the time for action approached, the tension
mounted. Even hardened combat veterans experienced
a period of anxiety before a mission commenced. They
would not have been human otherwise. A man was a
fool if he considered himself beyond those feelings.

Remsberg had met one or two men who refused to
acknowledge their fear. They were all dead now—dead
because they had lived in a fantasy world, walking a
tightrope balanced on the edge of insanity. Because that
was what a man had to be if he considered himself totally unafraid and unstoppable. Therein lay the differ-

ence between the reckless and the professional. The pro
considered the options and did everything in his power
to make certain he'd covered himself before jumping
into the firing line. The glory seekers went in without a
moment's thought, risking not only their own lives, but
the lives of those around them; they were the ones who
ended up dead and buried in quick time.

As Milt Peck entered Remsberg's office, the merc
leader glanced up. He was unshaven and looked tired.
Pushing upright, he stretched, glancing at his wristwatch.

"That time?"

"You all done?" Peck asked.

Remsberg nodded. He picked up a notepad and
tossed it to Peck. "Take a look. See if you agree."

While Peck read through the handwritten notes,
Remsberg moved to a coffee percolator that bubbled on
top of a small packing case. He poured himself a mug-
ful and stood drinking.

"Looks good to me, Cam," Peck said. "When do
you want to explain it to the guys?"

"After you get back from Manila," Remsberg said.
"Let's get the hardware shipped in first. Then we can sit
down and lay this all out."

"Yeah, okay."

Remsberg glanced at his second-in-command.
"Something biting you, Milt?"

The big Texan grinned crookedly. "Never could hide
it from you."

"So?"

"Hell, probably ain't nothing."

"How long I known you, Milt?"

"Ten, twelve years."

"Right. So I *know* when something isn't sitting right with you. We don't need to play games, so just spit it out."

"We could be walking into a heap of shit on this one, Cam. I just got me a feeling."

Remsberg laughed softly. "You and your fucking feelings. I wonder sometimes if you ain't nothing but an old woman under those damn pants."

"Hey, I've been right before," Peck said.

Remsberg perched himself on the edge of the big desk. "So convince me."

"Come on, Cam, you know it ain't as easy as that."

"So what is it that's eating you?"

"I don't like all this pussyfooting about with third parties passing information back and forth. We don't know from horse shit who it is paying the tab on this deal. Ain't seen him—or them. Just that skinny son of a bitch who came stateside and then met us in Manila. Just don't seem natural is all."

"I know it's not the way we normally operate," Remsberg said. "But this is the biggest contract we've ever had, and it isn't as simple as a straight hit-and-git operation. Way I read it, this coup could knock the whole Philippine government on its ass. So the guys running it have to lay low. If this thing doesn't run the way they expect, they're not going to have much of a chance if everybody knows who they are."

"Tough," Peck replied. "What about us? We're putting our asses in the bacon slicer. Who protects us if the game gets lost?"

"We do. Same as always," Remsberg said. "I wouldn't expect it any other way. We're getting paid to do a job, Milt, and we accept the risk along with the check. You know that."

"Sure I do. But most times we also know the face behind the checkbook. This time we don't know from nothing. And that's what's buggin' me."

"You're just being naturally cautious, Milt. Safest thing to be. Stop being cautious and you're a long way to being dead."

Peck nodded. He accepted that part of Remsberg's explanation. But he still felt uneasy about the deal.

And nothing Cam Remsberg could say was going to change that.

PART TWO

15

Phoenix Force, minus Katz, gathered in the room occupied by McCarter and James as dawn slipped into early morning. A thin mist, dispersed by the rising sun, drifted away from the green expanse of Rizal Park. The blue water of Manila Bay sparkled in the clean light of the new day.

Spread out before the hotel, Rizal Park was an oasis of greenery. Within its bounds were lagoons, gardens and playgrounds for children. Here, too, was the monument of José Rizal, the Filipino national hero whose name was given to the park.

An accomplished physician, poet, musician and artist, Rizal was also a man of the people. He used his creative skills to further the cause of his countrymen, who he thought were being exploited and brutalized by the Spanish. But his involvement with the liberationists naturally incurred the wrath of Spain; the Spanish saw Rizal as a revolutionary, though his intention was simply to give birth to reform. Finally, in an attempt to destroy the movement with which he was involved, the Spanish imprisoned Rizal in Fort Santiago, and on December 30, 1896, he was executed at the Luneta, which was renamed Rizal Park in his memory.

On the eve of his execution, despite the darkness of his hour, José Rizal found a way of expressing his love for his country and his people. He wrote the poem *"Ultima Adios"*—"Final Farewell"—which described his innermost feelings for his beloved islands. The Spanish succeeded in silencing the voice of José Rizal, but his spirit defied them and lived on in the words of his poem. Death claimed the flesh but the Filipinos held on to the dream of José Rizal. His execution made him a martyr.

Something of the lyricism of Rizal's poem lingered in the tranquil calm of the park, reaching out to ease—if only for a few moments—the frustration David McCarter felt as he gazed out the window.

A few dedicated joggers trooped around the park. In another area, totally oblivious to what lay around them, a group of Chinese of all ages performed the graceful movements of their tai chi exercises.

It all looked so normal, McCarter thought. Down there the daily flow of Filipino life carried on, most people totally unaware of what was taking place around them. The shadow people, hiding away in their secret rooms, were plotting and conniving to change that peaceful scene down there. While the ordinary folk—who for the most part simply wanted to get on with life—carried on the daily struggle to work and build and survive, evil men planned their coups and power ploys. They never considered for one moment asking the masses what *they* wanted, so convinced were they by their twisted logic that *they* knew best. Believing that their politics were the only ones worthy of a hearing, they were prepared to plunge their nation into chaos. To initiate violence and deceit on a massive scale. To kill and maim and destroy.

There was only one response to people like that, as far as McCarter was concerned. They had to be stopped. For good. Permanently. From past experience the British commando knew that there was little to be gained from negotiating with these people. They did not want to talk, except from behind the barrel of a gun or with a bomb in their hands.

They had to be met with their own brand of persuasion. Fighting fire with fire was the only way.

You located your enemy and took him out.

It was search and destroy.

GARY MANNING was on the telephone. He was in contact with Stony Man, absorbing the information Kurtzman was giving him. And true to form, the Bear had come up with the goods.

"Three groups, all male, flew from the U.S. to the Philippines within a four-day period. Two used regular U.S. airlines. The third took a PAL flight. That's Philippine Airlines.

"I managed to locate the travel agent who took their bookings. It was one in Albuquerque, New Mexico. Took some time, but when those three bookings popped up it seemed too good to miss. I knew it wasn't solid proof that we had our men, but it came close.

"I was going to run a make on the checking accounts used to pay for the three groups to see if I could establish a link there, but something came through to top that.

"I accessed the passport department in Washington—and guess what? Every passport in those three groups is false. None of them exist. No names. No photographs. No applications. Not a damn thing."

"Sounds like we're off and running," Manning said. "Can you give me a list of the names used?"

"Yes," Kurtzman said. "No problem."

"Any other information?"

"Accommodation was booked for each group in three different hotels in the Manila area. From what I've been able to establish, these were all pretty cheap hotels off the tourist track. Probably the kind of place where no questions are asked. I'd guess that by now each group will have moved on."

"Thanks," Manning said. "Give me the names of the hotels, as well, and we'll start doing the rounds."

Kurtzman read off the names he'd gathered from the travel agent's lists, finishing up with the names and locations of the three hotels.

When he finished writing down the information, Manning asked to be put through to Hal Brognola.

"How's it going?" the Fed asked.

Manning told him. There was a long silence as Brognola digested the information.

"All right," he said finally. "You know what you have to do."

Manning, tight-lipped, replied, "I know."

"It has to be this way," Brognola said. "Katz wouldn't expect anything else."

"You can't expect us to simply forget about him," Manning answered.

"The mission comes first," Brognola reminded the Canadian. "I know it's a lousy balance of priorities, but we have to accept that it's one life against many, and we have to go for the majority."

Manning's knuckles turned white as he gripped the telephone, making the plastic creak. His reaction to

Brognola's statement was caused by a feeling of help-lessness.

The Canadian also knew that Brognola was right, though accepting that knowledge didn't make it any easier to bear. Manning tried to exert some control over his emotions by quickly reviewing what little he knew: Katz had disappeared and had not kept in contact, which meant there was a major problem. But what kind of problem? He could have been injured and might, even now, be incapable of calling in. Or he could have been taken prisoner by someone, which would add a further complication, considering the complexity of the mission. Who could be responsible for kidnapping the Phoenix Force commander? Local Communists? Remsberg's mercenaries? The Morkrie Dela squad?

Any of those groups could have been responsible— which did nothing to make the situation any easier.

"You're right," Manning said finally. "The mission comes first."

"I know it hurts," Brognola sympathized. "And I know how much Katz means to you guys. If there was any way around this, believe me, I'd be the first to give you the okay."

"We'll keep in touch if the situation allows," Manning said.

"One more thing before you go," Brognola said. "There will be a special package arriving for you around midday, coming in to Clark Field—for use if you need it."

"That's good news," Manning said. "I've got a feeling we're going to need all the help we can get."

The special package Brognola was referring to hap-pened to be Dragon Slayer, a deadly combat helicopter capable of high-speed flight. Piloted by Stony Man's crack flier, Jack Grimaldi, Dragon Slayer had made its first operational sortie during Phoenix Force's earlier mission to Brazil. There, they had confronted a neo-Nazi group headed by Kurt Mohn, a fanatic who had envisioned a resurgence of the Nazi Reich through armed revolution and the use of a deadly bacteriological weapon known as the Armageddon Virus. Against superior odds, the Force had destroyed the madman's dream—and Dragon Slayer had proved its worth.

A state-of-the-art machine, Dragon Slayer employed the latest advances in technology; it was loaded with computer hardware. There was a rotary cannon in the nose coupled to a laser sighting device. This multibarrel weapon could deliver a devastating blast of fire that was capable of shredding a target out of existence. Under each stub wing were mounted rocket pods. Grimaldi had a selector in his cockpit that enabled him to choose the particular payload he wanted: HE missiles, heat-seekers or phosphorus.

To aid target location, electro-optical sensors were planted in each wingtip, and these were coupled to an air-data probe fixed in the front of Dragon Slayer. The probe measured airspeed, angle of approach and drift, feeding the data to the on-board computer that calculated the correct firing coordinates for the missile.

Since its initial introduction to the Stony Man arsenal, Dragon Slayer had undergone further assessment trials, and additional equipment had been installed. During the two weeks prior to Phoenix Force's arrival in the Philippines, Dragon Slayer had been called in for modifications. Now those refinements were complete, and Grimaldi and his awesome machine were back in service.

As Manning put the phone down, Encizo asked, "Did the Bear come up with anything?"

"I think we may have a lead on the Raiders," Manning said, relaying the information Kurtzman had uncovered.

"At least it's something to follow up," Encizo said. "What do we do? Try the hotels first?"

Manning nodded.

"Why don't you let Mahmud drive you around?" McCarter suggested as he turned away from the window. "He'll be able to find your hotels quicker than anyone."

"You sure you won't need him?" Manning asked.

"Cal and I will take the Blazer," McCarter said.

"All right," Manning agreed. "We'll move out as soon as he gets back from delivering the Torres girl to his friend."

It had been decided that Linda Torres would be safer in hiding. Before they had retired for the night, the Phoenix team had discussed Linda's relationship with the late Olivado Velasquez. The girl herself had been as helpful as she could be, but it soon became clear that she knew little more than she had already revealed. Velasquez had not included her in the business side of his life, except for a number of social evenings when she had accompanied him to parties given by his associates.

It had been at one of these functions that the photograph of Velasquez and Roces and Linda had been taken. As far as Linda could recall, the party had been held at a large house in one of Manila's expensive suburbs. She did not know whose house it was. Names were always scarce at the kind of functions Velasquez attended. At the time Linda never thought much about it. She had been too busy enjoying herself.

Linda Torres was from a poor background and it had only been through hard work that she had bettered herself. She worked for a garment manufacturer in Manila, obtaining the position of secretary to the owner. He had known Velasquez, who had met Linda during one of his frequent visits to the factory. One day while visiting, Velasquez had asked Linda if she would go out with him. Linda had accepted and the relationship developed from there. It had been going on for a few months, but during that time Linda had become uneasy about the kind of people Velasquez mixed with. His obsessive secrecy, which had increased over the weeks, also worried her. She had become concerned for Velasquez, but if she ever broached the subject, he became angry, refusing to discuss it.

Although it appeared that Linda knew very little, the Phoenix warriors found they were concerned for her safety. She could easily be in danger now. The people involved with Velasquez—judging from the way they had reacted to the Force's arrival in Manila—were plainly determined to silence anyone who even remotely posed a threat to their safety. If they were capable of killing Velasquez, they would not think twice about doing the same to Linda. The Phoenix pros decided to get the girl to a place of safety until matters were settled.

Mahmud came up with the specific answer. He had a good friend who lived outside Manila on a chicken farm. The man was a former policeman, a self-reliant, tough individual whom Mahmud trusted implicitly. In the early hours of the morning, Mahmud and Linda had driven from the hotel in the Blazer, with Calvin James riding shotgun.

Manning had become pensive. As he laid out his weapons on a low table, preparing them for the once-over that preceded any strike, he wondered if Mahmud had come up with any ideas on Katz's whereabouts while driving back from the farm with James. Or would the traitor in the embassy know something? The big Canadian looked up from the table and asked Mc-Carter, "You still going through with your charade?"

The cockney nodded. He was sitting on the edge of the bed, preparing to strip down his Browning Hi-Power. "If we can get this informer to show himself, maybe we can shake some info out of him."

"Let's hope so." With renewed determination, Manning turned his attention to the table in front of him. He fed 9 mm loads into the magazine for his Walther P-5, snapped the clip into place and cocked the weapon. Slipping on the safety, the Canadian laid the weapon down and began to load spare magazines. Once he had completed that he turned to the SA80, thoroughly checking the weapon. Satisfied, he loaded three 5.56 mm magazines for the rifle.

The Force had been trying new weapons over recent months, the experiment intended to get them all to use 9 mm caliber arms. The 9 mm cartridge had become so widely used that ammunition was always easier to come by, wherever Phoenix Force happened to be. The trial had worked to a degree, though on some missions the Phoenix warriors had returned to the weapons they had become used to and comfortable with. The only members of the team who did not have to change were McCarter and Katz. They were both already using 9 mm weapons. Katz had carried a SIG-Sauer P-226 for years and had always favored the Uzi 9 mm SMG. The irascible McCarter would never have changed his weapons, no matter what the reason, so it had been fortunate that both his Browning Hi-Power and Ingram M-10 were chambered for 9 mm rounds.

Rafael Encizo, on this mission, was using his replacement handgun, a Heckler & Koch P-9. His SMG, however, was still the same 9 mm MP-5 he had previously used.

Although Calvin James still carried his M-16 rifle, he was adjusting to using the Beretta 92-SB autoloader in 9 mm. However, he still held strong feelings for his .45-caliber Colt Commander.

Manning's attention to his weapons was momentarily disturbed by a light tap on the door. Encizo opened it to admit Calvin James and Mahmud.

When Mahmud saw the weapons being prepared he grinned. "You expecting trouble?" he asked lightly.

McCarter holstered his Browning as he glanced across at his friend. "You know how things are in this town."

"I know how *you* guys are," the Bajau replied.

"Us?" James asked as he took his M-16 from the aluminum case. "Now you know we're just peace-loving fellows."

"Of course," Mahmud agreed.

"Did you get the girl settled?" Manning asked.

Mahmud nodded. "She will be safe there."

"That farm is pretty isolated," James said. "In the time we had, I don't think we could have found anywhere better. And Mahmud's friend is one mean dude. Man, I'll bet he just tells those chickens to lay and they lay."

"Mahmud, I'd like you to ferry Gary and Rafael around. They need to check out a few hotels," McCarter said. "Okay?"

"That's fine with me," Mahmud said.

"We're set," Manning said.

"Only way we can keep in contact is by phoning in to the hotel and leaving messages," McCarter said.

Manning and Encizo placed their larger weapons in canvas zip-up bags, which they slung over their shoulders. Both men were dressed in lightweight, casual clothing.

"Watch your backs," McCarter said as the three left.

"And you guys," Encizo replied.

MCCARTER AND JAMES had a couple of hours to kill before making contact with Jack Milligan. The security man didn't get to his office until nine in the morning. While they waited the Phoenix warriors asked room service to send up breakfast, which they ate unhurriedly. It was not just a time-wasting exercise. Both McCarter and James knew that once they left the hotel and became involved with the mission, the opportunity for eating might be denied them for a long time. So it was wise to eat when time allowed. It was second nature to any soldier who had experienced the relentless grind of long spells of combat. A firefight wasn't run on an hourly basis, with time off for rest and food. In the sometimes frantic atmosphere of battle, a soldier learned to take his rest when he could snatch a few minutes. To eat during a lull. The rest of the time he was too busy trying to stay alive to worry about such mundane things. But the toughest warrior had to eat sometime. Had to rest. No man, hard or not, could carry on indefinitely.

At ten minutes past nine McCarter picked up the phone and dialed the number Milligan had given him the night before. It gave McCarter access to the American ambassador's personal office line—the same line that would have received the calls from Washington. The owner of the deep voice that answered the ringing phone identified himself as the ambassador.

"Mr. Ambassador, sir, this is Rawlinson. You may be pleased to know that we have the source of the leak at the embassy identified. I'm in a position now to provide photographic and documentary evidence to that effect. I can also say, with confidence, that by the end of the day we will be able to identify the informer's accomplices."

"Thank you, Mr. Rawlinson," the ambassador responded, playing his part in the charade.

"I'd be grateful, Mr. Ambassador, if you could ask Jack Milligan to meet with me in one hour so I can give him my evidence and discuss the matter further. He knows where to meet."

"Very well, Mr. Rawlinson, and thank you."

"Good morning, Mr. Ambassador," McCarter said, and broke the connection.

"Sounded good to me," James said.

"Let's just hope our embassy rat was listening in," the ex-SAS man replied.

James nodded. "And keep our fingers crossed that he's the kind who scares easy."

The Phoenix warriors picked up the canvas bags holding their SMGs and left the hotel room. They took the elevator to the ground floor and headed for the Chevrolet Blazer in the parking lot. Soon they were driving away from the hotel. They took Taft Avenue north toward the Jones Bridge, which spans the Pasig

River—which bisects Manila. Once over the bridge, they drove through the districts of Binondo and San Nicolas. Farther on, a right turn took them along the stretch of highway that runs behind the Tutuban railroad terminal and into the district of Tondo.

During the era of Spanish colonization, the Tondo district, separated from the walled city of Intramuros by the Pasig River, developed into a community of shopkeepers and craftsmen. Here the goods and skills were created that maintained the quality of life that the Spanish were accustomed to. The Chinese, with their usual flair for business, created industries designed to give the Spanish exactly what they wanted. The Oriental artisans established themselves as part of the Filipino fabric, blending into the culture with ease.

But among this heady throng the seeds of revolution were planted. The rebel leader Andres Bonifacio came from the Tondo district.

Born into a poor family, the son of a tailor, Bonifacio struggled to overcome illiteracy and devoured books with relentless ferocity. His desire for change led him along the path of revolution. The dedicated activist was the driving force behind the Katipunan, a secret society of men determined to nourish the dream of revolution. Better known as the KKK, this group gathered weapons and plotted revolution. In 1896, one of the KKK's own people betrayed the society to the Spanish. Bonifacio and his men fled to the hills of Balintawak near Manila. The promised revolution failed to gain momentum after this betrayal. Bonifacio, still faithful to his cause, was captured finally and, after a period of imprisonment in the Jesuit town of Maragondon, was clubbed to death in the hills above the town and buried on Mount Buntis.

Present-day Tondo has lost much of its former glory, having slid down the social ladder to attain its current reputation as a tough, no-nonsense slum area of corrugated-iron shanties. The old-town section of Tondo has become a crowded area of small stores and jammed streets. Situated close to North Harbor, with its complex of piers, Tondo is not ideally suited to the tourist industry.

However, as with most depressed areas clinging to the fringes of sprawling cities, Tondo did develop its own life-style, and remains entirely capable of looking after itself.

As McCarter drove the Blazer into Tondo district, entering by Juan Luna, the bulk of the Church of Santo Seng Kong rose against the brightening sky. Within this religious building are twenty-five icons, representing the major and minor religions of the world.

"Hey, don't upset the natives," Calvin James warned as McCarter kept slapping the Blazer's horn to clear the wandering pedestrians off the street.

McCarter smiled. "They won't get upset. This is the way they do it around here."

His declaration was punctuated by someone thumping the side of the Blazer.

"Oh, sure, man," James grumbled. "They just *love* you."

The chirpy Briton refused to be upset. He drove on through the busy district.

The sprawl of desperate shanties, crowding in on each other, said more about the plight of society's castoffs than any TV documentary. Here were the no-hopers: women aged beyond years; men who gazed at the passing Blazer with empty eyes, unable even to raise a spark of envy; children, grubby, wide-eyed, yet more worldly than their tender years should have allowed. There were some smiles, even waving hands, but McCarter saw the shadows behind the cheerfulness. It had to be hard existing in such deprivation when so much luxury could be found in other areas of the city.

Watching them as he passed, McCarter realized just how easy it was for the agitators, the trouble mongers, to create unrest in such a place. Though the masses huddled here were on the lowest rung, it was possible to start them on the ladder of revolution by playing on their vulnerability. A clever orator might easily supply a spark that could rapidly ignite a full-scale rebellion. When there is no hope—no salvation—any doctrine that promises to better man's wretched existence will be accepted with ease.

"Wouldn't our Soviet buddies just enjoy coming in here and playing to the gallery," James remarked, echoing McCarter's thoughts.

"You couldn't blame them for making the most of it," the cockney said. "The thing that makes me angry is the fact that we let places like this linger on. It's like saying come on in, Ivan, and make your pitch. We've even set up the punters for you."

As they drove on, McCarter spotted the narrow street Milligan had mentioned. He took the Blazer along its rutted surface. Every so often they were able to catch a glimpse of the sun-sparkling water of the harbor.

As they neared the outer limits of Tondo the Phoenix pair became instinctively alert. The area they were entering seemed even more desolate than that through which they had just passed.

The dock area looked abandoned and empty. A number of large warehouses stood silent and derelict. Loading bays were littered with debris. The burned-out shell of a car, long since stripped of anything useful, lay like a large black beetle.

"This kind of setup gives me the creeps," James murmured as he unzipped the canvas bag at his feet and removed his Uzi. The black commando quickly checked the weapon, snapping back the bolt on the SMG. He drew out a couple of extra mags for the Uzi, slipping them into the long inner pocket of his light jacket.

McCarter nodded. "I know what you mean, chum. Trouble is, there's no way you can organize one of these get-togethers with all the cards going your way."

"All we can do now is wait and see if your con trick works," James said, settling back in his seat.

McCarter parked the Blazer in the shade beside a dilapidated shed. He switched off the motor. After pulling his Ingram from its bag and giving it a quick inspection, the Briton settled down to wait, impatiently, wishing he had a couple of cans of iced Coke to ease his dry throat.

16

Katz was first aware of the pain. Waking slowly, his senses fragmented, unsure of his surroundings, he felt the overriding sensation of deep, nagging pain that pulsed with numbing regularity inside his skull. He remained still, wanting to be in more control of his faculties before he ventured on. Time meant nothing to him in his present situation, so Katz stayed exactly where he was, eyes closed because the darkness offered some security from reality.

Gradually he emerged from limbo, slipping further into the external world with each passing moment. Sounds and smells sharpened. His awareness became more acute. He realized he was lying down on a soft, yielding surface. A bed. Now he could feel the warmth of the sun on his body. He must have slept, or been unconscious, through the night. Or nights.

He still had not moved—so anyone nearby was probably not aware that he was awake. For the moment Katz preferred it that way. He needed time to gather his strength, both physical and mental. There was no way of knowing just what lay ahead. If he had been taken by the opposition, there was the possibility he could be in for a rough time. It all depended on how they viewed him. If he was considered a possible source of information, then his position could become extremely uncomfortable. There were many ways of extracting information from a captive, and many of them were crude and involved pain and suffering. Katz considered himself reasonably courageous in the face of personal danger, but there were limits to every man's resistance to pain.

The thought that he could be facing torture and possibly death did not throw the Israeli into a cold sweat of panic. He accepted his position with fatalistic ease. There wasn't much he could do about it—not until he had assessed the overall situation. Besides, death was inevitable—that was an inescapable fact. The most powerful man was as vulnerable as the most lowly peasant. Time was the only separating factor. The where and the when. But, in itself, the event was the same.

The fact that Katz accepted the final judgment of death did not make him a fatalist, ready to give up life and take whatever lay in store for him. To the contrary, Yakov Katzenelenbogen loved life and all the good things it had to offer. His intention was to live for a long time, Phoenix Force missions allowing. There were too many things to see and do before he died, and Katz was going to do his utmost to make his dreams come true.

His first priority was to assess his present position. To find out where he was and who was holding him.

There were a number of possibilities.

The Phoenix Force commander decided it would be easier to find out by waiting.

At that moment Katz heard a door open. Someone entered the room. From somewhere else in the room a chair scraped against the hard floor as it was pushed back.

"Is he awake?" snapped an authoritative voice in Russian.

A second voice replied in the same language, "He has not moved, Major."

"I didn't ask whether he had moved. Only if he is awake."

"There has been no indication, Major."

"No doubt you expect him to give you a call."

There was a taut silence.

"No, Major Testarov."

The name registered. Katz knew now who his captors were: the Soviet terror squad.

The Morkrie Dela.

The man named Testarov snapped, "Then let us look for ourselves."

Footsteps approached the bed on which Katz lay. The Israeli tensed in anticipation of a blow, then thought, *What the hell,* and rolled onto his back. He stared up at the two men standing beside the bed.

"I'll save you the trouble," the Phoenix pro said in Russian, and sat up slowly.

He was still conscious of the deep-seated ache in the back of his skull. Katz wondered in passing whether he had a mild concussion. Damage to the brain due to the shock caused by a sudden, heavy blow could result in long-term damage.

Sometimes the victim was unable to recall events just prior to being struck. In Katz's case, however, he was able to remember everything before the assault: the brief struggle in the gloomy alley; the flurry of blows; pain and anger. Then the sudden, stunning, enveloping blackness that had swamped him in the moments after someone had hit him across the back of his skull...and then nothing until he had drifted in and out of a deep, pain-filled sleep.

Still suffering the effects of the crippling blow, his mind had wandered and disjointed thoughts and images slipped in and out of focus until finally the merciful cloak of a deep and complete sleep had claimed him, holding him in its embrace while his body began the healing process.

And then he woke—to daylight and an awareness of his surroundings and his visitors.

The guard stood to Katz's left. He was tall and broad. His blond hair was cropped close to his skull and framed a wide face with a heavy bone structure. He was dressed in a lightweight tan suit and looked uncomfortable in it, but the squat Uzi SMG cradled in his large hands looked entirely at home.

The man who Katz knew instinctively was Leoni Testarov appeared completely at ease in his cream slacks and Filipino *barong*, a loose-fitting, long-sleeved shirt so thin it was almost transparent. The *barong*, a comfortable and practical garment worn over a white T-shirt and *never* tucked inside the wearer's pants, had been designed with the cloying heat of the Philippines foremost in mind.

The KGB operative, in his casual dress, might easily have been mistaken for a tourist out to see the sights. Yet a closer look into the man's dark piercing eyes allowed a glimpse of the inner hardness that was the core of Leoni Testarov. Despite his clothing, his firm, almost handsome good looks, the man was still KGB. An operative of the Soviet terror machine—the *Komitet Gosudarstvennoi Bezopasnosti*.

Over the years the Soviet secret police agency had changed its name but not its function. It was there to ensure the stability of the ruling class of the USSR within its borders, and to oversee clandestine operations on a global scale. This mandate gave the KGB wide-ranging powers. It was not wise to criticize the agency—or to do anything to provoke retribution, because when it came it would be swift and ruthless. The KGB had agents in dozens of countries, on many different assignments, though they all had the same goal: to assist the spread of global communism. The KGB advised would-be revolutionaries; it funded schemes aimed at destabilizing democratic governments, and supplied equipment and explosives to this end. Occasionally it sent out teams of its own to carry out particular operations. They worked efficiently and thoroughly, with little regard to the misery they caused. Cause and effect were given no place in the KGB book. The slaughter of innocents meant nothing to these highly trained but unfeeling cogs of the Soviet terror machine.

The most ruthless part of the vast KGB organization was the section designated as Morkrie Dela. Made up of hard-line killers, the Morkrie Dela squads were used for assassinations, murders and situations that called for mass killing, if necessary, in order to complete a mission.

Leoni Testarov had been given the Morkrie Dela unit as backup for the Philippine coup. His orders were to maintain stability in order that the proposed strike against the Filipino government could go off without a hitch. He was to stay in the background as much as possible, while overseeing the main business. If problems arose, his people were there to step in.

Problems had developed.

First, the idiotic attack on the American team at the airport, which had become wholesale slaughter. All because the local cell leader had initiated the strike without consulting Testarov. Although the entire attack team had died, the local police had announced the deaths as part of a gangland rivalry.

In order to maintain firm control over the Filipino communists, Testarov had repeated his earlier directive—that no one make any moves without first consulting him.

To hammer home the seriousness of his order, Testarov had sent one of his Morkrie Dela operatives—Ivan Gorovitch—to eliminate the erring cell leader, Olivado Velasquez. That had been on the previous evening. Only a short time ago Testarov had learned Velasquez was dead, as expected.

But so, too, was Ivan Gorovitch.

That had not been planned. The bearer of the news had not been able to throw any light on who was responsible for Gorovitch's death. The KGB agent had his own theories concerning that. He was certain that the American specialists were responsible. The partners of the man he was holding prisoner.

Something else had cropped up within the last few minutes. A telephone call had come through from Testarov's inside man at the American Embassy. He had overheard a conversation between the ambassador and a man identifying himself as Rawlinson. The caller had informed the ambassador that he had the identity of the embassy informer. There was photographic and documentary evidence ready to be passed over. The caller also told the ambassador that he would most likely be able to identify the informer's accomplices by the end of the day. Arrangements had been made for the security officer, Jack Milligan, to meet the man called Rawlinson at a prearranged location.

Testarov had listened to the informant with growing concern. But he was by no means ready to panic, or even to contemplate a withdrawal.

In the space of a few minutes, however, he had to make a decision based on his informant's report. That decision, once taken, would commit him to a course of action he was loath to take.

There were two ways of interpreting the information.

The call to the ambassador could be genuine. The identity of the inside man may have been discovered. In that case, Jack Milligan and the man named Rawlinson had to be dealt with before the information reached the wrong hands. This was doubly important if, as Rawlinson had stated, he had also got a line on the informer's associates, because those associates included Leoni Testarov and his team.

The KGB man, naturally, was anxious to protect his cover. He needed to stay in the background until the coup attempt was underway. There was too much at stake to allow some interfering American specialists to spoil things. This kind of situation was why the Morkrie Dela team had come to the Philippines—to step in and deal with anyone liable to upset the meticulous planning that had been prepared. Testarov hoped that his people could deal with the situation quickly and efficiently, without making a mess such as the local fanatics who had bungled the assassination attempt on the Americans had made.

On the other hand, Testarov realized, the call could be nothing more than a calculated bluff. Designed to do just what it had done. Scare the inside man into making some kind of incriminating move so he could be taken out of the game.

On reflection, whichever was the true story, something needed to be done. The Americans had been the catalyst for everything bad that had occurred from the moment they had landed. It was also true that they had been in contact with Milligan. The one-armed man, now Testarov's prisoner, had been with the security officer prior to his capture.

How deep their knowledge was of the Philippine situation Testarov was not sure. But of one thing he was certain—he could not afford to allow these Americans to meddle further. Whether by deduction or pure chance, they might come across something of vital importance. Something that might lead them to Testarov himself. Or to Castillo. Perhaps even to the band of mercenaries led by Cam Remsberg, waiting on their island for the signal to launch the attacks that would plunge the Philippines into revolutionary chaos.

Leoni Testarov had made his decision, instructing his informant to leave the embassy and join the Morkrie Dela agents staking out the embassy. They would follow Jack Milligan when he left the embassy to meet the man called Rawlinson. The Morkrie Dela agents were equipped with walkie-talkies, and through these they would be able to communicate with the additional members of the team Testarov had sent from their safe house.

Testarov's instructions to his men, before they left the house, had been simple. When they joined up with their comrades and reached the meeting place, they were to attempt to capture Rawlinson and anyone with him. Milligan, too, had to be taken alive, if possible. If there was any resistance, the Americans were to be eliminated. On no account were they to be allowed to escape alive. If the matter had to be resolved by killing, the embassy informer was to be eliminated, as well. It would be taking too much of a risk to allow him to go free. He knew too much, could identify too many people. It was not good practice to leave loose ends lying around, Testarov believed.

With all that arranged, the KGB man had made his way upstairs to the room where his prisoner was being guarded. He had been looking forward to meeting the man. When he had first gone to speak with him the previous evening the prisoner had still been unconscious. Then the team's medical man had looked him over and pronounced that he was in stable condition but probably suffering from a mild concussion, and would be better left till morning.

Testarov had enjoyed the sweetness of anticipation during much of the restless night. And now, finally, what a pleasant surprise it was to hear the one-armed man say "I'll save you the trouble" in perfect Russian.

Testarov smiled, inclining his head in admiration. "You speak my language well," he said. "Of course you also speak fluent French and Hebrew. English obviously. And you can also communicate quite well in Arabic. Am I correct—Yakov Katzenelenbogen?"

If Katz was surprised by the Russian's knowledge, he didn't show it. He simply raised a hand to acknowledge the facts.

"Quite correct, Major Leoni Testarov of the KGB, at this moment in time commanding a unit of Morkrie Dela."

Testarov laughed. "Very good," he said. "There is so much I want to know about you that our files do not show. And about your comrades. Although we have built up a dossier on your little group, there is much we haven't yet been able to fill in.''

Katz managed a smile. ''Save your breath if you expect me to help. I won't tell you a damn thing.''

''Of course,'' Testarov said. ''We both know you have to say that. We also know I have to have that information. You see, your group has caused us a great deal of embarrassment during the past few years. Moscow has issued a directive to the effect that you and your group must be eliminated. While my admiration for you as fighting men is genuine, as enemies of the Soviet Union you are detested. Heads have rolled because of the mounting toll of Soviet personnel killed by your group. Do you realize the vast sums of money wasted through operations being destroyed by your infernal interference?''

''Major Testarov,'' Katz said evenly, ''I don't give a damn how much money the USSR has lost. Or how many men. What do you expect the West to do? Just sit back and let you poison the world with your evil? Ignore the mischief you cause? The misery and suffering? As long as I'm able, I'll do everything in my power to combat you and your fanatics.''

''You may find that difficult to manage from a prison cell in Moscow,'' Testarov said glibly.

''You haven't got me there yet.''

''Give me time.'' Testarov glanced at his watch. ''In a while, you may have some of your comrades to keep you company.''

''They might not be as easy to take as I was.''

''We will know soon enough,'' the Russian said. ''Very soon, indeed!''

17

The sound of the approaching car reached the ears of the waiting Phoenix commandos. McCarter glanced at his wristwatch. Almost twenty minutes had passed since he had parked the Blazer. As the Briton sat upright, dropping his hand over the Ingram resting on his lap, he glanced through the windshield.

A light blue Ford nosed around the corner of an empty warehouse. The license plate showed the number Jack Milligan had given McCarter during their telephone conversation the previous evening.

"Heads up," McCarter muttered.

"I hope we haven't been wasting our time," Calvin James said.

"I've got a feeling our embassy rat has swallowed the bait," McCarter persisted.

"Does this ability of yours to see into the future tell whether he'll be alone or if he'll have company?" James quipped.

McCarter smiled without saying a word.

"I hate it when you do that," James muttered.

The blue Ford cruised across the warehouse loading area and stopped several yards from the Blazer.

Jack Milligan raised a hand to indicate that he had seen the Phoenix pair. He gave a thumbs-up sign, which

McCarter took to mean that the security man *had* been followed from the embassy.

Milligan's signal was confirmed less than two minutes later. A gray Dodge wagon appeared and came to a slithering halt on the far side of the area.

"I count six," James said.

"So do I," McCarter agreed.

The Dodge's doors swung open, disgorging its passengers. Five of the six were hefty, grim-faced individuals who looked as if they had been poured from the same mold. Clad in identical lightweight suits, each carried an Uzi SMG.

The sixth man, shorter than the others by some inches, was a lean Filipino with a gaunt face. When he moved he limped badly, favoring his left leg.

"If those blokes aren't Morkrie Dela," McCarter said, "then I'm a monkey's uncle."

Jack Milligan opened his door and stepped out of the Ford, his hands empty and in plain sight.

"Do we have business?" the security man asked.

One of the Russians stepped forward. He pointed at the Blazer.

"You two get out. You will all come with us."

As he spoke, the Morkrie Dela agent gestured and his companions began to spread out, their weapons covering Milligan and the Phoenix pair.

McCarter eased the catch on his door, pushing it open slowly. On the opposite side of the Blazer James did the same. Both Phoenix warriors held their SMGs at their sides.

"You will surrender," the Soviet demanded.

McCarter glanced at James. The black commando shook his head ever so slightly. Switching his gaze to

Milligan, the tough cockney caught the silent no that the security man mouthed.

"Throw down your weapons," the Russian ordered.

"No way!" Calvin James said loudly. "You get rid of yours."

The Morkrie Dela leader swung his head in James's direction. "*Chernozhopy,* you can die first then."

The Russian word for nigger did not upset Calvin James. He had been called worse things. What it did do was galvanize the Chicago warrior into action.

James took a quick dive toward the ground.

A split second later the Russian's Uzi chattered loudly as it released a long burst of 9 mm autofire. The hot slugs peppered the side of the Blazer, puncturing the body.

The Soviet's opening salvo was the signal for the other Morkrie Dela agents to open fire.

As 9 mm slugs crisscrossed the area, both McCarter and Milligan ducked for cover.

Dropping to a crouch beside the Blazer, McCarter ignored the bullets whacking the nearby concrete. Now that the situation had erupted into total combat, McCarter shook off the casual air he usually presented to the world and became his true self.

The tall fox-faced cockney from London's East End was a natural fighter. McCarter had learned early in life that he was never going to be satisfied with a regular nine-to-five job. There was a need burning inside David McCarter that could be satisfied only by danger and excitement. McCarter found both when he joined the army. He craved action like some men crave drugs. He also found he had an aptitude for the military life. He enjoyed being around machines and weapons, and quickly became an expert with anything presented to him. His world seemed almost perfect when he was accepted by the SAS and subsequently saw service in many parts of the world. One of McCarter's personal triumphs was to be part of the SAS team that initiated the action that ended the siege of the Iranian embassy in London in 1980. That had been a triumph for McCarter, but being asked to join Phoenix Force was a dream come true.

Twisting his lean body around the front of the Blazer, McCarter picked his target, bringing his MAC-10 into play. The Brit's finger stroked the Ingram's trigger. A short burst of 9 mm slugs caught a Morkrle Dela agent in the chest and slammed him to the concrete with brutal finality.

Almost in the same instant, one of the Soviets triggered his Uzi in McCarter's direction. A couple of the slugs snatched at the sleeve of his jacket.

Before the enemy could reaim or McCarter could respond, Jack Milligan triggered two shots from the big .357 Desert Eagle he had produced from under his jacket. The powerful slugs struck the Soviet in the side of the head, knocking him off his feet. He landed awkwardly, spilling blood onto the concrete, dying in silent agony while the firefight raged around him.

The moment he had hit the concrete, Calvin James twisted his long body, bringing his Uzi into play. The black Phoenix pro angled the Israeli SMG up at the Morkrie Dela leader who had just attempted to take him out.

The Russian had tracked James's dive with his weapon. He was about to trigger a second burst when James opened up. A stream of hot 9 mm lead burned into the Russian's body, causing extreme pain and severe shock. Still triggering his weapon, the Russian sent a blast of autofire into the Blazer. Windows shattered as the 9 mm slugs struck.

The two remaining Morkrie Dela assassins were contemplating a strategic retreat when another car roared into view and screeched to a dust-swirling stop beside the first Morkrie Dela vehicle. Doors burst open and a half-dozen armed agents entered the fight.

The newcomers were hastily waved into position by the surviving Morkrie Dela pair.

Watching the new arrivals, McCarter broke away from the side of the Blazer and sought cover beside Milligan's car. This gave him a clearer field of fire. The impetuous Briton engaged two of the new arrivals as they sprinted in his direction, firing as they ran.

The Russians sprayed the area with bullets but did little damage. Their Uzi SMGs were capable of quickly exhausting vast amounts of ammunition. Within its limits, the weapon was also fairly accurate, but trying to hit a target with one of the subguns while on the run—with the weapon jerking from side to side—was extremely difficult.

McCarter had none of these problems. He was in a stationary position, able to direct his aim with precision. When *he* pulled the Ingram's trigger, the weapon released its 9 mm flesh-shredders with deadly accuracy. The scything blast drove hot slugs into the Soviets' bodies, halting their forward motion and knocking them off balance. The light suits the Morkrie Dela assassins were wearing suddenly blossomed with flowers of fresh blood. Kicking and writhing, the fatally wounded Russians crashed to the ground, out of the firefight and soon out of life.

While McCarter was dispatching the two Morkrie Dela agents, Calvin James found himself at the receiving end of a three-pronged attack. The black ex-cop faced his adversaries with his usual calm, bringing his Uzi in line with a motion that was so smooth it looked almost lazy.

His first blast shot the legs out from under the leader of the trio, dumping him bloody and screaming to the concrete. One of the Soviet Uzis stuttered out its melody of hate, bullets zinging close to James's head. Ducking below the level of the Blazer's front fender, James triggered his SMG again. The Uzi crackled briefly then snapped empty.

Aware that he had only seconds before the remaining Russians had him in their sights again, James dropped the Uzi and snatched the holstered Beretta 92-SB from its resting place. Slipping off the safety, James gripped the autoloader in both hands, rose above the hood of the Blazer, snap-aimed and fired.

His first 9 mm projectile caught the closest Russian just under the jaw, angling up through the Soviet's mouth and into his brain. The Morkrie Dela agent ran on for a couple of yards before his legs stopped functioning and he melted to the ground.

After his first shot, James swung the Beretta's smoking muzzle onto the third Russian. This guy kept right on coming, his angular face taut with a mixture of rage and wild defiance. The Soviet's SMG spat flame as the enemy clamped down on the trigger and kept it down. Slugs whacked the Blazer's hood, clanging off the metal. One burned a thin, stinging line across James's right cheek, but the Phoenix warrior stood his ground and held his target.

James pulled the trigger twice in rapid succession. The first shot took a ragged chunk out of the top of the Russian's left shoulder, spinning him off balance. The second shot drove into the target's chest, puncturing his heart. The agent collapsed.

Milligan had traded a couple of shots with one of the Morkrie Dela agents, and though not hitting the man, Milligan was able to keep the guy under cover.

The security officer from the embassy had something else—in fact, *someone* else—on his mind.

That someone was José Santos. The middle-aged Filipino was the embassy janitor. He looked after the toilets and washrooms. Saw to it that fresh towels were available. Kept floors clean and performed a range of mundane tasks. He was a quiet, introspective individual who went about his daily routine in almost total silence. He was in the embassy every day, yet appeared so innocuous that he was hardly noticed. Santos had been involved in an automobile accident in his teens. Though he had survived, his left hip and leg had been badly smashed, leaving him with a permanent limp and an inner bitterness against life.

Now that he had the informer's identity Jack Milligan felt both relieved and angry. The relief was for the fact that the leak had been plugged. The security man's anger was directed mainly toward himself. On the one hand, the informer had been right under his nose. Milligan saw him every working day at the embassy, yet never associated him with the leak. Santos had become a part of the embassy, almost blending in with the fixtures and fittings.

Apparently, Milligan had neglected one of the basic rules of security, the need to look for the commonplace—the person so blatantly obvious that he or she just couldn't be the security risk. Santos had been that person, and Jack Milligan had overlooked him. Milligan's laxity had allowed the opposition to mount the

attack at the airport. Worse, this lapse had resulted in
Daniel Baum being kidnapped. If anything happened
to him, Milligan was going to feel plenty guilty. Upon
spotting the Filipino, Jack Milligan had made up his
mind not to allow the informer to escape.

Santos had remained beside the car he came in,
crouching behind an open door. The informer was unable to move because of the firefight, but he was obviously growing increasingly agitated as his Soviet
companions began to fall.

Still triggering their weapons, the surviving three
Morkrie Dela assassins retreated.

McCarter and James broke from cover, challenging
the Russians head on.

Gripping his Beretta with two hands, James dropped
one of the Soviets with a head shot, flipping the guy
back against the hood of the Dodge.

McCarter snapped a fresh magazine into his Ingram,
then stepped out to face the Morkrie Dela agents. He
arced the MAC-10's muzzle around and punched a line
of bloody holes across the broad chest of one of the remaining pair.

The last of the Soviet agents, aware of his fragile position, nevertheless remembered Leoni Testarov's directive not to allow the Americans to take Santos alive.

Knowing that his own life hung in the balance, the
Morkrie Dela killer swung around his Uzi to locate the
cowering figure of the Filipino informer.

As the Russian set his eyes on Santos, the Filipino
realized what the man was about to do. He threw out his
hands in a gesture of supplication, his lips forming
words of a prayer he had not uttered for years.

Jack Milligan, recognizing the situation for what it
was, ran forward. He lined up the Desert Eagle, trig-

gering a quick shot that took a bloody lump out of the Russian's left arm.

The Morkrie Dela assassin slumped against the Dodge, blood spilling from his wound down the fender. Despite the pain, he held on to the Uzi, still trying to bring it to bear on Santos, who was now curled up in a ball, whimpering like a beaten dog.

"Son of a bitch!" Milligan growled at the Russian's refusal to go down.

The .357's black muzzle centered on the agent again. This time Milligan kept right on firing, sending slug after slug crashing into the Soviet's body. The guy uttered a long yell of agony. His body twisted under the impact of the big slugs and he slithered along the Dodge. When he hit the concrete he stopped, and did not move again, save for one blood-streaked hand twitching momentarily.

Standing over the crouching form of José Santos with his Desert Eagle trained on the informer, Jack Milligan prodded the man with the toe of his shoe.

"Up on your feet, Santos. Make one wrong move and I'll finish what your Russian buddy started to do. Come on! Move it, pal!"

McCarter and James joined the security man.

"Bugger me if he doesn't look like a little rat," the blunt-spoken Briton remarked.

"Give me some time," Milligan said, "and we'll see if he can squeal like one."

"First thing we'd better do is get the hell out of here," James pointed out. "One thing we don't need is the local law breathing down our necks."

"They'll get here eventually," Milligan said, "but they'll take their time. Cops don't like dragging down to this area too quickly. It isn't their favorite beat."

"Next question," McCarter said. "Where do we go?"

"No problem," Milligan responded. "There's a safe house in the city. We maintain it for just this sort of situation."

"Let's go," James said.

"You ride with Milligan," McCarter suggested. "Keep a close watch on our chum."

James nodded. He followed Milligan to the embassy's Ford. The security man climbed behind the wheel. James prodded Santos, now sullen and showing some resistance, into the back.

When Milligan pulled away, McCarter fell in behind. As he maneuvered the Blazer out of the warehouse area, he wondered if Encizo and Manning had also come up with something.

One way or another, the cockney rebel decided, the ball was truly rolling. All they could do now was wait and see where it would bounce next.

18

Mahmud drew his jeepney to a halt at the curb, the tires rolling over the trash that lay in the gutters. He pointed along the busy back street to where a faded sign protruded from the upper story of a building.

"That's the place. The Star Hotel."

"It'll never get a mention in Fodor's guide," Encizo remarked.

Gary Manning smiled at the Cuban's words. This was the third hotel they had visited. The morning had been spent checking out the others, both of which had been similar in quality to this one. The visits had gained them nothing but grumbles and dark scowls from the proprietors of the seedy establishments. Their lack of helpfulness was obviously deliberate, as if they'd been primed to ward off strangers seeking information. Sensing the antagonism, Manning and Encizo had been left with growing frustration.

"This is a real sleazy street dive," Manning said, casting his eyes over the hotel frontage. It was flanked by an equally grubby bar on one side and what looked like an abandoned store on the other. The street itself, near the waterfront, was crowded with people. Mingled odors from numerous eating places drifted in the hot air. Cars and trucks hooted and crashed gears as they lurched and swerved along the busy thoroughfare. Down the street market stalls spilled out into the road.

"I thought the others were bad enough," Encizo commented.

"This is about as low as you can get without renting a basement," Mahmud remarked.

Manning glanced at the Bajau. "Now I know why you and McCarter get on so well," the Canadian said. "You both have the same lousy sense of humor."

The Phoenix pair clambered out of the jeepney.

"Hey," Mahmud called. "Take care."

Manning raised a hand as he followed Encizo across the busy street. They threaded through the crowds until they reached the entrance to the Star.

"You set?" Manning asked his Cuban partner.

"As much as I'll ever be."

They stepped inside, eyes adjusting to the semi-gloom after the bright street. The lobby of the hotel was stale and dusty. The odors of cooking and bad plumbing hung in the air.

A large Oriental-looking man behind the reception desk looked up from the newspaper spread out on the desk in front of him as the Phoenix pair entered.

"You looking for rooms?" he asked. His tone implied that he didn't care one way or the other whether the two strangers wanted rooms.

Manning shook his head.

"We're looking for some friends of ours. Heard they stayed here about a week back. Maybe a little longer."

"You don't sound too sure," the man said. He scratched his unshaven chin. "Just how well do you know these friends of yours?"

"Well enough," Encizo said.

"I don't think I can help you," the man stated flatly.

"We haven't asked you anything yet," Manning said.

The big man stood upright. His powerful chest threatened to burst the buttons on his tight shirt. So did the bulge of his large stomach where it hung over his trousers.

"I run a hotel, not a goddamn information bureau. Would you mind getting out of here? *Now?*"

"Not until we get some answers," Encizo snapped. He was fed up with being given the run-around at every hotel they visited.

"Yeah?" the big man snarled. "I'll give you answers, you asshole!"

He came lunging from behind the desk, wielding a thick wooden club he kept hidden in case of trouble.

Encizo stepped back, balancing on his left foot as the guy made a swing. The thick bat slashed the air beside his head. Pivoting his upper body, Encizo reached out with strong hands to catch the big man's arm and the collar of his shirt. Stepping in close against the guy, turning hip against thigh, Encizo executed a classic *seoie-nage* hip throw. As with most throws in judo, the defender uses the attacker's own momentum and body weight to do the work for him. In this instance it propelled the big man through the air and slammed him against the lobby wall.

Encizo followed the guy down, straddled his chest, crossed his wrists over the man's throat and took hold of his shirt collar on both sides. Then he put on the pressure, the insides of his fists compressing the carotid artery and the pneumogastric nerve, which stops blood circulating to the brain and causes spasmodic contractions of heart, lungs and diaphragm. Depending on the severity of pressure and the duration of the stranglehold, simple fainting can be induced, or death.

The big man struggled briefly, then lapsed into a state of semiconsciousness as Encizo applied more pressure.

Concerned about the noise the guy had made in falling, Gary Manning pulled his Walther P-5 from its underarm holster. His back to the wall, the broad-shouldered Canadian scanned the lobby for any signs of life.

Bending over the big man, Encizo waited patiently for him to come around. The guy opened his eyes, gulping air. He stared up at Encizo and made to get up. All Encizo had to do was reapply the pressure. When he saw the man slipping away again, he slackened off.

"Get the idea, my friend?" the Cuban asked. "I can do this all day. The trouble is, each time I do it I get a little more careless, until one time I squeeze too hard and you are *dead*!"

"What do you want?"

"Just a few answers to a few simple questions," Encizo said.

"What?"

"About eight, nine days back, more or less, you had six Americans staying here. Just for a couple of days. Remember?"

"Sure. They were here two days exactly. That's all I know."

"The hell it is," Encizo snapped. "Amigo, you'd better start to remember, and do it now."

To emphasize his point Encizo used his judo stranglehold to jog the big man's memory.

"Okay! Okay!" the guy gasped. "What do you want to know?"

"Where did they go when they checked out?"

"I don't know. And that's the truth." The man dragged air into his heaving lungs. "They stayed for two days, then paid their bill and left."

"They have any visitors? Telephone calls?"

"No visitors. No calls. They didn't do much of anything. Just hung around."

"Come on," Encizo demanded. "I need more than that."

The big guy's eyes flickered nervously. He seemed about to speak, then changed his mind.

"Well?" Encizo asked. "Say it. There's something you haven't told me."

The man stared into Encizo's eyes and must have seen the threat there. Whatever he recognized, it affected him.

"One of them asked about a boat."

"What sort?"

"Just a cabin cruiser. They wanted to rent one to go fishing."

"And?"

"I told them to try Mako's down on the jetty."

Encizo threw a glance in Manning's direction. The Canadian nodded, as if to say, *at least it's something.*

At that moment there was an angry yell from the far end of the lobby and a group of men burst into view.

"Company!" Manning called.

Pushing to his feet, Encizo turned in time to face the oncoming men.

There was no time to make a break for the door. The attackers were already on the Phoenix pair.

As the men advanced Encizo saw that there were five of them, all yelling wildly and flailing the air with wooden clubs.

Encizo ducked under the slashing club of the first attacker, then hammered his right foot deep into the guy's groin. The would-be hardguy folded up with a scream and crashed to the floor, clutching at his injured testicles.

Encizo turned to another thug who was lunging at him with a snarl. His thick club missed Encizo's head by inches. The Cuban powerhouse knocked the club aside, then delivered a stunning blow with his fist to the clubber's nose. Bone collapsed and blood spurted from the crushed nose. Before the guy could defend himself, Encizo struck him again. This time a sledging right caught the guy's jaw and snapped his head around. Thrown off balance, the thug was unprepared when Encizo snatched the club from his hand. The Cuban swung the heavy stick against the guy's head, driving him to the floor.

As Encizo was downing his first attacker, Gary Manning had launched himself at the thug closest to him. Still holding his P-5 automatic, Manning used the weapon as a makeshift club. Ducking under the first swing of his attacker, Manning slashed out backhandedly with the P-5. The hard metal caught the thug across the side of the jaw, tearing open the flesh in a burst of red. The dazed guy stumbled past Manning, who slammed the butt of the P-5 down on his skull.

Something hard connected with Manning's left shoulder. Pain flared, making the Canadian gasp. He instinctively dropped into a crouch, sensing the closeness of his attacker, and twisted his body around to meet the thug's next lunge. The Filipino's dark face loomed above Manning while his arm lowered the club toward the Phoenix warrior's head. Manning rolled back, breaking his fall with his left hand. His legs swept around, kicking the Filipino's feet from under him and dumping him hard on the floor. Even as the thug was going down, Manning sprang to his feet. He was already turning as the Filipino tried to rise. Manning's right foot shot out, the toe of his shoe cracking against the thug's jaw. The Filipino smashed back against the floor.

The remaining thug, already committed, drove in at Encizo, his club whipsawing back and forth. The Cuban waited for his moment, then struck. He reached out, caught the thug's wrist and twisted the arm. Swinging in toward the Filipino, he brought the club arm over his shoulder. The thug gave a pained yell as he felt the pressure on his arm, the pulling against the joint. He threw his other arm around Encizo's neck in an attempt to stop the pain. Encizo put more pressure on the already creaking joint. Bone cracked and the thug screamed. He slumped to the floor, moaning softly, gripping his broken arm close to his body.

"You get the feeling they were expecting us?" Manning asked.

"Yeah."

Encizo glanced down at the big man, who was still on the floor, hunched up against the wall.

"If we had the time," the Cuban said, "I'd like to find out who tipped these guys off."

"We can always come back," Manning said.

Encizo smiled. "I might do just that."

Manning put away his P-5. "Let's get out of here before we meet any more of the guests."

The Phoenix pair walked slowly from the hotel. The street carried on its normal business. The noise outside had drowned the sound of conflict in the hotel.

Mahmud saw them coming and started the jeepney. As soon as Manning and Encizo were settled inside, he eased away from the curb.

"Where to now?" he asked.

"Boat charter business on the jetty," Manning said. "Company called Mako's. You heard of it?"

"Only that it's a little on the shady side," Mahmud said. "Does that fit?"

Encizo nodded. "Sounds exactly right."

"Mako's it is, then," Mahmud answered cheerfully.

"Don't park too close," Manning suggested. "Drop us off and we'll walk in."

"You think somebody might be waiting for us?" Encizo asked.

"I'm damned certain they will be," the Canadian replied.

19

Boats of all shapes and sizes were moored along the jetty, rocking gently in the swell of the harbor. Various establishments, set back from the water, catered to the nautical trade. These included an open-fronted shed where minor repairs to marine engines could be carried out and where spare parts were stored.

The office of Mako Boat Charter was above the repair shop. The frontage needed paint; the old paint had faded over the years and was peeling from the bleached boards. The appearance of the business as a whole was one of neglect and untidiness.

Mahmud drove past the place and carried on along the jetty. He parked in front of an empty shed with a sign stating that the place was up for rent.

"Hey, you didn't tell me," Mahmud asked. "Did you guys have any trouble at the hotel?"

"A slight disagreement with a few of the owner's friends," Encizo explained.

"I'll keep the engine running," the Bajau said. "In case you need a quick getaway."

Manning and Encizo picked up the canvas bags holding their heavier weapons as they exited the jeepney.

"If anything heavy goes down, you stay clear," Manning warned.

The Phoenix warriors strolled along the jetty, looking like tourists out to see the sights. The only sights they were looking for were those indicating trouble. The way things were beginning to look, it seemed that the opposition was doing its best to block any moves Phoenix Force might make.

The more Manning and Encizo thought about it, the more convinced they were that the thugs at the Star *had* been waiting for them. Somebody obviously wanted to show them that they were not as secure as they imagined themselves to be.

As they approached the repair shop, Encizo turned to Manning. "How do we handle this one?" he asked. "Go in nice and polite and wait for the boot in the balls? Or kick the door down and scare the shit out of them?"

"Well, we went in the last place nice and polite, but still ended up in a brawl," Manning pointed out. "Maybe we should play the hardass from the start. Could save time."

As it happened the matter would soon decide itself.

They were almost at the top of the wooden stairs running up the front of the building when the howl of a hard-driven car reached their ears. Glancing around, they saw a dark sedan careening along the jetty, scattering people on all sides. A second car was close behind. Both vehicles screeched to a halt yards from the bottom of the stairs. Doors flew open and armed men jumped from the vehicles.

"You two on the stairs," yelled one of the men from the lead car. "Throw down your weapons, then raise your hands."

"What gives you the right to say that?" Manning challenged.

"We're from the ISAFP," the man stated. "You are wanted for questioning."

The ISAFP was the military arm of the Philippine secret-police network. On the Force's previous visit to the country they had clashed on a number of occasions with the Metropolitan Command Intelligence Service—known as Metrocom. The Metrocom squads had proved to be ruthless and trigger-happy, and Manning and Encizo had no reason to believe these ISAFP members would be any different.

One thing was certain—the Phoenix commandos had no intention of allowing themselves to be taken into custody by members of the secret police.

"Those mothers look like they're just itching to start shooting," Encizo muttered.

"I get the same impression," Manning said.

"Well," Encizo observed, "there's only one way for us from here, and that's up."

"It's going to give us the opportunity to see whether we can run faster than those guys can pull a trigger."

"Either surrender or we start shooting," the ISAFP leader called. "Make your choice."

"Go!" Manning said to Encizo.

The Phoenix aces broke into a run that took them up the last few steps to the small landing at the head of the stairs. There was no opportunity to observe the niceties of life—like opening a door by its handle. Gary Manning drove his powerful shoulder against the door and smashed it open, falling to his knees as he went through. Right behind him, Encizo barely avoided tripping over his Canadian partner.

The Phoenix pair had not fully entered the office when the ISAFP squad opened fire, raking the front of the office with a sustained blast of SMG fire. Bullets thudded against the planking, tearing off long splinters. Other shots put bullets through the windows, showering the interior of the office with flying glass. Dust, dislodged from the rafters, misted the air. After a few seconds of silence the autofire began again, riddling the office with bullet holes.

By this time the Phoenix pros were on the floor of the office.

Manning pulled open the zipper on his canvas bag and dragged out the SA80. A few feet away, his back against a desk, Encizo was giving his MP-5 a swift check.

Someone moved at the rear of the office. Encizo twisted around in time to see a dark figure rising from behind a double-fronted filing cabinet. It was a man dressed in a grubby T-shirt and jeans. His black hair was thickly greased and his face was covered in a scraggly beard.

What held Encizo's attention in particular was the hefty .45-caliber Colt automatic pistol in the man's hand. He extended his arm in Encizo's direction and triggered a wild shot. The blast of the .45 was deafening in the confines of the office. Encizo felt the wind of the bullet as it whizzed past his face and ripped a chunk of wood from a table across the room.

Skirting along the length of the desk, Encizo peered around the edge. The guy wielding the .45 was still staring in the same direction. Smoke issued from the black muzzle of the Colt automatic.

Aware of their delicate situation, Encizo realized there was not a great deal of time to play with. He made a decision and acted on it without further thought.

Raising the MP-5, the Cuban triggered a stream of 9 mm slugs in the general direction of the guy with the .45. The SMG chatter rattled around the office. The guy on the receiving end of the volley gave a startled cry and ducked as splinters of wood filled the air around him.

As the guy lowered his head, Encizo kicked away from cover and made a dash for the hunched figure. He was crouching beside the guy when the bearded gunman lifted his head. All Encizo had to do was press the warm muzzle of the MP-5 against the thug's head.

"Your choice," Encizo said softly. "Live or die."

The .45 dropped from the guy's fingers and clattered on the floor. He turned his head and stared into Encizo's face. "Don't kill me!"

Encizo recognized a plea from the heart when he heard it. The guy might have been ready to kill the two Phoenix commandos, but he drew the line when it came to losing his own skin. Which was the way with most people—excepting fanatics who consider it the most honorable way to further their cause. Given a choice, no sane man or woman would view death so casually.

"You knew we were coming?" Encizo asked sternly, making the guy believe the answers he gave would decide his fate.

"I was warned you might come—you were asking questions about the Americans who hired one of my boats."

"Who called the ISAFP?"

"It must have been the one who spoke to me by telephone. He said there would be people who would deal with you."

"Hey," Manning called from one of the shattered windows, "our friends down there are starting to move."

As if to emphasize the Canadian's warning, a burst of autofire peppered the front of the office. Window glass exploded inward, showering the interior with glittering shards. On the back wall of the office a framed photograph was hit. It bounced from the wall.

Through the open door Manning saw that a trio of ISAFP heavies had broken away from the main group. They had sprinted across the jetty toward the wooden stairs, and now, under the cover of the autofire from their partners, were climbing the stairs.

Manning swept the SA80 into position and triggered a short burst of 5.56 mm rounds. It caught the first of the ISAFP men in the left shoulder as he appeared near the top of the stairs. The police agent spun backwards, losing his balance. He crashed back downstairs, taking one of his companions with him. The surviving man ducked below the level of the top stair, frantically waving to his team on the ground to give him more covering fire.

"Is there a back way out of here?" Encizo demanded of his captive.

The guy shook his head. Sweat glistened on his brown face. He obviously hadn't anticipated this violent turn of events.

More gunfire erupted from the ISAFP squad on the jetty, and gouged holes in the walls and ceiling.

"This is getting hairy," Manning remarked. "For once I'd be glad to see that mad cockney and have him come up with one of his crazy schemes."

"Amen to that," Encizo agreed. "We damn well need something to come down out of the sky and . . ."

Manning caught Encizo's eye. He knew exactly what the Cuban was thinking.

"Do you think . . . ?"

Encizo shrugged. "What do we have to lose?"

Manning returned to the front of the office where he could keep an eye on the police squad.

"Turn over," Encizo ordered his captive. Puzzled, the man obeyed. Encizo unbuckled the guy's belt and dragged it from the loops in his jeans. Then he made him lie on his face again and put his hands behind his back. Looping the belt over the guy's wrists, Encizo secured his hands tightly.

"Be smart and stay there," Encizo warned him. "Because I'm going to be damn close."

Reaching up, Encizo grabbed the telephone and pulled it down to the floor. He dialed the number to the Special Operations Room at Clark Field. Information had been fed to the SOR regarding a top-priority operation and they knew what to expect. Encizo gave his cover name; that was enough to have him connected with the SOR administration officer handling the Stony Man operation.

"What can I do for you?" the taut voice asked.

"We need Dragon Slayer. Urgent," Encizo said.

"One moment," the voice requested.

Encizo couldn't hold back a smile. If the guy had been aware of the situation he would have realized how ridiculous his request was.

Bullets were still thudding into the front of the office, smacking against the back wall.

Manning was trading shots with the ISAFP squad, keeping them from rushing the stairs. It was nothing more than a holding operation. Eventually the secret police would rush the building and all hell would break loose.

"Hey, buddy, you in trouble again?" The familiar voice of Jack Grimaldi reached Encizo's ear.

"And how!" Encizo answered. "We didn't know whether you'd arrived yet."

"The flyboys landed me here two hours back. Soon as we got the lady unloaded I had her fueled up. Been waiting for your call."

"We're calling now, and we need a diversion," Encizo said.

"What's the situation?" Grimaldi asked.

"Somebody put a squad of the local spooks onto us," Encizo said. "Got us between a rock and a hard place, with no back door."

"Where?"

"Manila North Harbor area. A jetty where local charter boats are based. Be a couple of cars parked on the jetty with a bunch of guys shooting holes in a building signposted Mako Boat Charter."

"I'm on my way," Grimaldi said. "I'm just over fifty miles away. Should be with you in twenty minutes. Fifteen if I can do it. How many of you for pickup?"

"Just me and Callender."

"Hang in there, guys."

The line went dead. Encizo stared at the receiver in his hand, barely able to believe the conversation he'd just had. It seemed too easy to be true. But he knew he hadn't been dreaming.

Grimaldi and Dragon Slayer were coming.

"Over here," Manning called urgently. "On the double, partner."

Encizo joined him at the front of the office.

"They're up to something," Manning said. "Four of them went off along the jetty, then cut around the end of the block."

"They can't be trying for a back-door shot 'cause there isn't one," Encizo pointed out.

Manning considered the options open to the ISAFP men. He gave a grunt of annoyance. "No back door," he agreed. "But what about the roof?"

He indicated a glass skylight.

"They can pick us off easy from up there," the Cuban said.

"Not if we see them first," Manning exclaimed. "Did you reach Jack?"

Encizo nodded. "He needs fifteen, twenty minutes to reach us."

"Then we'd better see he gets it."

ISAFP guns opened up again as men broke away from the cover of the two cars for the stairs. A hail of bullets struck the front of the building, splintering more woodwork and knocking the last slivers of glass from the window frames.

Manning and Encizo returned fire, pinning a number of the secret police behind their cars. At the distance that was separating the two parties, accurate speed-shooting was not to be expected.

After a few minutes the firing slackened off.

"They're playing for time," Manning said. "Keeping us occupied while they get their boys on the roof."

"It'll help us," Encizo added. "Longer they stall, the closer Dragon Slayer gets."

Encizo watched the stairs while Manning scanned the jetty below. For a while nothing seemed to be happening.

A lone ISAFP gunman, for some reason believing he could reach the open office door before the two suspects could react, leapt into view at the head of the stairs. He carried a blazing Uzi in his hands, the muzzle swinging back and forth as he raked the entrance to the office.

A hail of slugs ripped through the air, chewing an office chair to tatters.

Encizo's MP-5 drove a wedge of 9 mm bullets into the reckless guy's chest. The agent staggered back into the rail at the top of the landing and plunged from sight. His body hit the jetty some twenty feet below with a sickening crunch.

"Trouble with these guys is they don't expect to be fired back at," Manning said.

The squad retreated for a hurried council of war.

"Their usual victims are dragged from bed in the middle of the night," Encizo remarked. He had experienced terror tactics in his native Cuba when Castro's regime had installed itself. The Cuban's beloved country changed to an island ruled by the brutal tyranny and terror of Castro's secret police. The memories of that time, forever etched in Rafael Encizo's brain, were one of the reasons he had dedicated himself to fight endlessly against such dark forces.

One of the goons went to a car and opened the trunk. The agent took out a stubby weapon and loaded a canister into its thick barrel.

"Tear gas," Manning warned as the man moved forward and took aim.

The gas gun fired a projectile toward the office. Fortunately, the operator had incorrectly judged the acute angle. The gas canister struck the edge of the landing, and bounced back down, exploding in a burst of white mist that began to drift away from the building. The light breeze coming inland from the ocean helped to pull the tear gas clear of the office.

Some of the drifting CS gas enveloped the ISAFP men concealed partway up the stairs. They began to cough as the gas affected their breathing and caused a terrible stinging in their eyes.

As the gas drifted away, Manning saw that the guy was loading another canister into the gas gun for a second try.

"No way," Manning muttered.

The Force's sharpshooter, the Canadian could take out targets at exceptional distances. Kneeling just inside the open doorway, Manning shouldered the SA80, utilizing the weapon's SUSAT optical sighting system. Manning acquired his target, held for a second, then triggered two quick rounds. The projectiles knocked the target to the ground, and a patch of red spread across his shirt front. As he struck the ground, the agent's finger closed against the trigger of the gas gun, blasting its load across the jetty. It hit the front of a parked car, spewing a thick cloud of noxious mist over the area, causing confusion among the assembled ISAFP agents.

One threat was removed, albeit briefly, only to be replaced by another.

Keeping an eye open for the rooftop attack group, Rafael Encizo picked up the faint sound of creaking wood. The Cuban moved across the office, studying the building's sloping roof. He caught another soft creak and noticed some pale dust sift down from between two overlapping roof boards. Glancing at the skylight, Encizo spotted a flickering shadow fall across the glass then hurriedly jerk back.

"Too damn late," Encizo murmured.

He angled the MP-5's muzzle up at the roof, judging where the agents might be standing, and pulled the trigger. A stream of 9 mm slugs ripped through the roof boards.

A man screamed in agony. There was a thump as a body crashed against the boards.

Encizo fired again, drawing a figure eight. Sunlight lanced through holes opened by the rounds.

Footsteps pounded across the roof as the attackers spread.

And then an automatic weapon began to fire, blasting splinters of wood from the boards as the bullets zipped down into the office.

Holding his ground, Encizo returned fire, locating his target by the angle of the enemy bullets, until he exhausted the MP-5's mag. A second one was taped to the empty one, so all he had to do was reverse the mags and snap in the fresh one. Cocking the weapon, Encizo opened fire again, raking the roof above him. He heard another body fall. There was a tumbling noise as the hit man rolled, then a cry as he fell over the edge.

Backing across the office, Encizo fished another double mag from his canvas bag and fed it into the MP-5, tossing aside the one he knew to be almost exhausted.

Above him the skylight was darkened as a figure appeared. All Encizo could see was a black shape. It was enough. The Cuban warrior snapped up the MP-5 and fired off a quick burst. The skylight's glass erupted into the gunman's face along with the 9 mm slugs. The fatally wounded agent fell through the skylight and crashed heavily to the floor.

Silence.

Manning watched the agents gather by their cars. One of them reached inside a vehicle and drew out a handset.

"Looks like they could be calling in reinforcements," the Canadian advised his Phoenix partner.

Encizo went to where the bearded man lay. The Cuban talked to the man while keeping an eye on the skylight. According to his calculations, it was possible there might still be an ISAFP agent up there.

"You feel like talking?" Encizo asked the man.

The man raised his head. Sweat was trickling down his face in streams.

"No," he whispered, his voice shaky with fear.

"Too bad," Encizo said. "It's good for you in situations like this. Helps you forget your anxiety."

"All I want is to get out of this alive," the man begged.

"Tell me what I need to know and maybe you will," Encizo encouraged him.

"What is it you want?"

"The Americans who hired your boat. How many were there?"

"I saw only three."

"What about the boat?"

"My largest. Seagoing cruiser. It could carry up to thirty people. I use it to take tourists on trips up and down the coast."

"Didn't you figure it strange, someone wanting to hire such a big craft?"

The man managed a crooked smile. "If somebody wants a big boat and pays well for it, should I care? Those men paid well. That's my business, mister. I work for cash and I don't ask questions."

"Try *answering* one," Encizo suggested. "Where were they heading?"

"I don't know. They didn't tell me and I didn't ask."

"They must have given you some idea. Did they ask for charts?"

"Only for a general chart of the currents out by Lubang—"

"Rafael! Above you!"

Manning's shout drew Encizo's eyes to the skylight, and he realized he had allowed his concentration to lapse while talking to the man on the floor.

There, framed against the light, was the figure of an armed man. The SMG in his hands spat fire.

Encizo rolled to one side. The bullets struck nearby. Wooden splinters peppering his face, the Cuban kept on moving, attempting to get the desk between himself and the ISAFP man.

The recognizable sound of Manning's SA80 rose over the clatter of the SMG. The enemy, losing his grip on the SMG, threw up his arms and stumbled away from the skylight. Seconds later he crashed down on the roof.

Encizo caught Manning's eye and nodded his thanks. He turned back to his prisoner.

And realized he would get no more answers from the man. Bullets from the agent's SMG had ripped across the prisoner's back. Blood bubbled from the gaping mouth. His eyes stared glassily across the bullet-scarred room.

On the jetty below a car screeched to a halt, disgorging a half-dozen police backups. They conferred with their comrades, then launched a full scale attack. Automatic weapons thundered loudly. Streams of bullets showered the office where Manning and Encizo took shelter, ripping chunks from the woodwork.

The Phoenix pair blasted the first agent who showed his face. His bloodied body tumbled to the ground.

The Stony Man warriors realized they could hold out for only a short time. They were running short of ammunition and, due to the heavy concentration of fire from the jetty, were having difficulty covering the stairs.

"This would be a good time for Jack to show up," Manning said, slamming home a fresh magazine into the SA80.

Encizo didn't reply. He was staring beyond the jetty at a black dot that appeared to be heading directly for them. It was getting larger with every passing second.

"Hey, Gary, make a wish," Encizo said. "I think it could come true."

Manning glanced up and followed Encizo's finger.

Out across the bay the sleek black shape of Dragon Slayer rushed toward them. It looked for all the world like some prehistoric bird sweeping in for the kill. Today its prey was the blood-hungry ISAFP agents.

20

Dragon Slayer came in low, rotor wash boiling the ocean to foam. The howl of the powerful turbo-boosted engine added to the combat helicopter's awesome appearance.

Grimaldi banked sharply as he reached the jetty, swinging his machine over the heads of the startled ISAFP squad. They scattered and dived for cover as Dragon Slayer turned sharply and drove in at them again.

This time Grimaldi brought the chopper down and held it ten feet from the ground. The hovering black machine swung gently to and fro. The gaping mouths of the rotary cannon's four barrels promised sudden death to any agent who attempted anything foolish.

One of the agents on the fringe of the group tried to sneak away. Dragon Slayer's nose drifted in his direction. The man stared at the 7.62 mm cannon aimed at him and forgot about moving any farther.

From their vantage point in the wrecked office, Manning and Encizo watched the scene below.

"I guess we can leave now," Encizo said.

Manning nodded. The Phoenix pros picked up their canvas weapon bags and slung them over their shoulders. They moved to the door and stepped onto the landing. The stairs were clear now.

Weapons held at the ready, the Stony Man warriors descended the stairs.

Ugly scowls disfigured the faces of the ISAFP heavies as Manning and Encizo crossed the jetty toward the hovering chopper.

The passenger hatch opened with the subdued hiss of hydraulics. Encizo backed in, closely followed by Manning.

The Canadian was drawing his legs inside Dragon Slayer when two agents broke to one side and opened fire.

Dragon Slayer shuddered as Grimaldi touched the rotary cannon's firing button, sending a withering blast of death howling across the jetty.

The bodies of the errant pair of agents, caught in the lashing gunfire, were reduced to sodden rags. Driven back across the jetty by the continuing hail of bullets, they were reduced to lifeless heaps.

Manning and Encizo sank into the cushioned seats and snapped the belt restraints into place as the hatch closed.

Jack Grimaldi boosted the power and Dragon Slayer shot forward, howling away from the jetty. Human figures and buildings shrank to tiny dots in its wake. Grimaldi poured on the power, sending the sleek combat machine out to sea, gaining altitude before he changed course for Clark Field.

"Hey, thanks, Jack," Manning said.

Grimaldi glanced over his shoulder. "No sweat." He grinned. "You guys okay?"

"We are now," Encizo said.

"What's the plan?" Grimaldi asked.

"Back to Clark," Manning said. "We need to contact David and Cal. They're trying to flush out an embassy eavesdropper. If they do, maybe we'll have ourselves a source of information."

"Sounds like you guys are up to your old tricks," the Stony Man flier said.

Leaning forward, Encizo asked, "What have they been doing to your baby?"

"Hell, I haven't had time to check it all out yet," Grimaldi answered. "I do know they've pepped up the communications. Better radio with a wider range. Tracking and homing is the best I've ever seen. There's a silent-mode option on the engine now. Cuts the sound down almost to zero so I can sneak up real close. Only works during low speed flight and I can keep it engaged for about fifteen minutes before the overheat light comes on."

"Sounds handy," Manning said.

"Hey," Encizo said, "do you think we could get one to fit McCarter? Just imagine him in silent mode."

"I couldn't stand that," Manning said. "Too unnatural. Be spooky."

They made Clark Field without incident. Grimaldi put Dragon Slayer down outside the small building that had been assigned to Phoenix Force.

Inside they found Air Force efficiency up to standards. There was a telephone sitting on a military issue desk. On a small table was a percolator holding hot coffee and plates of sandwiches. There were a couple of made-up camp beds against one wall, and a portable color TV set across from them.

"These guys think of everything," Encizo remarked as he poured himself a cup of coffee.

Manning picked up the phone and found it had a direct line. He dialed the Manila Hotel. When he got through, he was informed by the desk that Mr. Rawlinson had phoned in earlier, leaving a number where he could be contacted. Manning took the number and hung up.

"Trouble?" asked Encizo as he handed Manning a cup of coffee.

"I don't know," the Canadian replied. "We'll find out when I reach McCarter."

21

The safe house was a white-painted wooden villa, surrounded by extensive grounds, in a quiet residential area of Manila. Tall palm trees overhung the front of the building. A gravel drive curved up to the house, and when Rafael Encizo drove the borrowed Toyota wagon through the open gateway he spotted the Chevy Blazer parked alongside Milligan's Ford.

"Looks like this is home," Gary Manning remarked.

"For us?" Encizo asked. He shook his head. "There are times when I think I don't have a home. Just places I move from. You know?"

The Canadian nodded. He knew exactly what the Cuban was trying to say. The Phoenix Force warriors were constantly on the move from one country to another as their missions took them around the world. They spent long hours on planes and other forms of transport. When they booked a hotel in yet another strange city, they might only be there long enough to grab a quick meal and a couple of hours sleep. Then, usually, they were off and running, facing all kinds of odds, and having to fight simply to survive against the terrorists and the fanatics.

Encizo braked the Toyota beside the Blazer, noting the bullet scars on the other vehicle. He and Manning climbed out, lugging their canvas bags. As they headed for the house the front door swung open and McCarter grinned out at them.

"Been having a busy day?" the irrepressible Briton asked. He sounded like a housewife chiding her husband for being home late.

Manning entered the house, with Encizo close behind. McCarter closed the door and followed them.

"In there," he said, indicating an arched entrance.

The arch led into a large lounge that opened, via sliding patio doors, onto a paved area.

Calvin James and Jack Milligan were bent over a table that held a scattering of papers and an IBM computer.

"You got anything?" Manning asked.

James glanced up. "Maybe," he said. "We're trying to pin it down."

Encizo dumped his bag and slumped into a low chair, stretching his legs. "Exactly what are you trying to pin down?" he asked.

Milligan straightened up, grateful for the chance to take a break. "Our trap netted us the embassy informer who gave away your arrival. We met some opposition but got the informer out alive and back here."

"I checked him out and he was a prime candidate for a dose of scopolamine," James added.

Scopolamine, a colorless alkaloid extracted from such plants as henbane, was used as a muscle relaxant and also as a truth serum. Calvin James, as the Force's medic, was trained in its use. He had employed the serum a number of times to obtain information from reluctant captives.

Manning helped himself to coffee from a bubbling percolator and asked, "So what did you get?"

"He told us everything he knew," James said.

"Which wasn't much," McCarter butted in. "Whoever is running this show doesn't give much away to the hired help."

"The information we got from Santos was fragmented," Milligan explained. "But we managed to fit bits of it together. He gave us the address to the base where he reports. And other information concerning an arms cache. Even under the influence of the serum Santos wasn't too clear about its whereabouts."

"Don't let him kid you," McCarter said. "Milligan took what that little rat gave him and played around with it until he came up with a likely location."

Manning joined the security man at the table. Interested as well, Encizo dragged himself out of his chair and crossed to the table.

"The information came out in bits and pieces," Milligan explained. "In the end I fed it all into the computer and played around with it. Eventually we had a logical assumption based on the facts."

"What he means is the bloody computer came up with a location that fits the bill," McCarter interrupted. "An abandoned cannery on the Pasig River. Tied in with an old mate of Santos, as well. The late Velasquez."

Milligan nodded. "I accessed some of Velasquez's bank statements. He once made a payment to an agent who holds the title to the derelict cannery. Velasquez slipped up there. If he had paid cash to this guy, we never would have made the connection."

"Looks like a visit to the cannery is on the list," Manning said.

"How did you guys make out?" James inquired.

Between them, Manning and Encizo detailed their visits to the hotels and finally the boat charter company. The firefight with the ISAFP squad added yet another twist to the Force's complicated current mission.

"The ISAFP can be a hard bunch," Milligan commented. "They play pretty nasty games. If they're involved, it looks like we've got some military types mixed up in this coup."

"Which is par for the course around here, I'd say," Encizo said. "From what I've learned, there are one or two discontented characters in the Philippine military."

"Power plays are pretty regular," Milligan agreed. "Things have been quiet since the last attempt to overthrow the government, but you never know what's around the next bend in the river. This damn country runs hot one minute, cold the next. Hard to tell where the next surprise is coming from."

"If we have anything to do with it," McCarter stated, "it'll be coming from us. I think it's time we started kicking some ass and getting this job done."

"We didn't get a great deal from the guy at the boat charter," Manning said. "We were in the middle of a firefight at the time."

"Excuses, always excuses," McCarter muttered as he popped the tab on a chilled can of Coke.

"The only bit of sound info we got from the guy before he died was that the Americans who hired his largest boat asked for charts showing the currents around Lubang Island."

"Lubang?" Milligan thought about the information. "I can't see your mercs using Lubang itself. Maybe they just wanted to know the area. Let me see what I can dig up.''

The security man returned to his computer.

''We've got the location of this house Santos gave us,'' Manning said. ''Maybe Katz is there. I suggest we pay it a visit this evening.''

''I'll drink to that,'' McCarter agreed, raising his can of Coke.

''We'll go and get freshened up,'' Manning said, indicating Encizo. He turned to McCarter. ''We had to call in Dragon Slayer to get us out of that firefight. There was no way we could contact Mahmud. He was parked on the jetty pretty far from where we were, so I reckon he would have taken off. You want to give him a call? Check if he's all right?''

''I'll do that.'' The Brit picked up the telephone. ''Knowing Mahmud, he'd scoot out of there once he saw you were okay.''

McCarter got through to his friend after a few rings. Mahmud assured the Phoenix warrior that he was fine. McCarter gave Manning the thumbs-up in order to pass along the message.

''Give us a half hour and we'll be ready,'' Manning said. ''Then we'll see if we can find Katz.''

MANNING'S HOPE was not to be realized.

When Phoenix Force arrived at the large house and grounds just off E. De Los Santos Avenue, beyond the Manila Golf and Country Club, they found the place dark and deserted. Inside the mansion they found evidence of recent occupation.

But whoever had been in the house was gone. And with them, the Phoenix warriors were certain, had gone the chance of an early reunion with Katz.

22

The room was long, with a high ceiling. The walls were richly decorated with carved wood panels and oil paintings hung in artfully lit, recessed niches. The floor was covered with glazed tiles laid out in a mosaic of deep reds and browns. Two large glittering chandeliers were suspended from the high ceiling. In the center of the room stood a long dining table, capable of seating at least twenty people, surrounded by that many high-backed, handcrafted chairs, their seats covered in rich velvet. The wooden chairs and table gleamed with that deep luster only obtained over long years of careful polishing.

Leoni Testarov waited impatiently as the others seated themselves for the hastily convened meeting.

On the KGB man's left was Major Diego Castillo. The Filipino military man had not spoken a word since entering the house. He appeared to be in control of his emotions, yet Testarov sensed that he was extremely tense and close to anger.

Beside Castillo, looking extremely uncomfortable, was Lee Harun. The pudgy negotiator had been instrumental in making contact and subsequent arrangements with Remsberg's Raiders. An expression of sheer terror showed in his normally greedy eyes. Although he had been an underworld fixer for many years, Harun's usual clients were strictly minor league. The moon-faced negotiator had jumped into the big time by accepting Testarov's offer. Not only were the financial rewards extremely generous, but Testarov had indicated that after the overthrow of the present government, there could well be a position for Harun in the new administration. Lee Harun had been secretly overwhelmed. Here, he realized, was a prime opportunity to move up the social ladder.

Harun had ambition. He didn't give a damn that Testarov was planning to overthrow the government and make way for a Communist regime. No matter what the system, there were always deals to be made, people to manipulate and influence. Harun knew he could help Testarov and simultaneously help himself. It was a once in a lifetime deal. And it was one that Lee Harun could not refuse.

Now, though, with all that had happened over the last couple of days, Harun was watching his golden opportunity sliding down the tubes. The entire deal seemed to be in danger of falling apart, and Harun realized that when these things happened certain people had to take the blame. They were usually the least important members of the team, the ones who could be dispensed with and forgotten.

Harun was feeling very unimportant right now. He also had the feeling that he might become instantly disposable once the meeting got underway. The knowledge sat heavily on his soft shoulders.

Leoni Testarov allowed himself a wry smile as he glanced at the perspiring fixer. Let the gullible fool squirm, the Soviet thought. The man was unaware that he had been under sentence of death from the moment

Testarov hired him. Part of the plan had been to have Harun eliminated the moment his work was completed. Tonight's meeting would decide his fate. If Harun could offer little more to the overall scheme, then he would not leave the house alive.

At the far end of the table sat the political conspirators—the men who would gain the most from the coup if it were to succeed.

Armand Serratto was a wily, experienced politician who had cajoled and bribed and coerced his way through twenty-five years of Filipino administrations. He had survived instability and personalities, even remaining untouched when the Marcos regime was toppled. Now he served under the leadership of Cory Aquino.

The Serratto family had always been rich and influential. They had interests in a number of diverse businesses, from which they had acquired property and wealth.

Yet Armand Serratto wanted more. His major obsession was power. He desired no less than the ultimate power in the Philippines—the presidency.

He was also a dedicated Communist, and had been since his teens. Serratto was smart enough, however, to keep his socialist tendencies well concealed, though over the past few years he had been secretly funding the NPA rebels.

Over the years Serratto had made contact with others who felt that a Communist takeover was the Philippines' only hope of salvation. As time went by they began to formulate their plan for a coup. After many months the talk had evolved into a cohesive plan of action.

Which had been set in motion.

It all seemed to be going so well at first, but then a wild card, in the form of a mysterious group of American specialists, had appeared on the scene.

From the moment they arrived on Philippine soil, they had caused havoc.

Not only had they survived every attempt to wipe them out, they had also inflicted extreme injury to the various squads sent out to handle them.

A group of local Communist hard-liners had attempted to assassinate the specialists on their arrival, and had died to a man.

Then a team of Testarov's Morkrie Dela killers had faced up to two of the Americans. They, too, had been defeated. To add insult to injury, Testarov's informer, planted in the U.S. Embassy, had been taken prisoner by the Americans.

Castillo, using the influence of one of the conspirators, had arranged for an ISAFP squad either to capture or kill two of the Americans. They had failed.

The entire affair was turning into a farce of gigantic proportions, and it had been decided to hold a council of war in order to bring some sanity to the proceedings.

With Serratto were his constant companions. Hector DiCenzi, a spare man with piercing eyes behind large spectacles, was a member of the judiciary, a man involved with the legal department who liked to bend the law when it suited his purpose. The third member of the unholy trio was Marcus Rufio. He held the dubious honor of having once been associated with the ISAFP. Now Rufio worked as a close adviser to Serratto, and also looked after the man's personal protection. Rufio was not a man to trifle with. It was hinted that he still had great influence within the country's secret-police organizations.

As he watched the group settling, Testarov consoled himself with the knowledge that, despite the disappointments, he still had the man named Katzenelenbogen as his prisoner—something he had kept to himself and intended to continue doing. Whatever else happened, Testarov would be able to present this man to his superiors in Moscow. That triumph was his alone and could not be taken from him.

"All right," Testarov snapped. "Let us begin."

Every eye around the table focused on the KGB man.

"We are all aware of the current situation, I presume," Testarov prompted.

There were nods of acknowledgment.

"Our plans have been ruined," grumbled DiCenzi in a display of self-pity. "All the money we have poured into this grand scheme may be wasted."

"Money!" Testarov shouted. "This is not about money. We are deciding on the fate of a nation. A nation that has for too long been held by the throat by the most corrupt capitalist empire ever to have existed—the United States of America. Or have you forgotten, Comrade DiCenzi?"

DiCenzi's face darkened with anger. "Do you doubt my loyalty, Major Testarov?"

Serratto held up his hands. "Please, my friends, let us not allow this matter to get out of control. The events of the last day or so have been stressful, to say the least, but we must not fall out among ourselves. If we cannot agree around this table, then we are helping the enemy to win."

Castillo nodded. "I agree with Armand," he said. "This band of American assassins has caused us a great deal of embarrassment—plus an increasingly large number of men.

"It would be easy to allow ourselves to become disillusioned. To let the defeats we have suffered break us apart.

"Surely we can overcome these setbacks. We cannot allow these five Americans to destroy our grand plan. There is too much to lose."

"Exactly!" Testarov said forcibly. "Do we abandon everything simply because of the intrusion of these American killers? We must not. If we are prepared to give up so easily now, what would happen in the face of a real threat? There is only one policy to adopt—that of total dedication to the cause and a refusal to be intimidated. Any threat must be dealt with ruthlessly."

"I am in full agreement," Marcus Rufio said. "However, time is not on our side. The operation schedule dictates that we commence in forty-eight hours. There can be no deviation from that time. Everyone is committed. Can we guarantee to contain these Yankee specialists in the hours left to us?"

"I believe we can," Castillo stated. "Admittedly, we have underestimated them up to now. They are experienced combat specialists, capable of facing superior odds and surviving such an encounter. Now that we are aware of this we can deal with them."

DiCenzi allowed himself a faint smirk. "Are you sure? From what I gather they wiped out a whole squad of your ISAFP men."

There was a discernible stiffening in Castillo's shoulders as he stared at DiCenzi. "You don't have to remind me," he said. "It would be more helpful if you could come up with a useful suggestion instead of adolescent sneers."

"Gentlemen, gentlemen," Serratto soothed. "Please, let us confine ourselves to the matter at hand.

"What concerns me is the fact that the two Americans who went to Mako Boat Charter may have talked to the owner before he died. Shouldn't we be worrying about what information Mako has given them?"

"As far as we are aware, he knew nothing," Castillo said. "Remsberg simply hired a boat from him. He did not divulge his reasons for hiring the craft, or his destination. Mako was interested only in making money. His reputation was well known."

"Can we be absolutely certain he told them nothing?" Rufio insisted.

"No," said Testarov, "we can't. So we must take precautions." The KGB man turned to the perspiring Lee Harun. "Harun, you will fly out to the island immediately and inform Remsberg. Tell him of the need for extra vigilance in case the Americans turn up."

"In the meantime, what do you intend to do here?" DiCenzi asked.

"As already stated," Testarov said, "we must attempt to contain these Americans. I had hoped to keep our involvement with them as low-key as possible. That objective, however, does not appear to apply any longer. So instead we must try to deal with them as quickly as we are able."

"What about the man Santos?" Serratto asked. "The Americans took him prisoner. Surely they will make *him* talk? Are you not concerned?"

"Santos was *my* informer," Testarov informed them. "He dealt with me and no one else. He was strictly confined to the American embassy. He knew nothing about the main plan because I told him nothing. Rest assured that he knows nothing about any of you.

"I decided to move here as a precaution, as Santos knew the location of the other house. But he does not know the whereabouts of *this* house."

"So you feel we are still secure?" Serratto asked.

"Yes, I do."

There was a considered silence before Serratto nodded slowly. "As unfortunate as these episodes have been," he said, "I refuse to abandon the operation. Too much has gone into it, and we may never have another chance. I feel we should go ahead as planned." The Filipino smiled. "We are strong enough to endure a few minor setbacks. Especially with the prize that awaits us."

"I believe Comrade Serratto has spoken for us all," Testarov said, taking the initiative once again. "Risk is an integral part of life, and we must take our chances if we wish to further our cause."

Serratto stood. He gazed around the table, like a father bestowing his blessing upon his children.

"In a few days, when we are in control of this beloved country of ours, we will wonder why we worried so. Have faith, dear friends, and we *will* triumph."

"There is food and drink in the lounge," Testarov informed the group. "Please help yourselves. I will join you in a few moments."

As the conspirators moved from the table, Testarov caught Diego Castillo's eye. The Filipino joined him.

"I feel we have satisfied them," Testarov said. "For the time being."

"This is one of the problems when you align yourself with civilians," Castillo remarked. "They have such a confined mentality."

"Is everything in order?" asked the KGB man.

"Yes. My troops are standing by. We have men assigned to move in and take control of key installations throughout the major cities and towns. Each group will concentrate on a specific target. At the appropriate time I will send out a single radio message which will be relayed to them all. After that nothing will be able to stop us."

"What about the slight difficulty you were having at Villamor?"

Castillo smiled. "That has been resolved satisfactorily," he said. "The commander at the base will no longer offer any resistance."

Villamor Air Base was the headquarters of the Philippine air force and also controlled the international airport. A squadron of assault helicopters based there was an important part of the coup operation. Castillo had been faced with a stumbling block in the shape of the base commander, a staunch Aquino supporter. However, the deputy commander, one of Castillo's people, had arranged to step in and seize the base—with the aid of his own loyal personnel—at the appropriate time.

"Excellent," Testarov said. He gestured toward the door. "I think we should join the others before they start to imagine we're plotting against them."

Castillo laughed heartily. "We mustn't allow them to think that!"

With that the KGB terror monger and the Filipino conspirator strode from the room, like two boys sharing secrets.

PART THREE

PART THREE

23

Katz opened his eyes. Warm sunlight filtered through the shutters of the room in which he was imprisoned. The Israeli sat up slowly, conscious of the fact that his headache had gone. He still felt sluggish and a little weak, but he put those symptoms down to a lack of exercise and good food.

Pushing the covers aside, Katz slipped out of bed. He located his shoes and put them on, then crossed to the window. He reached through the iron scrollwork that covered the window and pushed the shutters wide open.

This was only his second opportunity to view the outside of his new prison. Testarov's departure from the previous house had been swift. A cloth hood had been secured over Katz's head and his hands tied behind his back. He had been rushed from the house and bundled roughly into a car. There had been a long drive. Katz, aware of the delicacy of his position, had remained silent and cooperative. He heard the sounds of the city fading away, leaving only the soft hum of the car's tires on the road. From the smells and the occasional sounds of birds, Katz assumed they were out in the country. Finally the car drew to a halt, tires crunching across gravel. Doors were opened and Katz was manhandled from the car and into a house. He was taken upstairs, along a passage, into a room. There he had been dumped on a bed and left. A door had banged shut and a key turned in a well-oiled lock.

Katz was alone with his thoughts—and his fears. These were not enormous. It would take more than a car ride in the dark to worry Yakov Katzenelenbogen.

During his life Katz had seen and experienced too much to allow himself to be intimidated by such tricks as being left encased in a hood with his hands tied. He had long since accepted the inevitability of death. So he had lain on the bed and waited for his captors to tire of their game.

They left him there for two hours. Finally the door opened and someone came in. The hood was removed and Katz's hands untied. He sat on the edge of the bed, blinking against the bright light in the room.

"Here is your food," the burly Russian standing in front of Katz intoned.

A tray was placed on a table. The Russian left the room and the heavy, carved wooden door slammed shut, the lock clicking as the key was turned.

Katz crossed to the table, examined the food. There was rice and fish on the plate. Next to the plate was a large mug of what looked like extremely strong coffee. The thought crossed Katz's mind that the food might be drugged or poisoned, but he could see no reason why his captors should subject him to such treatment. From what he had deduced from Testarov's conversation with him, the KGB man wanted Katz alive and well and delivered to Moscow. Sitting down, Katz ate the food and drained the coffee mug.

Afterward he explored his room. The place reeked of money. The furnishings, even the paintings on the walls, were expensive. There was a great deal of Spanish influence in the decor and design of the room. Katz spent a long time going over the room. He was unable to find anything remotely helpful. Nothing to help him break out. He had discounted the window the moment he had seen it. The wide opening was covered by a grille of scrolled iron, effective as any iron bars. The room probably hadn't been designed as a prison cell, but it certainly could stand in for one.

Beyond the window, rolling lawns were bordered by gently swaying palm trees. A curving drive cut its way from the house to a white stone wall and high gates. On the far side of the wall lay more trees and thick vegetation. Katz realized that his earlier guess had been correct. This place, wherever it was, was not in an urban setting. They were well away from Manila.

Movement caught the Phoenix commander's eye. He watched a man appear near the closest stand of palm trees. A hefty figure, dressed in light slacks and a short-sleeved shirt. Hair cut short above a broad Slavic face. One of Testarov's Morkrie Dela agents. The Russian was carrying a stubby SMG.

Katz's room was on the second floor. Jutting out from the main body of the house, at right angles, was a stable and garage extension. The stables appeared unoccupied, but there seemed to be some activity around one of the garages. The double doors were partway open and figures could be seen moving around inside. There was no way for Katz to see farther in, but he decided to keep an eye on the place. Something had aroused his curiosity, though he couldn't put his finger on it.

Now that he had a night of reasonable sleep behind him, Katz decided to take another look at that garage. Who could say what a fresh mind would come up with?

This time the double doors were wide open. Katz was in time to see a sleek white ambulance roll out of the garage. It was fitted with all the regular accessories—roof lights, a siren and lettering indicating that the vehicle belonged to the Manila Medical Center Emergency Squad.

A small group of men appeared. They stood around the ambulance, discussing something. Katz spotted Leoni Testarov. The KGB man seemed to be leading the discussion. Eventually some kind of concensus was apparently reached. Testarov leaned through the ambulance window and spoke to the driver. Moments later the vehicle moved off along the drive, passed through the gates and drove out of sight.

Katz stepped away from the window. His mind was working busily, trying to recall a scrap of information that had come out of Hal Brognola's Stony Man briefing. Something to do with the Philippine president.

Something she was going to do on a certain date.

An official function.

The Israeli paced the room, angry at himself for not being able to lock in on the whole story.

And then it came rushing in to crowd his mind.

Suddenly, chilling, the connection was there. Katz knew where and when and how the assassination of the Philippine president would be staged.

But unless a miracle took place to release him, there wasn't a single thing he could do to warn anyone about it.

24

The derelict cannery was situated near the Pasig River in an area that had once been a busy trading section. The section had outlived its usefulness and as the businesses had dwindled and pulled out, the whole area fell into a state of disrepair. The people moved out and the derelicts and rats moved in.

During its heyday the cannery—handling locally grown pineapples—had boasted its own loading dock, where ships had moored to be loaded with boxes of tinned pineapple that were either sliced, cubed, shredded or turned into juice. The dock stood empty now, its timbers slowly rotting as they were washed by the dirty river.

Phoenix Force arrived at the cannery complex in the early morning. The sun was already up, though it had not reached its zenith yet. Adjacent to the cannery was a section of undeveloped land where palm trees and vegetation grew in abundance. It was deep in this section that David McCarter parked the Chevrolet Blazer and cut the motor.

The Force was ready for combat. Every member of the team was dressed in camouflage gear and carried full weaponry.

As well as handguns and heavy weapons, each of the Phoenix warriors carried grenades, knives, and additional ammunition for their particular firearms.

McCarter, as usual, had his 9 mm Ingram MAC-10, plus his favorite Browning Hi-Power autopistol.

Backing up his H&K MP-5 subgun, Rafael Encizo wore his P-9 pistol in a shoulder rig, and had a Cold Steel Tanto fighting knife sheathed on his belt.

Gary Manning's Walther P-5 9 mm pistol was partnered by the Canadian's newest acquisition, the SA80 5.56 mm.

Although Calvin James had accepted the replacement pistol—a Beretta 92-SB in 9 mm—he still favored his 5.56 mm M-16 rifle. In addition, he still carried his G-96 Jet-Aer dagger.

"Check watches," Gary Manning said as the Force assembled on the fringe of the treeline and studied the seemingly deserted cannery.

They had agreed to carry out a recon of the place first, to establish whether their information was correct, that something actually was being stored in the empty factory. Milligan had come up with some old plans of the complex, showing the layout of the buildings. From these the Phoenix pros had devised their recon strategy. Each man had a specific section of the site to check. When the recon was accomplished they would return to a predetermined rendezvous point to exchange information.

Watches were synchronized.

"Let's move out," Manning said. "Rendezvous in thirty minutes."

Without another word, the four Phoenix Force warriors broke cover and went their separate ways.

The area appeared deserted. The buildings were empty, many with broken windows. Some doors had been secured with thick wooden planks, while others gaped wide open. The spaces between the buildings were littered with debris left behind when the buildings had been stripped of salvageable scrap. Weeds had sprouted in abundance, pushing up between cracks in the concrete walkways and at the bases of the walls.

To the casual observer, it was a derelict site. Abandoned and left to decay.

Close inspection, however, highlighted a block in what had been the cannery's storage area, in which the neglect was far less apparent. Here a set of high double doors were supported by new hinges. Traces of grease on the door catches revealed that these doors had recently been oiled.

It was Rafael Encizo who spotted the doors. The Cuban, carrying out his part of the recon, had worked his way into the complex, finding nothing to indicate recent occupation—until he reached the storage area.

It was a puzzle. There was a long row of warehouses, each with its own set of high doors. But only one of them showed signs of recent use.

Encizo, crouching in the shadow of a metal fire-escape platform bolted to the wall, inspected the area carefully. His keen eyes moved from the doors themselves to the concrete fronting the warehouse.

Dark streaks showed where vehicles had recently been reversed up to the doors. There was even a stain of oil from a leaky engine.

Encizo remained where he was. It would have been too simple to accept the scene at face value—to make an assessment of the situation based on an all-too-brief surveillance.

Rafael Encizo was too much of a professional to fall into that trap. So he watched and waited, allowing the minutes to slip by.

He could feel the hot sun on his face, taste the dust in the air that was also tinged with the smell of the nearby river. Above everything else was the silence crowding in on him.

The faint scraping sound came from above him, and ahead. Shading his eyes from the hard glare of the bright sky, Encizo scanned the parapet that jutted from the roof of the warehouse. At first he saw nothing. Then he caught a glimpse of a man's head and shoulders.

A rifle of some kind leaned casually against the guy's right shoulder. He gave the impression of being bored by the duty he had to perform. Lulled by the monotonous task of having to continuously patrol the roof. Given the unrelenting heat, the guy was probably losing concentration.

He was becoming lax.

Distracted.

Which was good news as far as Encizo was concerned.

The Cuban spent another ten minutes in careful observation. The guy on the roof disappeared from the parapet and returned again in about six minutes. During that time Encizo did not see or hear anything else to arouse his suspicion.

Encizo quietly slipped back the way he had entered the complex, eventually reaching the dense foliage edging the area.

The others were already there, waiting. McCarter was prowling back and forth across the clearing, a dark scowl on his face.

"And about bloody time," the Briton muttered ungraciously. "Where the hell have you been? Having tea and bleedin' biscuits?"

"Don't mind him," Manning said. "I think it's his old age that makes him crotchety."

Calvin James, trying to keep from grinning at McCarter's grumbles of disgust, asked, "You find anything?"

"I think so," Encizo replied.

"Well, are you going to tell us, or do we have to bribe you?" McCarter asked testily, his attention aroused by the possibility of action.

"I located the storage area," Encizo said, totally ignoring McCarter's rudeness. "A block of adjacent warehouses, each with its own set of high double doors. The whole complex looks deserted—except for one warehouse. It has new hinges on the doors, and the catches and handles have been greased. There are signs of vehicular movement around the doors. And there's a guy on the roof keeping watch. I think he does circuits of the roof. He's carrying some kind of rifle."

"Sounds like it might have possibilities," McCarter remarked cheerfully. "How are we going to handle it?"

"Let Rafael lead us in so we can assess the place, then act on what we find," Manning suggested.

McCarter glanced at him with a disappointed expression on his face. "The trouble with you Canadians is no sense of adventure. I suppose it's having to live with all that snow. Slows you down."

"Come on, David," James argued. "You know Gary's right. We have to do it right. We can't go crashing in without knowing how many we're up against."

McCarter nodded. "Of course. Like I said, Gary's been right all along. We do exactly what he said."

James shook his head in exasperation. There were times when he failed to understand McCarter at all. The Briton had the strangest sense of humor, confusing everyone around him, then just as swiftly transforming into the ultimate professional. Then he would defy them to pick a flaw in his logic. And there was no one to match the Briton's skill and fighting fury when the chips were down.

"Okay," Manning said. "Let's move out."

The Phoenix quartet slid into the dense foliage, Encizo in the lead, Manning directly behind him, Mc-Carter next, James in the rear. When they reached the edge of the greenery Encizo indicated the path they would take through the complex.

Again the Cuban went first, moving to the first building without a sound. He crouched at the base of the wall, checking out the area before he signaled to his waiting partners. Manning crossed the same stretch of ground with Encizo covering him, as James and Mc-Carter watched. The procedure was repeated for Mc-Carter, then for James; his safety was covered from the new position.

"Gets a little easier from here," Encizo said. "There's plenty of cover provided by the buildings, so we can just jump from place to place. We're heading in that direction. Should take us about ten minutes to reach the warehouse block."

As before, the Force made the trip in a series of carefully covered moves from point to point. Not one word was spoken during that time. Hand signals were employed to move someone forward, to stop, to change direction.

The men of Phoenix Force possessed combat skills that made them one of the most deadly commando strike squads ever to exist. Now all the casual banter ceased. The true professionalism of the Stony Man warriors shone through as they silently, almost invisibly, worked toward the enemy stronghold. Each man a separate yet vital cog in the functioning machine known as Phoenix Force. In just under ten minutes they were assembled beneath the fire escape Encizo had used previously.

The Cuban pointed out the warehouse and the parapet edging the roof, just as the armed guard appeared. The guy laid his rifle along the parapet, took a pack of cigarettes from his shirt pocket, and lit one. He stood smoking, gazing around as if he was on a sight-seeing tour.

"We could do with him out of the way," Manning said softly.

"I'll handle it," James volunteered.

Manning nodded. "How long do you want before we move in?"

"Give me fifteen minutes, then go for it," James said.

As the black commando edged forward, preparing to cut across to the warehouse, McCarter touched his arm.

"Take it easy, chum. We want you back."

James nodded. He waited until the guard turned away, then ran across the wide alley between the buildings, flattening himself against the wall of the warehouse. Turning, he moved quickly along the frontage until he reached the corner, then vanished.

25

Calvin James spotted the metal ladder bolted to the side of the warehouse. It reached to the parapet, and had probably been intended for maintenance crews to inspect the roof. It was quite a distance from where James crouched, so he took his time checking out the area before he approached.

Reaching the ladder, James slung his M-16 over his shoulder, grabbed the rusting rail of the ladder and started to climb. He moved swiftly. The ex-Chicago street-tough didn't want to risk being spotted while in the vulnerable position halfway between ground and roof. Near the end of his climb, James slowed, keeping his head below the parapet. When he did expose himself it was gradually, his movements slow and deliberate, so as not to attract any attention by suddenly popping into view.

The expanse of flat roof spread out before him. The tarmac-covered area was dotted with metal ventilator hoods and the raised blocks of skylights.

He couldn't see the guard, which was not surprising. If the guy was at the far end of the roof, the numerous ventilator hoods formed effective obstacles for the Phoenix warrior's line of sight.

Seizing the opportunity, James scrambled over the parapet, dropping to the surface of the roof. He crouched and made his way across to the closest ventilator hood, pressing close. He sat in the hood's shade, eyes and ears straining to pick up the slightest hint of the guard's whereabouts. A good three or four minutes dragged by before James heard the soft crunch of footsteps on the tarmac.

He turned in the general direction of the sound. The black-haired Filipino, an AK-47 in his hands, was no more than twenty feet away.

And by one of those infuriating quirks of fate that often occur, the Filipino just happened to look in James's direction at the same moment.

To his credit the Filipino did not yell. Or pause to take a second look. Or hesitate.

He simply lifted the Kalashnikov and opened fire, sending a rain of 7.62 mm bullets at James. They clanged against the ventilator hood, some penetrating the rusting sheet steel.

James responded with the instincts of a true survivor, twisting his body away from the hood and throwing himself prone. He knew he wasn't going to have much time to bring his M-16 into play, so he didn't even try.

Even as he was dropping to the tarmac, James's right hand was reaching for the Beretta 92-SB slung in its shoulder rig. He yanked the 9 mm autoloader free and arced the muzzle around, pulling the trigger and sending a deadly message winging toward the Filipino triggerman.

The 9 mm parabellum drilled through the guy's left shoulder, clipping the bone and knocking him off balance. The Filipino stumbled back, the shock of the bullet already clouding his reactions. He wasn't even aware that James, after firing once, had steadied himself, realigned the Beretta and fired once more. The second and third bullets entered the target's chest cavity and terminated his life functions within seconds. The Filipino hit the tarmac on his back, kicked a couple of times, then became eternally still.

As the guy went down Calvin James rose to his feet, aware that the short but deadly exchange of fire had most certainly alerted everyone in the vicinity. He sprinted across the roof toward the front of the building. At the parapet he leaned over and caught Gary Manning's eye. When the Canadian spotted him, James spread his hands, palms turned upward in a gesture that said, *sorry, I couldn't help it!*

THE SOUND OF GUNFIRE had alerted Phoenix Force. They were already preparing to move in on the warehouse when James appeared at the parapet.

"Quiet time's over," Encizo said, hefting his Heckler & Koch MP-5.

"You said it, mate," McCarter affirmed as the warehouse doors swung open and a trio of gun-wielding Filipino hardcases burst into view.

The three were armed with AK-47s, as had been the guard James had downed. The moment the Filipinos were out of the door they separated, each covering a different section of the warehouse frontage.

The middle man in the trio ran toward the building concealing Phoenix Force. There was no way they could withdraw to deeper cover in time. The Filipinos were obviously highly agitated, tense and under strain from having to sit and guard whatever was inside the warehouse. It showed in their frantic reaction to the gunfire. These men, whatever else they might be, were not professionals. It made them unpredictable, and that much more dangerous, because there was no way to anticipate what they might do next.

"Hard choice time," Manning said.

"Like bloody hell it is!" McCarter growled. The uncompromising Briton knew a back-to-the-wall situation when he saw it, and in the ex-SAS man's book there was only one way to handle such a crisis.

You hit the enemy before he hit you. It might have seemed hard to some, but as far as David McCarter was concerned, it was better to be alive and considered a bastard than dead and called a hell of a nice guy.

The cockney stepped around his Phoenix Force buddies, confronting the oncoming Filipino, who seemed highly surprised as he yelled a warning to his partners.

The Filipino angled his bouncing Kalashnikov in McCarter's direction, his finger fumbling to touch the trigger. It was as far as he got. The MAC-10 in McCarter's hands spat a burst of 9 mm slugs that ripped into the Filipino's chest and slammed him to the concrete.

Close on McCarter's heels, Manning and Encizo burst from cover. They turned in different directions, each taking one of the remaining Filipinos, as McCarter himself ran toward the warehouse's open doors.

Encizo traded shots with the Filipino he'd drawn. Both men missed with their first burst. The Filipino seemed to be having problems with his weapon, an AK-47 on full auto. The line of slugs he aimed at Encizo smashed into the brick wall behind the Cuban.

As the Filipino's volley echoed between the walls of the complex, Encizo fired again. His burst was short but effective, catching the guy in the throat and ending his career as a local hardman.

Dropping to one knee and ignoring the shots being pumped at him by the third Filipino, Gary Manning shouldered the SA80 and took steady aim. He pulled the trigger twice, feeling the butt of the weapon slap back as the 5.56 mm slugs streaked from the barrel. His first shot took the guy in the chest, spinning him away from Manning so that the second shot, slightly higher, burned its way into the Filipino's neck. In doing so it severed the main artery. The guy flopped to the concrete, his body twisting in ugly spasms as he bled to death.

AWARE OF THE EXCHANGE of shots behind him, McCarter burst through the warehouse doors, instantly breaking to the left and dropping to a crouch.

From ahead of him full auto fire raked the doors with bullets. Splinters of wood went flying.

"You'll have to be quicker than that, my lads," McCarter murmured.

He scanned the interior of the large warehouse. Twenty feet from him were a couple of parked forklift trucks. Beyond that all the British commando could see were tall stacks of crates. Long rows of them ran deep into the warehouse. The crates had a certain familiar military look, and McCarter knew they had hit pay dirt.

Before the concealed occupants of the warehouse could readjust their aim and pin him down, McCarter cut a zigzag course for the closest forklift truck. As he curled up behind it, one of the hidden gunners opened up. Bullets whacked the thick steel sides of the truck, clanging dully against the tough metal.

McCarter's keen eyes had picked out muzzle flashes coming from high up in the warehouse.

To his right, a set of metal stairs led up to a walkway fronting several glass-fronted offices aligned halfway up the inside wall of the warehouse. As his eyes adjusted to the light he found he was able to make out a figure crouched on the walkway, a Kalashnikov clutched in his hands.

Edging to the front corner of the forklift, McCarter angled the muzzle of his Ingram up toward the walkway. He pulled the trigger, spending half the magazine's ammunition. His hail of bullets drove the gunman back from the rail, permitting the Briton to lunge to his feet and make a dash for better cover near the stairs.

The gunman made a swift recovery. He opened fire with his AK-47, sending a spray of slugs at McCarter's weaving figure.

Had the guard taken a few seconds to aim, he might have hit his intended target. As it was, the stream of slugs erupting from his chattering weapon went wild. They struck the floor and the wall, feet away from the Phoenix warrior.

Ignoring the spray of bullets, McCarter suddenly stopped, raised his Ingram and took steady aim. Then he pulled the trigger. The blast from the MAC-10 planted a half-dozen slugs in the Filipino's chest. Even before he could utter a stunned cry, the gunman found himself hurled back by the impact of the slugs chewing through his chest. He struck one of the office windows, his torso breaking the glass.

McCarter continued on, briefly ducking for cover next to a stack of crates marked in Russian. The Brit knew enough about the language to decipher the stenciled marks. The crates held more AK-47s.

Releasing the spent magazine from his Ingram, McCarter snapped a fresh one and recocked the SMG.

He heard the rush of feet across the concrete, and knew there were more of the enemy still around.

MANNING AND ENCIZO entered the warehouse to see McCarter handle the gunman on the walkway. Before they could join their Phoenix buddy, however, they were confronted by a bunch of Filipino thugs who burst into view from around a high stack of boxes.

The Stony Man warriors, reacting as usual, matched fire with fire with deadly accuracy.

Manning turned toward the oncoming Filipinos, bracing his powerful form as he raised the SA80 and pulled back on the weapon's trigger. The SA80's muzzle spat flame and 5.56 death. Each pull on the trigger sent another howling projectile toward the rushing thugs, the bullets cleaving flesh and splintering bone. The men became screaming creatures who tumbled to the concrete, spilling blood as they died in the dirt. In an instant they were transformed from raging fanatics into writhing objects, yearning for an end to their terrible pain and suffering. Their deaths made a mockery of those who pictured combat as something glorious and welcoming. Something that would make men from boys and heroes from ordinary men. In truth there was nothing glorious or remotely romantic about dying on a dirty concrete floor while squirming in pain and agony.

No one knew better than Rafael Encizo of the indignity of suffering and death. He had seen his share and had sent many an enemy on that final plunge into the abyss. Each time he took on a mission, he accepted the risk of ending up in such a condition himself, as did all the others. Yet he still accepted each call to arms, because he had decided that the values he was protecting were worth far more than a single life. Too many innocents around the world were suffering untold horrors each day of their lives because of the evil that men do. His small part in trying to eradicate the evil ones gave Encizo the satisfaction of acting rather than sitting still—and that was as much as any man could hope to do.

Evil this day came in the form of Filipino thugs trying to deprive the Cuban of his life. Encizo could not, would not, accept such a threat.

His MP-5 chattered loudly as he returned the fire. His aim was as true as ever and the two leading Filipino thugs were knocked off their feet by the unrestrained volley of 9 mm parabellums. A short burst at a heavy-set Filipino, who had been drawing a bead on Gary Manning, caught the thug in the head, splitting his skull.

As the last Filipino hit the concrete, staining it with blood, Encizo and Manning ran across the warehouse, reloading as they went, knowing full well that the battle was far from over.

CALVIN JAMES SWUNG the skylight cover open and peered down into the cavernous warehouse. Hearing the rattle of gunfire, he knew that his partners were in the thick of it.

He scrambled over the edge of the skylight, hanging from the frame by his hands. Some eight feet below where he hung suspended was the top of a stack of crates. With a shake of his head at his own recklessness, the Chicago hardass let go. He relaxed his muscles just before he hit the crates, letting his body roll. He felt the stack sway and totter under the impact. When the motion ceased the Phoenix warrior realized he was lying full length on the top crate.

Sitting up and unlimbering the M-16 from around his shoulders, James scrambled to the edge. From there he jumped down to a smaller stack, and from there he made it to the floor. He realized he was at the far end of the warehouse, so he headed through the rows of crates to the front of the building.

Figures darted in and out of the crates. They were not Phoenix Force.

The gunfire continued.

Cutting between two high stacks of crates, James found himself confronted by a trio of SMG-wielding Filipinos. They were obviously in no mood for answering questions—or asking them. They separated the moment they set eyes on James, then opened fire.

The black Chicago hardass dived to the floor, breaking his fall with his left hand and arching his supple body in a roll that took him away from the spray of bullets. The slugs snapped viciously as they struck the concrete floor. Coming out of the roll James snapped his M-16 into firing position and triggered a burst.

The closest Filipino thug caught the full blast of James's volley in his stomach. He screamed. The sound was a protest against premature death and also a way of expressing sheer terror. His shrill cries rose to the rafters of the warehouse. Abandoning his weapon, he clutched the ball of fire that seemed to engulf his body and tried to staunch the flow of blood issuing from his perforated flesh. Sinking to his knees, he toppled face-down on the concrete, dead.

After firing on the first Filipino, James swung his M-16 to the second attacker. The guy had the presence of mind to drop into a crouch so as to present a smaller target. But the Phoenix warrior—who knew every evasive tactic in the book, plus a few he had invented himself—generally expected an adversary to do the unexpected, so his senses were slightly ahead of the action. As he saw the Filipino drop, James altered his aim, tracking the target. He touched the trigger before the Filipino thug could realign his own weapon. Slugs perforated the guy's chest and head, kicking him off balance. He hit the concrete face first, bouncing slightly before settling like a deflated balloon. Thin fingers of blood from the guy's shattered skull spidered out across the concrete.

The surviving Filipino, more than a little shocked by the rapid demise of his buddies, suddenly realized he was holding a weapon himself. Out of sheer instinct, allied with a tremendous desire to live, he turned his AK-47 on the black devil who had eliminated his partners. He yanked back on the trigger—nothing happened. A knot of cold fear twisted the Filipino's gut as he realized he had not released the safety. He never got a chance to rectify that elementary mistake.

Calvin James touched the M-16's trigger for the third time, catching the Filipino in the chest. The thug was propelled against a stack of crates. His shirt was shredded by the shots and rapidly drenched with blood. He hung against the crates for what seemed an eternity before falling.

As James gained his feet he replenished the M-16's magazine slot.

Rounding a stack of crates, the black warrior came up behind two men preparing to open fire. Beyond the thugs James caught sight of his three Phoenix buddies, firing at some unseen targets.

James's 3-round burst severed one guy's spine and dropped him instantly. The thug's partner spun on his heel, bringing his AK-47 to bear on James's face. The American ducked under the muzzle, feeling the heat from the bullets that screamed from the barrel. Now he triggered a shot and took a meaty chunk out of the Filipino's left shoulder.

The Communist stumbled away, blood pouring from his pulped shoulder. But he was still in a fighting rage. He tried again to line up his Kalashnikov. James batted it aside with his own weapon, then slashed the butt of the M-16 across his adversary's jaw. It struck with a solid whack, spilling the man and his AK-47 to the floor. James kicked the Russian-made assault rifle well out of the guy's reach. Leaning over him, James jabbed the M-16's warm muzzle against the guy's face.

"Try any kind of sneaky shit on me, man, and you are dead," James snapped. "Understand?"

The man nodded.

From the pocket of his combat pants James pulled out plastic riot cuffs, which he looped and secured around the Filipino's ankles. He also riot-cuffed the man's hands behind his back.

"Don't go away," James said softly before he moved on.

The gunfire was slackening off. A final burst from what James recognized as McCarter's Ingram was followed by silence.

Moving toward the front of the warehouse, the black warrior called out, warning his partners of his presence.

Moments later the four Phoenix commandos were reunited.

26

"Anyone hurt?" Gary Manning asked as the Force regrouped.

McCarter shook his head.

There was a similar response from Rafael Encizo.

"Few bruises is all," James offered. "Nothing to complain about."

"So why are you?" McCarter asked brusquely.

James shot his head around. "Hey, get off my back, man!"

"See?" McCarter said, all defensive. "You offer a mate a little sympathy and he bites your head off."

"Sympathy? You call that sympathy, you..."

At that moment the black Phoenix pro caught Manning and Encizo grinning at him, and he realized he'd been set up. Glancing at McCarter he saw that the Briton, leaning casually against a stack of crates, had a wry smile on his face.

"Anyone ever tell you what a lovely color you go when you're angry?" McCarter asked.

James couldn't help but grin.

The light moment helped to release the tension of the heated combat they had just survived. Later they would all realize how lucky they were—again. But right now they needed something to drain away the high-voltage rage and the adrenaline that was pumping frantically through their systems.

"As the old saying goes," McCarter intoned, "they've stored enough weapons here to start a bloody war."

"Exactly what they want to start," Manning said. "Once the coup gets underway, whoever's running the show could hand out weapons to every sympathizer in need."

"I spotted grenades back there," James said. "Explosives. Rocket launchers."

"It appears our Russian friends have invested heavily in this deal," Encizo said. "Don't you guys feel we should knock a few points off the value of their shares?"

Gary Manning nodded. "Watch them go down with a bang?"

"Exactly," the Cuban said.

"You want to give me a hand?" Manning asked.

The pair wandered off to select the explosives and other gear they were going to need.

"I'll amuse myself, don't worry," McCarter called after them.

"Listen," James said. "I've got a live prisoner back there. He took a slug in the shoulder, but he is alive. Maybe we can get some info out of him."

"Sounds like a worthy pastime," the cockney remarked. "Do you think he'll be ready to talk?"

"I don't know. He could be easy. On the other hand, he might turn out to be a mean bastard."

McCarter smiled. It was the kind of smile that suggested he had some evil trick up his sleeve.

James led the way to where the wounded prisoner was tied.

"This him?" McCarter asked, his voice hard and devoid of feeling.

James caught on to the Briton's act, nodding in answer.

Between them James and McCarter pulled the man to his feet.

"All right, mate, you're coming with us."

The Filipino, face glistening with sweat brought on by the pain in his shoulder, stared at the grim-faced McCarter.

"Where are you taking me?"

"Our mates are starting to lay some explosives around this place. It's going to look like fiesta night when all this lot goes up." McCarter nodded. "And you're going to have the ringside seat. Be able to experience what an explosion is like from the inside."

"You will not leave me in here?" the Filipino asked, his eyes bulging in terror.

"Look, pal, we don't want you," McCarter snapped. "If anybody thinks I'm going to drag some bullet-wounded victim around Manila, looking for a doctor, then they can kiss my ass."

"Well don't look at me," James protested. "Ain't my fault the sucker moved when I shot him. If he hadn't he'd be dead and we wouldn't have this problem."

"I keep telling you," McCarter went on, "it ain't a bleedin' problem. If he could be considered useful to us, okay. But this guy ain't got anything to tell us, so he can sit next to one of the explosive packs and go up with the place. Easiest solution all around."

The Filipino stared at one, then the other Phoenix pro, getting nothing but hard glances from both. He saw no hope of salvation—unless he could bargain with them. He decided it was worth a try. "Maybe I do have information," he began.

"What can *you* tell us?" James asked harshly.

"I could tell you that even if you destroy all the weapons stored here, a shipment has already gone out."

"When?"

"Yesterday. Midmorning."

McCarter took a gamble.

"That would be the shipment for the Americans," the Briton said to James.

"Yeah. The one that went out by boat."

Their prisoner looked dismayed. He had been about to impart the same information himself, but these two seemed to know it already.

"How did you find out?" he asked.

McCarter smiled thinly. "Sometimes we just have to listen and people give the answers without even realizing."

The Filipino's mouth dropped open with surprise at being so easily caught out. He viewed his captors with respect, aware of his own shortcomings, and saw that his only way to survive this day was to give them what they wanted.

"You feel like finishing the story for us?" James asked.

"What do you wish to know?"

"Who came for the weapons?"

"Four Americans. Three came with the boat. The fourth came on his own, much earlier. He flew in by helicopter. He personally selected the weapons that were to be used by his people."

"He have a name?" McCarter asked.

The prisoner-turned-informant shook his head. "He did not give it. And no one would have asked. He was a bad man. Very big. Very tough. I believe he would be a very violent man if angered. I can only tell you he spoke like those cowboys in American movies. The ones they call Texans.''

McCarter nodded. He glanced at James.

''Milt Peck. Remsberg's second-in-command,'' James confirmed.

''Anyone tell you where the boat was heading when it left here?'' McCarter asked.

''No.''

The Filipino suddenly swayed and sank to his knees, his body trembling with delayed reaction to his wound.

''He isn't going to tell us much more,'' James said after giving the man a swift examination.

''Give us a hand, then,'' McCarter said, ''and we'll get him outside. Can't leave the little bugger in here after everything he's told us.''

''You're all heart,'' James murmured as he helped McCarter carry the semiconscious man from the warehouse.

''I just can't help it,'' McCarter replied.

''Do something for me, then,'' James said. ''Stay here and keep your eyes open while I go get the Chevy.''

''Make it quick, chum. The sooner we get away from this place the better I'm going to like it.''

As James vanished, McCarter, leaning against a wall, took a pack of Players from the top pocket of his combat jacket. The Briton frowned when he saw that the pack was squashed. He fished one of the bent cigarettes from the pack and stuck it in his mouth. From another pocket he produced a lighter.

The Phoenix commando had almost finished the cigarette when Manning and Encizo joined him.

''Where's Cal?'' Manning asked.

"Bringing the transport," McCarter said. "How long do we have?"

"I set the timer for fifteen minutes," Manning replied. "We've got about thirteen left."

Five minutes later James rolled the Chevy Blazer to a stop in front of the warehouse. The wounded man was placed in the back, then the Force climbed in. James gunned the motor and drove away.

The factory complex was far behind them when the explosion dully sounded. A number of sharper explosions followed as the stored ammunition and explosives detonated. Twisting around in his seat, McCarter spotted a ball of flame and smoke rising in the blue sky.

"Head for home," the Briton told James. "Let's hope that Milligan's located that bloody island. If he has it's our next stop."

27

The return to the safe house was without incident. Shortly before the Phoenix team arrived it began to rain. There was little warning. One minute warm sunshine flooded the sky, the next, heavy raindrops appeared, turning swiftly into a torrential downpour.

"Just like home," McCarter muttered. "A British summer at the seaside."

At the safe house the wounded Filipino was transferred to a bed. Calvin James, making good use of an available medical kit, tended to the man's injury. While he carried this out, Manning briefed Milligan on the events at the warehouse.

James eventually returned to the living room, where everyone had gathered.

"Can you arrange proper medical attention for him?" the black Phoenix commando asked the security man.

Milligan nodded. "I'll fix it," he said, and went to make a phone call.

On his return the embassy man poured himself a mug of coffee and stood drinking it, watching the Stony Man team replenish their ammunition pouches and check their weapons. They were, he realized, true professionals. Men who put their lives on the line on a regular basis. He ran through the list of confrontations they had been involved in since arriving in the Philippines, and he silently saluted their dedication and stamina.

"What have you got for us?" Encizo asked, glancing up from his MP-5.

"I believe I've located your island," Milligan said.

"Good man," Gary Manning said as he and the others gathered around.

A large maritime chart lay on the table. Milligan stabbed a finger at a red circle he had marked.

"Twenty miles from Lubang," the security man said, "is an island all on its own. Never been permanently inhabited. Doesn't even have a name. It's ten miles long by four miles wide. Pretty wild place. Lots of vegetation and trees. Rough ground."

"Fine," McCarter said. "*National Geographic* would love that description. But apart from being in the vicinity of Lubang, what else is there that puts *this* island at the top of the list?"

"Three years ago it was used by the Philippine Army as a weapons training area. The army used the rough terrain to simulate jungle conditions in exercises. The island has a small base camp with offices and barracks. When the Marcos government hit a bad financial patch the island was abandoned as too costly and left to rot."

"Be ideal for Remsberg and his bunch," James pointed out.

"And if—as we now suspect—there is military involvement in the coup plot," Milligan added, "we can assume there is someone with enough clout to keep the occupation of the island under wraps."

"Sounds good to me," Manning agreed.

McCarter studied the chart. "Have to admit it's got possibilities." He glanced at Milligan. "You wouldn't know whether there's a loading dock or jetty?"

"For the boat to unload?" Milligan asked. He nodded as he unrolled another chart. "I got this through Naval Intelligence at Subic Bay. All I did was mention the code name your people gave us and everyone jumped.

"This is a detailed layout of the island and the base camp. The base is located close to the landing jetty here in this natural bay at the south-east corner of the island. To the north and west is a lot of rough country. Nothing has been developed. It's very primitive."

McCarter grinned. "So are we, chum."

"If we make a landing up-country from the base camp we could walk in and surprise them," Encizo said.

"Ah, don't ye just love the boy's simple faith," McCarter intoned in an excellent Irish accent.

"First thing we need is a telephone," Manning said.

A couple of minutes later he was speaking to Jack Grimaldi at Clark Field.

"I can be airborne in ten minutes," the flyer said. "Hey, we heading for the action?"

"Most likely," Manning admitted.

Grimaldi listened as Manning gave him a rough location. "Okay, you switch on that homer I gave you, and the lady will land right in your backyard."

While they waited for Grimaldi, the Force grabbed a quick meal. McCarter drained a couple of cans of Coke, and stuffed a couple more in his pockets to drink during the flight.

McCarter also took the opportunity to call Mahmud. He was lucky enough to catch his friend at home.

"Are you all right?" Mahmud asked.

"Fine," McCarter replied. "Look, Mahmud, we'll be disappearing for a while. Understand?"

Mahmud did. It meant that McCarter and his friends were going to be involved in another dangerous encounter.

"Take care, my friend," the Bajau said. "I may have some news for you when you return. News that may help to locate Mr. Baum."

"Thanks," McCarter said. "You watch out for yourself. Don't do anything foolish."

"Coming from you that is very funny."

"I suppose you're right. But I mean it."

"I know you do. And the same goes for you."

"One of these days I'll visit you for a proper holiday and we'll have a hell of a time," McCarter said.

Mahmud laughed. "David, any time you visit the Philippines, we have a *hell* of a time."

"You know something? You're right."

"David, *mabuhay*," Mahmud said.

THIRTY MINUTES LATER Dragon Slayer settled on the lawn behind the house. As the wheels touched the grass, Phoenix Force appeared from the building and climbed inside the combat chopper. As the access hatch was being closed Grimaldi took Dragon Slayer up and away.

"Where to?" the pilot asked.

Gary Manning moved up and slid into the seat next to Grimaldi. "It's an island to the northwest of Lubang. About twenty miles off."

"Okay, pal, let's see," Grimaldi said. He punched in instructions to the on-board computer and moments later a screen lit up in front of them. On it was a section of a map. Grimaldi tapped in additional information. The image changed. Now they were looking at the island of Lubang. More input scrolled the image down the screen until it stopped on the outline of the island Milligan had shown them on his chart.

"One of the new gadgets they fitted while the lady was grounded," Grimaldi remarked. "All I do now is lock onto that island and the computer gives me the course."

"I'm impressed," Manning said.

"I wish to hell it could give us a location for Katz," Grimaldi said.

"So do we all," the Canadian agreed.

28

Grimaldi approached the island at high altitude, swinging in to bring Dragon Slayer down at the western tip.

The terrain was as Jack Milligan had described. The undulating landscape was covered by thick vegetation and trees. Here and there the lush greenery was relieved by brilliantly colored flowering plants.

First out of the helicopter, Rafael Encizo moved ahead a few yards to check the area.

Shutting down the chopper, Grimaldi removed his headset and released his hatch so he could climb out to stretch his legs. The flier carried a 9 mm SIG-Sauer P-226 in a shoulder rig and had an Uzi fixed in a clip next to his seat.

The weather had cleared during the flight and the sun was high overhead. A slight breeze came in from the ocean but did little to relieve the sullen heat.

"Bloody horrible weather for a hike," McCarter grumbled as he jumped to the ground from Dragon Slayer. "I can tell you right now I'm going to be pissed off by the time we get where we're going."

James, checking his gear, said, "Look at it this way, David. You perform better when you're mad at something."

The cockney rebel brightened at that thought.

Gary Manning turned to Grimaldi. "As soon as we know if we've hit the right island I'll activate the homer, Jack. Then you can come in making as much damn noise as you want."

"Just make sure you're aiming at the bad guys if you decide to use that bloody rotary mincer," McCarter said.

Grimaldi smiled. "Don't worry. Good luck, fellows."

THE DENSE, LUSH VEGETATION closed in around Phoenix Force. Beneath the green canopy formed by the trees and high plants the heat gathered, creating a hothouse effect. The ground underfoot was soft and spongy, moisture oozing from it.

Within minutes of entering the greenery the Phoenix warriors were sweating heavily as the cloying heat drew the natural moisture from their bodies.

"Try and get us out of this soon as you can," James called to Encizo.

The Cuban raised a hand in acknowledgement.

The Force had to traverse the dense forest for another half hour before they broke free. On a high ridge they sank to the ground, grateful to be able to breathe in the comparatively fresh air of the open terrain.

Manning slapped at the insects buzzing around his wet face. He pulled a pair of binoculars from his backpack, stretching out on the ridge as he scanned the distant landscape.

"Anything?" James asked.

"Nothing moving," the Canadian replied. "The land must drop away beyond that last stretch of forest to the east. My guess is the base camp will be below there."

Manning continued using the binoculars for a few more minutes, thoroughly checking the way ahead. He finally sat up, returning them to his pack.

"I figure we'll be safe from being spotted until we're right on top of the place. It's so damn hard to move around on this island that I can't see Remsberg and his bunch straying far from their base."

McCarter was stretched out on the ground with his camouflage beret tipped across his face; he grunted angrily.

"You say something?" Manning asked.

McCarter sat up, swiping the beret aside. "I said, let's hope you're right."

The British ace was becoming increasingly touchy. Manning didn't respond because he was feeling tense himself. It was a combination of the climate and all the pressure they had been under since their arrival. It seemed almost like one continuous firefight. The Force had jumped from confrontation to confrontation, with little breathing space in between. And it was far from over yet.

And on top of everything else they carried their concern for the missing member of the team.

Being without Katz was like being without part of their own bodies. The tough, hard-fighting Israeli was held in great esteem by the rest of Phoenix Force. He was a guiding light and a good friend, as well as their commander. Each man in the team felt his absence strongly. They would carry out the functions of their mission as normal, but no one would rest comfortably until Katz returned to their midst.

"Come on, you guys, let's head out," Manning said a few minutes later.

In single file the Force followed the long slope that took them off the ridge and into a narrow valley. On either side the valley's green walls rose into the blue sky. Near the far end they came across a clear, fast-flowing stream. The water flashed over smooth stones in the stream bed, catching the bright sunlight.

Each man in turn knelt by the stream, sluicing the fresh water onto their hot faces, splashing it down their chests in an attempt to cool themselves.

Moving on again, they cleared the valley and turned slightly south. Their intention was to reach the edge of the island and follow the coastline as much as possible.

The plan proved wise. Although in places the dense thickets grew right up to the shoreline, there was generally less vegetation along the coast. Now they had the ocean in sight all the time. The terrain rose and fell, so that sometimes they were only a few feet from the white beaches, and other moments they would ascend a steep slope and the beaches would lie at the foot of cliffs eighty to a hundred feet high.

Time seemed to pass slowly. Overhead the sun had advanced beyond its zenith and was commencing the relentless fall toward the western horizon.

Encizo, still in the lead, raised his arm and signaled for the others to stop. Crouching, he stroked his hand toward the ground, telling them to keep low. One by one the Phoenix pros edged closer to the Cuban.

Inches from shore, they stood atop a fifty-foot cliff overlooking the natural bay that curved away from them. It was a good half mile across. In the center of the curve, set some two hundred yards back from the white sand beach, was the abandoned base camp. Just as Milligan's chart had shown.

What the chart had not shown were the men moving about the base. Or the large cruiser tied up at the jetty that extended out into the bay.

For a few moments the Force studied the scene.

Then McCarter gave an exaggerated sigh of relief.

"What was that for?" James asked.

A smile creased McCarter's face. "I'd almost resigned myself to believing we'd come all this way for nothing. But I can say with confidence now that I was wrong."

29

"I'd say those guys are expecting company," Calvin James observed.

"Why?" Manning asked.

James pointed out the perimeter guards, all well armed, and the machine gun post in front of the main block. There were two men lounging on the foredeck of the cruiser, as well.

"Probably someone on the mainland tipped them off about us, so they're taking precautions," Encizo said.

"They've also got some transport," McCarter said.

He indicated a couple of Bell Huey helicopters parked behind the main building. Nearby was a mat-black Loach—the nickname for the Hughes OH-6 Cayuse.

The Force retreated from the skyline and hunched down to discuss tactics.

"Before we get involved in a shooting match," Manning said, "we need to identify the undercover man, Jim Dexter, and get him clear."

"We all got a look at his photograph during Hal's briefing," Encizo reminded everyone.

"All right," McCarter said. "I'll stroll down and give him a shout."

"David!" Manning said sternly.

McCarter held up an apologetic hand.

"What we could do is snatch one of the sentries," the Briton said soberly. "Get him to tell us where Dexter might be."

"I never know when he's serious," Encizo remarked.

"This time he is," James said "Right?"

McCarter nodded.

"Cal," Manning said. "We need you and your grenade launcher in a position to take out that M-60."

"On my way," the black warrior said. He shrugged out of his backpack and checked his equipment, making certain he had additional ammunition for his M-16 and Beretta 92. From deep in his pack he produced a walkie-talkie, clipping it to his belt.

"Let me know when you're in position," Manning said as his combat associate departed.

James studied the slope on the far side of the ridge, planning his route. When he was satisfied, he eased over the rim and vanished from sight.

McCarter gave his MAC-10 a final check, glancing at Manning.

"One talkative sentry coming up," the SAS veteran said. He too dumped his backpack after fishing out his walkie-talkie. "See you chaps in a while."

"Hey, take it easy," Manning warned.

McCarter flashed his confident grin. "Me? I always take it easy."

Without another word the tall Briton disappeared into the undergrowth.

"So what do we do?" Encizo asked.

"I guess we go and do some sneaking around, as well," Manning said. "Try and get in close so that when the time comes we can back the guys up."

"Sounds good to me," the Cuban said.

CALVIN JAMES, flat on his stomach, wormed his way down the steep slope toward a wide ledge some twenty feet above the beach. It had taken him close to a half hour to reach his present position. The slope, heavy with tangled foliage, had been difficult to traverse, especially since James was attempting to crawl down it without being seen or heard. The fact that he was carrying his M-16, plus all his other equipment, didn't make the task any easier.

Not that the Chicago warrior wanted it easy. The challenge of being part of Phoenix Force was a great test of his skills, of his endurance under supreme pressure. And his ability to face and conquer great odds. Calvin James wouldn't have had it any other way. It was the uniqueness of the Force and the missions it undertook that distinguished it from any other fighting force. The Stony Man concept was one of unending resistance to the forces of evil, in whatever shape or form they took. There could never be any form of compromise with the destroyers of life and hope. For as long as any of them were able to draw breath, the warriors of Phoenix Force and Able Team would fight on. No matter that each time they cut down one forest of evil another grew in its place. Stony Man would strike again and again, until the evil in the world saw it was not going to win. It was a daunting task. There was so much to be done, so many hot spots in the world bursting into flame. Flame that would spread and devour everything in its path—unless someone came along to extinguish the fire.

Well, Phoenix Force was doing its damnedest to put out the fires, James thought. With the help of Stony Man and Hal Brognola.

And with the shadow of the big guy himself seeming to follow them around. It was often in times of stress that James thought about Mack Bolan. The Executioner, the guy who had started the whole ball rolling, was still out there himself. Chasing around the world, still a loner, handing out his own direct justice in a way that had never been done before. Bolan, the most human of men, carried a great deal of compassion around with him, despite having to walk the hellgrounds most of the time.

It was one of those ironies of life that Bolan— brought in out of the cold by the government to head the Stony Man project—was finally declared an outlaw by that very same administration. Through no fault of his own, save his desire for justice in the world, Mack Bolan became a hunted man again. He refused to quit, though, carrying on his fight by his own efforts—albeit secretly helped by the Stony Man personnel whenever they could. Bolan struck time and time again. At the criminal element in society. At the terrorists who were determined to make a whole world suffer for their twisted beliefs. He fought corruption and violence on a global scale, racking up one hell of a score for the better values of man.

Which was also where Phoenix Force fit into the picture, doing pretty well the same thing by their own efforts, though sometimes the situations they landed themselves in were so damn hot...

James eased himself down onto the wide ledge, crawling around the thick foliage that grew there. From his new vantage point he could see clear across the bay. The moored cruiser was closer now. James could see that the two men on the vessel were armed with AK-47s. Dressed in combat fatigues and boots, they were sprawled on the foredeck, long-peaked caps pulled low over their faces to protect them from the sun.

Turning to look inland, James studied the machine gun emplacement fronting the main building block. The M-60 was set up behind a wall of sandbags. Two men stood by the gun. James calculated that the distance to the gun emplacement was around two hundred meters, which placed it within range of the M-203 grenade launcher. He was extremely familiar with the M-203, having employed its destructive power on numerous occasions, and having mastered the weapon's firing technique to perfection.

He pulled out several 40 mm rounds for the launcher, but decided to load an M-397—the technical specification for the Bounding fragmentation round. He decided this might serve him best, since the machine gun was behind a three-foot sandbag wall. The M-397 would not explode on impact. Instead, it was fitted with a small explosive charge that blew the round back into the air, taking it to around five feet before it detonated. The grenade's sizzling fragments were then spread over a wider radius, and were infinitely more effective when dealing with enemy troops concealed behind barriers or in open holes. As well as the M-397, James also had some standard M-406 high-explosive rounds. This was a point-detonating round; it exploded on impact, spreading its 325 fragments over an effective injury radius of five meters. As a precaution against exploding too soon, the M-406 did not actually become explodable until it had traveled between fourteen and twenty-eight meters. This gave the round its "semismart" designation.

With his weapon loaded and ready to fire, James unclipped his walkie-talkie. It was time to contact Manning and let him know everything was set.

WHILE JAMES WAS still moving toward firing position, David McCarter spotted a patrolling sentry and started to stalk him.

The British commando, concealed in deep foliage, spent some time watching the sentry. He wanted to work out the farthest limit of the man's range so that he could take him with the least possible chance of alerting anyone else.

As soon as he had established the extent of the guy's circuit, McCarter slipped from the undergrowth and circled around so that he would be waiting for the sentry on his next approach.

McCarter put his MAC-10 behind a thick clump of grass and slipped the Gerber Predator from its sheath. He waited patiently, his senses alert for any untoward sound or sign that might indicate things were not as they should be.

Crouched in the undergrowth, the cool Phoenix warrior showed a tenacity that would have done an Apache of the New Mexico badlands proud. Though the Briton came from a totally different cultural milieu, his ability to remain immobile and silent was worthy of those formidable warriors of the Old West. The fighting chiefs such as Geronimo and Mangas Coloradas would have welcomed McCarter as a brother. He was as they had been—a natural warrior, born with the spirit of combat and a fearlessness that permitted risks that others might consider reckless. For McCarter that kind of daredevilry was daily fare. Life was full of risks. If you debated each move before it was made, life might become safer—but by McCarter's reckoning it would also become depressingly dull.

He heard the approaching sentry well before he saw the guy. The merc was clumping through the undergrowth with all the stealth of an elephant walking over glass.

McCarter picked him out while he was still yards away. The sentry was tall, with heavy shoulders and chest. Under his combat shirt his muscular biceps pushed tightly against the fabric. Instead of a hat the guy wore a sweatband around his head and his hair hung down to his brawny shoulders. McCarter grinned at the sight. Stallone had a bloody lot to answer for, the Phoenix commando thought. The Remsberg merc carried a Beretta 92-F in a high-ride holster on his right hip and an AK-47 in his hands.

McCarter let the sentry step by, then rose silently and came up behind him. With his left hand, the Briton grabbed the guy's thick mane of hair and yanked his head back while the right swept the glittering blade of the Predator around to the sentry's taut throat. McCarter applied just enough pressure to nick the skin.

"You can die right now, chum," McCarter said evenly, "or you can go down on your knees and live a little longer. Your choice."

The merc knew he had no choice. The knife at his throat could kill him long before he could carry out any kind of evasive move. He sank to his knees, feeling McCarter follow him down. The pressure of the knife at his throat didn't waver a fraction.

"Put the safety on the rifle," McCarter ordered, "then toss it over to the left into the grass." The sentry did as instructed. "Now the Beretta."

With the sentry disarmed, McCarter told him to lie facedown on the ground and spread his arms and legs. The guy did as he was told, still feeling the cold steel of the Predator pressed against his sweaty skin.

"That's better," McCarter said cheerfully. "Now we can have a little chat."

"About what?" the merc asked sourly.

"No sulking, mate," McCarter chided. "You lost, so don't be...difficult about it."

"Fuck you," the merc spat.

"Language," the Brit remonstrated. "Let's get this over with. All I need is a simple answer to a straight question."

"Yeah?"

"Where do I find Arnie Ryker?"

The merc was silent for a moment, then he began to chuckle, as if McCarter had cracked a funny joke.

McCarter let the Predator's blade slice into the guy's throat a fraction more. Just enough to make the wound sting and allow a thin finger of blood to trickle down his throat.

"You're making me nervous, chum," McCarter warned. "Just let me in on the joke."

"The joke is you've come a long way for nothing," the merc said. "Ryker was caught snooping while we were still stateside. He took a long time to die. When it was over he was buried somewhere away from the base."

"You really are a miserable bunch of bastards," McCarter growled, his anger threatening to get the better of him.

Perhaps the Briton's rage resulted in a slight increase in pressure of the blade against the merc's neck. Or perhaps the guy figured he'd said too much. Whatever the motivation, the merc attempted to extract himself from his restricted position. He arched his powerful body up off the ground and grabbed McCarter's knife wrist.

Tipped slightly off balance, McCarter almost lost his advantage. He managed to hang on to the Predator, despite the iron grip of his adversary. As he moved to one side, lifted by the merc's body, McCarter reached out to catch hold of the guy's long hair, but his fingers were unable to make contact.

The brawny merc made a Herculean effort and managed to unseat McCarter from astride him. With a burst of reserve strength the merc twisted his body, dragging himself partially clear. His steady grip on McCarter's wrist still prevented the Phoenix warrior from using the deadly blade.

The merc rammed his left elbow back and up, a hard blow that bruised McCarter's ribs on his right side. In retaliation McCarter sledged his left fist in a short, sharp arc that clouted the merc behind the ear. The guy grunted, stunned by the blow. McCarter hit him again and again. The merc ducked, released McCarter's wrist and rolled clear to avoid further blows.

McCarter kicked to his feet and confronted the angry merc, who was cursing in a low monotone. He rubbed a big hand across the sore area of his head. When he took his hand away the palm was slick with blood.

Without warning, the merc charged McCarter, tightly grabbing the cockney's knife wrist again. As they smashed together the merc drove his right knee into McCarter's groin. The Phoenix pro expected such a move and blocked it with his leg. McCarter punched the merc in the face, feeling the guy's nose crumble under the blow. Blood burst from the crushed organ. Before the merc could react McCarter struck again, crashing his hard fist against the exposed face. The merc's head rocked under the powerful blow.

McCarter felt the iron grip on his wrist begin to slacken. The British brawler kicked out, the toe of his combat boot driving in between the merc's legs. It struck with a solid thud, drawing a shuddering moan from the hired gun. With a sudden wrench, McCarter freed his wrist, stepped back, then whirled, delivering a brutal snap-kick with his right foot that connected with the merc's skull.

There was an audible crack. The merc slid sideways, his body losing all coordination. He flopped to the ground in a dead heap.

Muttering to himself, McCarter unclipped his walkie-talkie and keyed the transmit button.

"Rawlinson," he growled when Manning acknowledge. "I bagged my man. He talked. Ryker is dead. They tagged him before they left the U.S. I'm all through here. Ready to go in when you are."

"Stay put," Manning said. "I'm waiting for Jackson to call in. Soon as he does I'll have him take out the machine gun. The minute he does that, we all go in."

"Tell him to make it fast," McCarter snapped, and switched off.

"Is HE PISSED OFF," Manning exclaimed as he finished speaking to McCarter.

Encizo smiled, well aware of the Briton's volatile nature. He could live with it, because there was no better man than McCarter to have at your side in a firefight.

The Canadian and the Cuban were concealed in a shallow depression on the edge of the concrete apron that jutted from the building complex.

Manning's walkie-talkie clicked with a metallic sound. The Canadian thumbed the receive button.

Calvin James's voice echoed from the instrument.

"I'm in position. You want me to take out that MG?"

"Affirmative," Manning said.

CALVIN JAMES planted the butt of the M-16 on his shoulder, sighting through the special attachment of the M-203 grenade launcher. As he zeroed in on the distant machine gun emplacement, he calculated range trajectory. He slipped his finger through the M-203's trigger guard and fired.

The M-397 round described a perfect curve as it rose, reached the apex of its flight, then sank gracefully. It struck the concrete within three feet of the emplacement. There was a sharp crack as the internal charge exploded, hurling the canister back into the air. The main charge threw a heavy blast of sound across the concrete apron. The metal fragmentation load lashed out and down, shredding the top layer of sandbags and puncturing the flesh of the two Remsberg mercs who had been manning the machine gun.

30

McCarter saw the flash and heard the thud.

He was moving before the sound died. Because he was close to the helicopters, the Briton took them as his priority. He felt pretty sure that the two big Hueys were for transporting the Remsberg mercs to the mainland. Since helicopters are useful only as long as they can be flown, McCarter decided to put the three choppers out of action.

He cleared the greenery and hit the concrete apron, boots thudding against the hard dusty surface as he broke to the left. A crackle of autofire came from the direction of the beach.

Ahead of him a pair of armed figures in combat fatigues moved away from the Hueys. One raised a Kalashnikov and opened fire. The harsh report of the Soviet weapon preceded the stream of 7.62 mm slugs that peppered the concrete at McCarter's feet.

McCarter turned, his MAC-10 tracking the carrier of the AK-47. The Brit fired a 9 mm reply at the merc. His first volley cut the guy's left leg from under him. The merc yelled and fell facedown to the concrete, his weapon slipping from his fingers. Cursing wildly, he clawed at the automatic pistol leathered on his hip, only to be denied that option by a second burst from Mc-

Carter's crackling SMG. A trio of slugs slammed into his skull. The dying merc twitched, then went limp.

Turning toward the second merc, McCarter heard the vicious crackle of autofire. The British commando felt the urgent tug of bullets snatching at his clothing. There was a sudden burning sensation over his right hip. McCarter swore viciously as he threw himself full length across the concrete. Slugs hissed overhead. Ignoring the pain throbbing in his shoulder, McCarter concentrated on bringing his Ingram into play. He jerked the muzzle around, seeking the remaining merc.

Both weapons fired simultaneously.

McCarter heard the Kalashnikov rap out its sound. The concrete exploded all around him.

His MAC-10 exploded with a sound like tearing cloth as McCarter emptied the magazine in a brief, continuous burst. The stream of slugs hammered into the target's torso. The wounded merc fell in a spasm of jerks and twitches.

Rolling to his feet, McCarter fed a fresh magazine into the MAC-10, cocking the weapon as he made a dash for the three helicopters.

The figure of a stocky Filipino, dressed in dark coveralls, appeared in the open hatch of one of the Hueys. He was in fact one of the pilots. The guy was brandishing a heavy automatic pistol, and the moment he laid his eyes on the armed trespasser he opened fire. McCarter was too quick for him. The pilot died in the very flying machine he had sought to protect.

Reaching the first Huey, McCarter tossed a grenade inside the open hatch. He repeated the operation with the second chopper, then ran on, his long legs taking him swiftly away from the doomed aircraft.

One explosion followed the other with only a second between them. The Hueys rocked with the detonations, Plexiglas windows blew out, riveted seams burst, and spilled fuel was ignited, the flames spreading quickly. When the mass of fuel blew, there was a ragged, heavy thump. The helicopters were ripped apart in boiling, seething balls of fire. Hissing tentacles of flaming fuel lashed outward from the center of the inferno, streaking the concrete with black fingers. A rain of debris rattled and thumped to the ground.

The shock waves from the explosions flung McCarter across the concrete like a leaf in a windstorm. Fortunately, he had the presence of mind to relax his muscles and roll with the pressure.

Regaining his feet, the cockney commando glanced over his shoulder at the ruined Hueys. Then he sprinted across the littered concrete apron, heading for the Loach, which sat far enough away from the other helicopters to escape being damaged. McCarter intended to alter that.

A Kalashnikov opened up to McCarter's right. The bullets whipped through the air inches from his body. McCarter turned in the direction of the gunfire. A merc clad in combat gear was taking aim for another shot. The Phoenix commando returned fire, his Ingram rattling out its shots at blinding speed. The merc jerked to one side, his chest showing blotches of red as he crashed to the concrete.

Nearing the Loach, McCarter lobbed a grenade beneath the parked helicopter and retreated, making for the main block of the base buildings.

MANNING AND ENCIZO encountered resistance almost immediately.

As the Canadian broke from cover, with his Cuban partner close behind, a trio of Raiders appeared from a side door, all fully armed. Their weapons were turned immediately on the Phoenix pair.

Bullets whacking the concrete around him, Encizo tackled Manning to the ground, then returned fire with the MP-5, catching the leading merc in the upper body, and slamming him against the wall. Their companion hit, the other two mercs held their fire in order to spread out. They never resumed the battle. Changing tactics in combat is risky. Momentum has to be maintained, the enemy kept under engagement, even while changing position. Their brief hesitation cost the mercs their lives.

Manning had rolled twice upon hitting the ground, and as Encizo took out one of the mercs, the Canadian aimed his SA80 at another. When the guy broke to the left Manning's weapon followed, stuttered, and propelled a stream of 5.56 mm slugs into his chest. The guy went down with a bone-jarring crash.

The remaining merc fired his Soviet rifle once before Encizo took him out of the game.

Manning, back on his feet, sprinted to the front of the main building. Encizo followed in the Canadian's shadow.

They hugged the wall of the main block, weapons ready, each man covering a different direction.

From across the complex came the twin cracks of exploding grenades. A spiral of smoke and flame shot skyward.

"David," Manning said softly.

Encizo nodded. "I'd guess we scratch the choppers."

"Company!" Manning yelled.

He triggered a burst at the four armed figures in combat gear who burst into view around the corner of the building. The group split apart, turning their weapons on the Phoenix pair.

The stutter of AK-47s filled the air where Manning and Encizo had stood only seconds before. Now the two were crouched below the firing line, their own weapons tracking the mercs.

Manning's SA80 ripped into one of the mercs at hip level, shredding flesh. The merc found himself dealt out of the action. During the few protracted seconds of intense agony before he slipped into merciful unconsciousness, he realized that despite the money he earned and the thrill of violence, none of it was worth this kind of suffering.

As the merc hit the concrete, Encizo delivered a double blow, taking out two more of Remsberg's Raiders. Manning picked up the fourth guy. The merc toppled over, blood bubbling from his chest.

WITH THE MACHINE GUN rendered inoperative, Calvin James turned his attention to the cruiser moored at the jetty. He fed a second round into the grenade launcher. James used the M-406 HE round this time, needing point-of-impact detonation.

With the grenade loaded, James aimed the launcher at the boat. Just then, two mercs on the cruiser opened up on James's position.

Gouts of earth spat into the black warrior's face as the Kalashnikov slugs dug into the slope and the rim of the ledge.

Wiping the dust from his eyes, James understood how vulnerable he was on the ledge and that it was in his best interest to leave it as soon as possible.

Easing to the far end, he peered over the edge.

One of the mercs had left the cruiser, sprinted across the curve of beach and was already clawing his way up the slope. The other merc, remaining on the boat, scanned the ledge with his AK-47 to his shoulder.

James calculated the distance to the cruiser, aimed the grenade launcher and pulled the trigger. The M-406 round howled toward the cruiser.

James knew instinctively that he had misjudged the shot. The grenade clipped the cruiser's stern, the blast ripping large splinters from the woodwork.

The merc climbing the slope below James had braced himself against the high bank. Now he pumped 7.62 slugs up at the Phoenix commando, driving him back from the rim.

From the slightly damaged cruiser the second merc opened fire again.

James lay flat against the ledge as the two guns hammered his position. While the ledge protected him from a direct hit, it also restricted his movement.

Stretched out on the ledge, the black warrior loaded another round into the M-203. Then he took two standard grenades from his combat harness.

Inhaling deeply, he braced himself, then pulled the pins on the grenades. He released the levers, held the grenades for three seconds, then dropped them over the ledge.

The moment the grenades detonated, James brought his weapon into firing position. The merc on the cruiser, seeing him, swung his AK-47 in James's direction. He was sighting along the Kalashnikov's barrel when a puff of smoke gushed from the muzzle of James's weapon.

An instant later the grenade struck the cruiser no more than a foot from the merc. The world erupted in the guy's face. There was no time even for pain to register as the fragmentation load reduced him to a bloody and lifeless rag doll. The grenade blasted a hole in the cruiser's hull through which water began to pour.

Before James could withdraw from the rim, the harsh crackle of the unseen AK-47 rang out. The Phoenix pro felt a terrific force strike the grenade launcher, almost wrenching it from his grasp.

"Damn!" James muttered.

He rolled to the back of the ledge. A swift check of the rifle showed that the barrel of the grenade launcher had been badly distorted by the strike. At least, the Stony Man warrior realized, the M-16 itself hadn't been damaged.

Not that the knowledge gave him much comfort. He was still boxed in, his movements restricted by the range of the merc's AK-47.

The thought did not sit easy with James. He hated being bested by anyone, and especially by some money-hungry killer with a gun. James considered the matter for a few seconds and decided it would have to be corrected.

He made his decision and acted on it without further thought.

Laying down his M-16, James produced his Beretta 92-SB pistol. He scrambled over the ledge, hitting the slope and digging in his heels to slow his descent. He had also snatched his Jet-Aer dagger from its sheath with his left hand. He stabbed the blade deep into the earth, using it as an anchor, and brought himself to an uneasy halt.

The Raider was slightly above James, some twelve feet away across the slope.

The merc attempted to get his AK-47 into line as James plunged into view, but he was too slow.

The Beretta emitted two silvery messengers of death that burrowed deep into the merc's chest and threw him down the slope with a strangled yell. Hurtling to the bottom, he came to a tangled stop on some jagged rocks.

James put away his Beretta and climbed back to the ledge. He retrieved his M-16 and slung it across his back. Then he climbed down to the beach.

═══ 31 ═══

Manning and Encizo, skirting the destroyed machine gun emplacement, climbed the steps and entered the main block. They found themselves in what had been a large office, now being used to store the weapons the Raiders had brought over from the mainland.

A number of crates had been opened and their contents laid out on canvas sheets on the floor. There were Kalashnikovs, a number of M-60s, half a dozen RPG-7 launchers and, to one side, boxes of ammunition, grenades and rockets for the RPG-7s.

"Jackpot!" Encizo said as he cast his gaze across the armaments.

"Game isn't over yet," his Canadian partner warned.

The creak of a door emphasized Manning's words. The Phoenix warriors parted company, each making for opposite sides of the room.

Seconds later the interior of the building reverberated to the thunder of a Kalashnikov. Bullets whacked the wall just above Encizo's head, blowing chunks of plaster away. The Cuban's back was peppered by flying splinters.

An instant before joining the fray, Gary Manning slipped one of Grimaldi's homers from his pocket. He activated the device and laid it on the floor against the wall.

Out of the corner of his eye the Canadian commando spotted movement in the shadowed rectangle of the open doorway. Light glinted on a metal barrel.

Manning triggered the SA80, sending a spray of slugs toward the Kalashnikov. Wood splinters exploded from the frame and the AK-47 was hastily withdrawn.

"Cover me," Encizo yelled.

The Cuban fireball sprinted across the room, dodging and weaving. He skidded to a halt, slamming against the wall close to the doorway where the AK-47 had shown. Encizo slipped a grenade from his harness, popped the pin and tossed the grenade through the opening. Then he pulled back to hug the wall.

There was a loud crash. Smoke billowed through the doorway. Debris pattered from the ceiling.

Encizo ducked low and burst through the door. Ahead, filled with swirling smoke, stretched a passage with several doors leading off it.

Through the smoke Encizo made out the shape of a merc slumped against the wall some yards away. The guy was badly wounded, but he was still able to support the AK-47 and track Encizo the moment he showed through the door.

Encizo brought his MP-5 up and triggered a burst into the plaster over the wounded merc's head.

Moving to one side, the merc pulled the trigger of the AK-47. Because he was holding the weapon with one hand, the recoil lifted it so that the slugs hit the ceiling.

Down on one knee, taking careful aim, Encizo fired again. This burst crashed into his opponent's chest and throat, terminating him.

Getting to his feet, Encizo slapped plaster dust from his clothes. He fed a fresh magazine into his MP-5.

Manning came through the doorway, his SA80 up and ready.

"You okay?" he asked.

The Cuban nodded.

"Come on," Manning said. "Let's clear this damn rats' nest."

CALVIN JAMES SAW Encizo and Manning vanish inside the main building. They had moved too quickly for him to call, and he figured they were probably busy enough without being distracted.

The black commando sprinted across the beach. The fine sand, slipping away beneath his boots, slowed his progress.

Behind him the cruiser had begun to list as the shattered hull filled up with water.

Dark clouds of smoke were rising into the sky at the rear of the complex.

From inside the building came the dull boom of an exploding grenade, followed seconds later by a burst of gunfire.

He had almost reached the concrete apron when an armed figure appeared on the roof and opened fire.

James took three long strides and dived across the sand. He landed and rolled, conscious of the bullets thudding around him. Finding a shallow dip that hid him from the rooftop merc, the former cop located his target, pulled his M-16 to his shoulder, snap-aimed and fired three times.

His first shot missed. The second caught the target in the left shoulder, spinning him sideways. The third shot, rising a couple of inches, blasted his skull. The merc plunged over the roof and crashed on the concrete below.

James raced toward the building, entered and flattened against the inner wall. He remained there while his breathing returned to normal.

The Phoenix pro advanced into the room. Seeing the arms cache, and a bloody corpse sprawled against the wall, and smelling the stench of a recent explosion, James moved on, his weapon at the ready.

At that moment the rattle of automatic fire echoed through the building. It came from up ahead, deeper in the building.

THE DOOR BURST OPEN under McCarter's boot, slamming back against the wall. The Phoenix warrior went in fast, breaking to the right and flattening himself against the wall.

The room measured twelve feet by twelve feet and contained only a low cot and a chair.

A round-faced, tubby Filipino, dressed in civilian clothes, shot up off the chair as McCarter burst in. He didn't look anything like a mercenary or a rebel, or even remotely threatening to the Briton. In fact the guy looked scared. His eyes were almost popping out of his sweating face.

The Filipino took one look at the tall, grim-faced McCarter, clad in combat gear and armed to the teeth, and made a dash for the door.

The ex-SAS man reached out and caught hold of the Filipino's coat. Hauling him back into the room, McCarter slammed the tubby guy against the wall. The Filipino gave a groan and slumped to the floor.

McCarter looped plastic riot cuffs around the Filipino's wrists and ankles. Then he dumped the moaning figure on the cot.

"Talk to you later, chum," McCarter said.

He crossed to the room's other door and opened it. Seeing that the passage beyond was clear, he moved on.

He was at the far end when a grenade went off. Then gunfire erupted.

"Sounds like the fight's come home to roost," the cockney murmured.

He booted open a door. It opened on a large room that contained five armed men, including two in blue coveralls.

The five were halfway across the room, heading in McCarter's general direction when one of them saw the Phoenix commando and yelled a warning. All five faced McCarter directly.

"Oh, shit!" the Briton muttered.

Behind the five, a door crashed open and Manning and Encizo burst into view.

One of the guys in the blue coveralls opened fire, with his Uzi in McCarter's direction.

As the British hell-raiser lunged to one side, his Ingram was already tracking the five. Seeing the Uzi moving to pick him out, he realized he had to retaliate quickly. His finger touched the MAC-10's trigger. The guy in the blue coveralls stopped a chestful of 9 mm slugs.

An eruption of fire filled the large room.

Encizo took out one of the Remsberg mercs, Manning another. Aware that his rifle was now empty,

Manning snatched his Walther P-5 and triggered two shots into the face of the second guy in blue.

The remaining merc snarled his defiance at the Phoenix warriors and reached for a grenade on his combat harness.

Aware of his intentions, both Encizo and McCarter opened fire. The combined power of their two weapons blew the merc apart, driving him to the floor in a bloody, twitching heap.

The sound of gunfire drifted away.

Pale wreaths of smoke hung in the warm air.

The Phoenix trio stood still, weapons raised and ready. The fury and speed of the firefight had been too much, even for the experienced pros of the Force. It left them stunned, still on a high of combat readiness. For long seconds they remained in position, bodies taut, nerves strung out.

They were only beginning to relax when Calvin James appeared in the doorway behind them. The black warrior assessed the situation quickly. He saw the position of the bodies on the floor and knew what had happened. And he had heard the furious blast of fire—all over in a matter of seconds—which told him how tight it had been for his partners.

James slid quietly into the room.

"It's over, guys," he said evenly. "Let go. It's over."

His soothing words broke through.

McCarter ran a hand across his face and managed a taut grin. "Trust you to miss the main event," he said.

"Hey, you know me," James replied. "I never was one to crash a party."

Encizo slowly turned his head and looked toward a window. "You hear that?" he asked.

"Yeah," Manning said. "Sounds like Dragon Slayer."

James grinned. "See. I ain't the only dude who's late."

32

Even as Phoenix Force waged battle on the island, Mahmud was fighting a war of his own.

It began after the Bajau had spoken to McCarter. Upon replacing the receiver, Mahmud drove his jeepney to the chicken farm where Linda Torres was hiding. Certain that the girl had calmed down and would be getting over the events culminating in the violent death of Velasquez, Mahmud hoped she might now recall in more detail the house she and Velasquez had visited.

Mahmud was hoping that this house might be where McCarter's friend was being held. He knew it was a long shot, but anything was worth looking into. If Linda Torres could perhaps give him some idea where the place was located, Mahmud intended to do some snooping.

He was well aware that he could easily place himself in danger. That made little difference to Mahmud. He was quite prepared to put himself at risk for McCarter, and he knew that his friend needed as much help as possible.

Two hours later Mahmud was returning to Manila. His visit with Linda Torres had proved to be extremely fruitful after all. The Filipino girl *had* provided some useful information. She had described the trips she and Velasquez had made to a large estate an hour's drive northeast of Manila, in the lush countryside. The mansion, she explained, stood on an estate surrounded by a high white stone wall with tall gates. The visits had always been at night, but she remembered isolated landmarks.

As soon as Mahmud reached the city, he stopped at a pay phone and called Jack Milligan. The security man tried to talk Mahmud out of what he intended, but the Bajau was determined to carry out his plan.

"Wait until they get back," Milligan suggested. "Let them handle this kind of thing, Mahmud. It's what they're good at."

"You don't understand," Mahmud explained. "I'm only going to have a look at the place. It will save my friends time."

"It could be dangerous," Milligan said. "You must realize the kind of people we're dealing with. They wouldn't think twice about killing you."

Mahmud laughed. "I am only going to have a look. I intend to be in and out very quickly."

Before Milligan could present any further objections Mahmud replaced the receiver. He returned to his jeepney and drove on.

He took the North Expressway out of the city environs, driving steadily for close to forty-five minutes. Mahmud looked out for the back road off the expressway that Linda Torres had described. He identified it by the three palm trees standing on the left. Turning onto this road, Mahmud continued driving. He was in the country now. On each side of the road the lush forest grew thickly. Deep greenery battled for supremacy with the towering trees.

Mahmud slowed the jeepney. It was quiet out here, a great contrast to the twenty-four-hour noise of Manila. He glanced at his watch. According to Linda's time-table he should soon see the side road leading to the estate.

He almost missed it. The dusty track was practically hidden by the dense undergrowth. Mahmud drove by, pulling the jeepney off the road a couple of hundred yards farther on. He eased the vehicle into the greenery until he was certain it couldn't be seen from the road. Then he killed the engine.

From the flip-top locker between the jeepney's front seats Mahmud took a .45-caliber Colt Commander. He checked the automatic pistol's load, snapping the seven-shot magazine back into the butt. He worked the slide to load the first cartridge, then slipped on the safety. He took an extra magazine and slipped it into his shirt pocket.

Mahmud left the jeepney and moved into the undergrowth. It took him almost ten minutes to reach the estate boundary. The high stone wall ran east to west, as far as he could see in both directions.

Mahmud crouched in the shade of a huge palm, studying the wall. He followed the wall east until he saw the tall wooden gates that closed off the estate to outsiders. The information that Linda Torres had given him was proving very accurate. However, there was no evidence yet that the people David McCarter and his friends were after were behind the stone wall. Mahmud decided that he needed more proof before he allowed his friends to waste their valuable time.

He moved a reasonable distance from the gates, then approached the wall. The heavy stones used in its construction had gaps between them that allowed him to gain handholds. The Bajau scaled the wall quickly, reaching the top and peering over. At its top the wall was three feet wide. Mahmud drew himself onto the flat ledge and looked down into the grounds.

A wide drive curved up from the gates, with lawns on either side, until it widened into an oval before the imposing house. This was a sprawling two-story building constructed along traditional Spanish lines. The white walls of the building contrasted neatly with the red-brown roof tiles. Between the high wall and the house, tall palm trees dotted the lawns. A number of expensive cars were parked near the house.

Mahmud studied the scene for some time. His curiosity was aroused now, and he wanted to probe further. To find out more. He knew this was what David would have done. His mind made up, Mahmud climbed down the wall and crouched at its base. The Colt Commander in his hand, the Bajau checked the area. He saw no movement.

Mahmud ran for the cover of the closest palm tree, pressing himself tight against the rough trunk. Once again he checked the grounds. Saw nothing. Heard nothing. He moved to the next tree, then the next, each time pausing to examine the way ahead before moving on.

Soon he was close enough to the house to identify the makes of the parked cars. The Bajau surmised that the drivers must be inside the house.

Now he faced a problem. There were no more trees between himself and the house. Only a curving sweep of open lawn. At least a hundred yards of exposed terrain. Mahmud examined the area. Some twenty feet to the right of the entrance was an arched opening that led to an inner courtyard. Mahmud figured that was the ideal place to head. If he crossed the open lawn he would be able to hide behind the parked cars before making the final dash to the arch. It was not the ideal solution, he admitted, but it was the best he was liable to find.

And it was time he made his move, Mahmud decided. He eased away from the palm, preparing to sprint across the lawn.

Something hard jabbed into his back, prodding insistently.

Mahmud began to turn, the Colt Commander ready in his hand.

A harsh voice snapped a command the Bajau was unable to understand. When he failed to respond as quickly as the owner of the voice obviously expected, something hard cracked against the back of Mahmud's skull. Hurt, but still very conscious, and growing angry, Mahmud spun around to face his attacker.

He received a quick impression of someone very big. Broad. With a hard face beneath short-cropped hair. The figure was dressed in casual, lightweight clothes that somehow didn't seem to fit his bulky shape.

There was something dark and metallic in the guy's hands. Mahmud couldn't identify the make of the weapon but he knew it was an SMG. Sunlight glinted on the cold steel as the weapon slashed up and around, connecting solidly with Mahmud's jaw. His head snapped to one side, a burst of pain engulfing his brain. Mahmud tasted blood on the inside of his cheek where the flesh had caught his teeth. He fell against the palm, feeling the coarse trunk scrape his back through his shirt.

Trying to overcome the swell of sickness threatening to engulf him, Mahmud pushed away from the palm.

Again something hard struck him. The Colt Commander dropped from his fingers. He made a last desperate attempt to resist. All it got him was yet another brutal blow across the side of the face. He fell to his knees, his strength gone. Mahmud's head hung low, blood dripping from the gashes on his face.

Dimly he felt himself being dragged across the lawn. He knew he was being taken to the house. Then inside. He tried to focus but his vision swam. Every time he attempted to see where he was going his sight faded to gray. Pain mushroomed inside his skull. Mahmud gave in to the darkness that swirled about him.

Sounds reached him from far off, echoing with a deep hollowness. He seemed to have lost touch with reality. Everything was so far away. Voices swelled and receded.

Then he seemed to be floating. The brutal hands were gone from his arms. He suddenly realized the floating sensation was caused by his falling. He tried to throw out his hands to stop himself. But the hard floor rushed up to hit him in the face and he lost consciousness.

He came out of the darkness slowly, aware of being talked to. The voice was familiar. Mahmud could not place it. He tried to concentrate. The voice came again. Firm but gentle. Drawing him slowly back to reality.

Mahmud blinked his eyes. A blurred face swam in and out of his vision. Mahmud concentrated on that face, trying to bring it into focus.

It came abruptly. The graying hair above the tanned face. Concern showing in the light blue eyes.

The face of Yakov Katzenelenbogen.

The Israeli commander of Phoenix Force was relieved when Mahmud slowly came around. He helped the Bajau to his feet and got him settled in a chair. He stared at Mahmud for a few moments.

"Is this just a social call?" Katz asked. "Or have you joined the club?"

Mahmud touched the raw spot on his cheek, feeling the blood ooze from the gash.

"I think I've joined," he said. "In fact, I'm sure I've paid all my dues."

Katz sighed. "It might not be the most appropriate thing to say—but welcome aboard."

33

Four of the Raiders and one of the helicopter pilots were still alive. Calvin James attended them, using the medical kits the Raiders had with them on the island. Some of the wounds, however, needed hospital treatment.

"I'll get in touch with Clark Field," Grimaldi said. "Have them send in some medevac units."

Clark Field, under orders from Washington via the Stony Man-White House link, had units on standby just waiting for the word from Phoenix Force.

"Jack," called Gary Manning, "when you get through tell them to bring body bags and to leave enough room to haul all these weapons out of here."

Grimaldi nodded. "Will do," he said, and went out to where Dragon Slayer stood on the concrete apron.

"Right," McCarter said. "I think it's time to go talk to our fat little Filipino chum."

"Any thoughts on who he might be?" Manning asked.

Rafael Encizo said, "He's no fighter. The guy dresses too fancy and he's soft like a woman."

"Then what is he doing out here with Remsberg's bunch?" Manning questioned.

"You want to know what I think?" McCarter said, daring anyone to say no. "I think he's the gofer for all the parties involved. He delivers messages. Makes arrangements. Does all the running about. He's the go-between. The organizer. The bloody fixer."

"Could be," Encizo mused. "How are you going to find out?"

McCarter gave him a wide grin.

"I'm going to scare the shit out of that fat little bugger," the Briton said. "If he doesn't talk after that I'll give up drinking Coke."

"There goes a confident man," Manning said.

MCCARTER ENTERED the building and went to the small room at the back. As he got near he began to march, deliberately smashing his boots down hard on the floor. Reaching the room, he slammed the door open and strode in with a hammering of boots on the floor.

Without a word he drew his gleaming knife and severed the plastic strips securing the Filipino's ankles. Then he pulled the dazed man to his feet, leaving him standing awkwardly in the center of the room.

"All right, my lad," McCarter roared in his best sergeant-major voice. "Outside, and be damn smart about it. We can't keep people waiting like this. Isn't good enough."

The Filipino stared at the surly-looking Briton.

"I don't understand. Where are we going?"

"I've told you, chummy. Outside. Nice clean wall for you to stand against. Got six of my best lads. All armed and ready."

"For what?"

"Your execution, my lad. By firing squad. All be over in a few minutes. Now move!"

McCarter shoved the trembling figure toward the door that led outside.

"No!" the moon-faced Filipino screamed, sheer panic gripping him. "I will not go! You cannot kill me! You must not kill me!"

Lee Harun had been frightened enough when McCarter first crashed into the small room and tied him up like a pig being prepared for market. With the abrupt return of the terrifying figure, the Filipino go-between convinced himself that he was seconds away from death.

Harun had already recognized that his jump into the big time had been a mistake. He was a small fish wallowing around in a large pool full of killer sharks, and in time they would devour him.

He should have stayed with his own kind. In his own element, far away from the bewildering and sinister shadow world of secret meetings and antigovernment plots. He had been dazzled by offers of money in large amounts and promises of things to come when the new administration came to power. His eyes had been closed to the reality of the situation, and it had been only here on this desolate island—where he had been forced to spend a miserable night because the helicopter that had brought him developed a fuel-line blockage—that he had found time to consider his unstable relationship with his employers.

So much had been happening over the past couple of days. So many things that had caused panic and uncertainty in the minds of some of the principals involved in the coup plot. It had taken the emergency meeting, called by the KGB man, Testarov, to calm the jittery nerves and smooth over the problems.

As always Testarov had remained unshaken, a stabi-
lizing influence always ready with the right words and
gestures. He had the knack of talking around thorny
problems and reducing them to minor inconveniences.

But Harun had also seen the Russian's other face.
The mask had slipped to reveal the Soviet's ruthless
streak when he had been dealing with the errant Olivado Velasquez. Testarov had ordered the man's sum-
mary execution as casually as one might brush away a
fly.

At the time Harun had seen that act as evidence of
Testarov's strength. But the previous night, turning
restlessly on the narrow uncomfortable cot that had
been provided for him, Harun replayed that scene again
in his mind. This time he arrived at a different conclusion about the Russian.

The more he thought about it, the less secure Harun
felt. His position within the organization was finely
balanced, to say the least. Velasquez provided an example of this. He had made a mistake, true. But the way
he had been eliminated began to worry Lee Harun. It
made him begin to question his own security. Was he,
too, expendable? Would he, too, be cast aside as soon
as his usefulness was done?

Harun asked himself these questions.

And did not like the answers.

He worked out how much he actually knew about the
people and places involved in the plot. The answer
confirmed his fears. He knew too much. He knew many
things that Testarov would not want divulged to third
parties. With that in mind Harun reached another conclusion. Because of his knowledge there was no way he
would be allowed to withdraw from the group. If he
even hinted he was thinking of quitting he could just as

well shoot himself on the spot. Trying to back out was
equivalent to signing his own death warrant. Like it or
not, Harun was in the game until the end.

His dreams of achieving some high position through
his connections with Testarov and company began to
evaporate. He saw an empty future without promise or
reward—save sudden death.

Leoni Testarov, the Soviet manipulator, would see to
it that Harun had no future. The KGB man was using
them all to further his own country's cause. He was not
really interested in the Philippine cause. He was devoted to his communist creed, and would use and abuse
whoever and whatever he could to advance the state.
The man was clever, extremely clever. He had engi-
neered a plot to overthrow the government and install
a regime that would ultimately be nothing more than a
puppet administration dancing to Moscow's tune.

And they had all fallen for his clever words. None
more than Harun himself, greedy for money and power.
He had walked right in with both eyes open, running
around to arrange matters for Testarov. It had been
Harun who had initially contacted the mercenary group
in the United States, who had liaised with Remsberg all
the way along. Passing information. Fetching and carrying so that Testarov and his fellow conspirators would
remain no more than shadow figures.

And now, with this sudden invasion of the island, it
seemed to Harun that his time was quickly running out.

"COME ON, you miserable little sod," McCarter yelled.
"Up off your bloody knees and outside!"

"But I have nothing to do with these people," Harun exclaimed. "I'm simply a messenger boy."

"As far as I'm concerned, chum, you're one of them," McCarter snapped. "You were caught in the presence of paid mercenaries involved in a plot to overthrow the official government of the Philippines. That's treason, and punishable by death. In your case there are no extenuating circumstances. You're a Philippine national so you've been working against your own people."

"It isn't like that. I haven't . . ."

McCarter shook his head. He jerked a hand toward the door.

"Wait!" Harun shouted. "We can make a deal. Information for my life."

"You haven't got a damn thing I want to hear," McCarter replied.

"Yes I have. There are names. And places. I *can* help you. You have to listen!"

34

Lee Harun gave McCarter exactly what the Phoenix pro had been hoping for—the names of the conspirators and their subordinates, and the location of the house where Leoni Testarov had retreated after the American Embassy infiltrator had been exposed.

He also revealed that Cam Remsberg and Milt Peck were not on the island. The head of the Raiders and his second-in-command had flown from the island to an unknown location in Manila the evening before. The two mercenary leaders were to stay undercover until the time of the strike against Aquino. The others were to have flown—in the helicopters destroyed by McCarter—to the mainland to be in position for the next phase of the operation. It had been decided to keep the main body of the mercs out of sight until the last possible moment. A large group of armed men would have been difficult to conceal with complete security in an urban area.

McCarter asked Harun if he knew of any prisoners being held at the KGB man's base. The Filipino said he had not seen any and had not been told of any such person or persons.

When he was certain the Filipino had given him everything he knew, McCarter hauled Harun from the room, pushing him across the concrete.

The moon-faced fixer turned on the cockney, his face glistening with sweat. "You promised no firing squad if I helped you," he yelled.

McCarter gazed at him. "What firing squad?"

Harun looked around. He and McCarter were the only ones standing on the concrete. The Filipino turned to the Briton.

"You lied to me," he said in a hurt tone.

"Didn't I just," McCarter replied.

Harun shook his head slowly.

"You were finished anyway, chum," McCarter said. "Look at it this way—at least you don't go down on your own."

Lee Harun managed a mocking laugh. "You don't know these people. They are powerful. They have influence. Money. They can buy anything they want."

"They can't buy us, mate," McCarter said. "And all the money and power in the world didn't help the bunch of so-called mercenaries here on this island."

Harun couldn't argue with that. As he and McCarter moved along the concrete apron he saw for himself the deadly aftereffects of Phoenix Force action. The dead lay where they had fallen. Smoke still drifted up from the wrecked helicopters, leaving dark smudges against the clear blue sky.

"Who are you?" Harun asked.

McCarter didn't reply and Harun decided not to press the point. The Filipino knew he was truly out of the game now, and in a way he welcomed the fact. At least with these people he might live a little longer. His eventual fate was yet to be decided. He might very well end up dead. Regardless of his motives or any other reasons, he *had* committed treason against the country of his birth. Whether he accepted it or not, that was how the authorities would view his part in the attempted coup.

Oddly, despite his position, Harun felt relieved that it was over. He had been feeling increasingly uncomfortable with the whole affair. Becoming the prisoner of the men who had defeated Remsberg's Raiders didn't seem as much of a burden.

Reaching the front of the main block, McCarter saw Jack Grimaldi climbing out of Dragon Slayer. He nudged Harun to go to the helicopter.

"Cavalry's on its way," Grimaldi said.

"I hope they make it fast," McCarter grumbled. "Sooner we can get away from here the better."

Grimaldi glanced at Harun. "He been singing?"

"You could say that."

"Helpful?"

McCarter nodded. "Keep an eye on him," he asked the Stony Man flier. "I want to talk with the fellows."

McCarter entered the main building and found Manning and Encizo.

"Cam Remsberg and Milt Peck left the island yesterday by chopper," he informed them. "They were heading for Manila. Location unknown. They'll lie low until the time for the hit on Aquino. The rest of the group would have been lifted out tomorrow in those Hueys and dropped at prearranged locations in time for the follow-up to the assassination.

"I've got the names of the ringleaders of the planned coup. And the address where they'll be gathered waiting for the result of the attempt. It's up-country from

Manila. Some big coconut plantation. Walled-in grounds, armed guards.''

"Any news about Katz?" Encizo asked.

"This guy doesn't know anything about any prisoner," McCarter said. "But this place is where our KGB chum Testarov can be found. He decided to quit his first base when Milligan flushed out the embassy informer."

"Sounds like this has to be our next target," Manning said.

The others acknowledged the fact silently. Words were not needed at times like these. The men of Phoenix Force accepted that conditions often dictated that they move directly from one conflict to another with little or no respite. They lived on nerves and adrenaline. Yet even the Phoenix commandos were human. They could not hope to function properly without some rest—a period of time for their bodies to recover from the battering they received.

"As soon as the Air Force teams touch down, we go," McCarter said. "I think we should get back to the safe house and give Milligan all the info we have. Let him try to come up with any backup detail we might need. It'll give us a chance to grab some rest and gear up for the next round."

Encizo nodded. "Sounds good. I think we all need some rest. No point risking our lives when we're too tired to stay alert."

McCarter rubbed a hand across his dry throat. "I could murder for a Coke right now," he said.

THE HELICOPTERS came thumping down out of the afternoon sky, settling on the concrete around the base like huge squat beetles. The powerful machines looked awkward and clumsy against Dragon Slayer's sleek shape.

The officer in command came over to meet Phoenix Force. He was a lean young man with the tanned features of a professional. He treated the Stony Man commandos with respect and listened in silence to the details of the report Manning gave him.

As soon as the briefing was over the officer passed his orders to the waiting teams. James led the medical squad inside the building where the wounded mercs were ready and waiting.

"We'll clean up here," the young officer said. "By the time we leave, there won't be much evidence left behind. Nothing much we can do about the choppers. Our main concern is to remove any evidence of American involvement. The wounded men will be detained at the base hospital until they're fit enough to be shipped back to the U.S. The Filipino pilot and your fixer will have to be handed over to the Philippine authorities when this affair is all over. In the meantime they'll disappear at Clark Field."

A few minutes later James rejoined the Force by Dragon Slayer.

"Okay," he said. "Everything's taken care of."

The Force boarded the combat helicopter. As the hatch thumped shut Grimaldi poured on the power. Dragon Slayer's already pulsing motor accelerated. The moment he had enough power Grimaldi took the helicopter up, banking sharply out across the water, away from the island and back toward the mainland, Manila, and yet another confrontation.

35

"The bad news is that Mahmud has gone missing, too," Milligan said. "When he called me and said he'd located the place Linda Torres used to visit with Velasquez, I told him to leave it until you got back."

"But he wouldn't." McCarter shook his head.

Milligan shrugged. "He was all strung out. Excited because he figured he was helping you. He was convinced the house was where it was all happening."

"The trouble is he was right," Manning said.

"I'll bet he walked right into trouble," McCarter said. He was upset—not at Mahmud's interference, but because he was concerned about his Bajau friend's safety. He knew he would probably have done exactly the same thing himself. Impulsive behavior was something the two had in common.

Manning poured himself a second mug of hot, rich coffee. He slumped tiredly into a deep armchair, rubbing his eyes.

"Before you say anything," the Canadian interrupted as McCarter opened his mouth to speak, "I know it's important to go in after Mahmud. We all feel the same about him. He's done a lot to help us and we aren't going to desert him. All the same, we still need some rest before we jump into another firefight."

Encizo put a hand on McCarter's shoulder. "He's right," the Cuban pointed out. "None of us are going to give our best if we go in half-tired. Do that and we're no damn good to Mahmud or ourselves."

McCarter held the Cuban's unflinching stare. The Briton's face was taut and Encizo could feel the tense muscles of his friend's powerful shoulder beneath his hand.

"Right?" Encizo said very softly.

Slowly McCarter eased off, allowing the tension to drain away. He released a sigh of resignation.

"All right," he admitted. "I guess I was letting my feelings get in the way."

Milligan took the moment to step in with some information.

"So, now you've confirmed that Mahmud was right about the place. After he told me about it I figured it might be wise to keep one step ahead, and in case he had picked the right location, I pulled everything I could lay my hands on about it.

"The house is located on a large estate up-country. Coconut plantation. Place has had a number of owners over the years. Most recent is a company named Sapphire Inc. They also own other businesses on the islands. Sapphire is diverse if nothing else. The company is involved in a dozen different things. It owns property. Runs a franchise organization. Owns a number of gas stations. Shipping. Aircraft. Even has a stake in the record and movie industry. The owners are lost in a tangle of holding companies that I managed to trace back as far as the Bahamas. One thing I did verify. One of Sapphire's subsidiary companies owns the first house the opposition used."

"I get the feeling we've done all this before," James said. "You know, tracing back through holding companies to find the real owners."

"It's because people have something to hide," Milligan pointed out. "In order to cover their illegal activities they try to conceal them under a shield of respectability. To do that they have to work within the law to a degree. That means proper documentation, contracts. Which means that somewhere there are files with names on them. They might be halfway around the world, but they do exist. And that means they can be located. And if they are, we sometimes get surprises."

"Any links with the names we gave you?" asked Encizo.

"Nothing yet," the security man admitted. "Not that we need it desperately. Lee Harun has pointed the finger so we know who to expect."

"Any of those names surprise you?" Manning asked.

"I've learned the art of not being surprised at anything this country throws at me. The Philippines have this habit of turning themselves inside out regularly."

"This Serratto character," McCarter said. "There ever any suspicion he might be a closet red?"

"Nothing we've ever been able to come up with. Armand Serratto has always been an eccentric in Filipino politics. The guy has survived a number of regimes and managed to keep himself covered each time. The man is a true political survivor. Rich as hell. Knows a lot of people. Can pull strings."

"Wait until he sees the way *we* pull strings," McCarter muttered darkly over the rim of a can of Coke he'd located.

"What about the others?" asked James.

"Marcus Rufio used to be involved with the ISAFP," Milligan explained. "Rumor has it he was—and still is—a nasty piece of work. I wouldn't be surprised if he turned out to be the one who had you staked out when you visited those hotels, and set the ISAFP goon squad on you. Rufio still has a lot of influence with the secret police.

"The one called DiCenzi is pretty much a non-starter. Member of the judiciary. Not much else known about him, but he could be a handy guy to have on your side. Diego Castillo is our military man. He'll be the one who organized the island for Remsberg and probably the arms. There could be a lot of support for him throughout the armed forces. He's likely to have sympathetic groups waiting all over the country for the word. The Raiders would have moved in and done the groundwork, leaving everything ready for the military to step in and take control."

"And all of it being watched over by our KGB friend, Testarov," Manning said. "Neat little setup."

"The only missing piece of the puzzle is what Cam Remsberg and Milt Peck are up to," Encizo said. "We know they're in Manila somewhere. Hiding out until when? To do what?"

"Harun admitted the target is Aquino," McCarter volunteered. "And tomorrow seems to be the big day. The how and where is the bit we don't know."

"The president has a busy day tomorrow," Milligan said. "She has to open a new research facility at the Manila Medical Center at ten a.m. Then attend a civic lunch. In the afternoon she goes to a meeting of local bankers to discuss financing for some proposed housing projects."

"An assassination could be carried out at any one of those functions," Manning said.

"That gives us a couple of problems," James said. "When we were getting our briefing it was made clear that President Aquino would not cancel any public appearances, even if there was the threat of an assassination attempt. She refused even to discuss the matter with the President of the U.S. despite his making a personal call to her. Her decision was a matter of principle. She won't back down under any circumstances. Death threats or whatever."

"That isn't so unusual," Manning suggested. "It's happened before. High-profile politicians can't be seen to shy away from personal danger. Especially when they're trying to persuade the public to resist terrorism and the like."

"You've got to admit the lady has guts," McCarter said.

"Agreed," James answered. "I just wouldn't like to see them spilled all over the sidewalk."

"What's the other problem you wanted to mention?" Encizo asked James.

"We may have the names of the principals involved in this proposed coup. But how many others are involved? Are any of them close to the president?"

"What you're asking is whether we can risk telling anyone in the government to look out for the president's safety," Manning suggested.

James nodded. "We could be talking to a sympathizer to the antigovernment plot. Someone who just might do everything he can to make certain the president stands in the right spot for the assassin's bullet."

"Oh boy," McCarter murmured. "Ain't life complicated?"

Manning rose from his chair and crossed to refill his coffee mug. He took a sip of the hot brew before he spoke.

"As I see it, we have two objectives. First, we go for the house. Put out of action as many of the conspirators as we can, including our Russian overseers. We also try to free Mahmud and Baum if they're there. We must also try to find out just what Remsberg intends, and where.

"Second, we try to stop Remsberg. And we do it through our own initiative. We can't afford to tell anyone. We just have to do it the only way we can."

The others nodded in agreement. Manning had said it all. There were no other options. As had happened many times before, Phoenix Force was faced with an unenviable task—one that had to be accomplished by direct action. There was no room for negotiation. No time for official sanction or for clearing red tape. Life or death situations could be solved only by life or death decisions, and Phoenix Force had just made one, for better or for worse.

"Let's get our equipment organized," Manning said. "Then we can clean up, get our cuts and bruises seen to before we catch some sleep. Dragon Slayer can have us on site by dawn."

THE FINAL DAY

36

Leoni Testarov glanced up as Serratto entered the paneled study. The Russian agent did not allow his thoughts to show as he watched the Filipino politician cross to a small table on which stood cut-glass decanters containing expensive whisky and brandy and rum.

The KGB man was secretly concerned at the way the whole affair was going. His earlier confidence had been shaken when he had learned of the attack at the cannery where the arms cache had been hidden. He knew, without having to be told, who was responsible. The American force who kept appearing out of nowhere to hit and then run. They were, Testarov decided, more devils than men. He could not fault their fighting skills or their ability to survive against great odds. He wished his own Morkrie Dela squad had such qualities.

The arms cache was no more. The Americans had destroyed it. That was a ghastly blow. The stored weapons would have been extremely useful during the uprising. Once the coup began, the guns and explosives would have been vital in supplying local sympathizers. Now they were gone, and with them went a strong advantage the insurgents might have had.

Testarov had yet another cause for concern. His negotiator, the fat, perspiring Lee Harun, had failed to return from the island after delivering his message to Cam Remsberg. Harun should have been back in Manila the day before last. His failure to return made Testarov wonder if there was a problem on the island.

Unfortunately, there was no way of contacting the island. By conscious decision, no form of radio or telephone link had been set up. There were too many ears listening to radio waves. A single short message picked up by the wrong party could have disastrous consequences for the conspirators. Despite the difficulties arising from the lack of communication, it was infinitely more acceptable than any of the alternatives.

So Testarov was left to speculate as to why Harun had not returned.

Had the man's helicopter crashed?

Or had Harun decided to get out and hide?

Were the Americans involved? Testarov felt this to be the most likely explanation. The Americans had discovered and destroyed the arms cache. Had they also found out about the island and the Raiders? Was it possible they had invaded the island and eliminated the mercenary force?

That brought yet another question.

If the island had been attacked and the Raiders wiped out, where was Cam Remsberg? Dead? Or in his secret hideout in Manila? If the mercenary leader had died or been captured on the island, then the catalyst that would have started the coup's chain reaction had been neutralized.

And if that was fact, then the whole scheme had been ruined. Remsberg and his Raiders were vital to the commencement of the uprising. Without them the planned assassination would not occur, and so—Testarov had to accept it—the coup would flounder. Everything had been planned around the assassination. It was to be the spark to ignite the firestorm that should have burned the islands and destroyed the democratic power base, leaving the way open for the socialist wind of change.

But now?

Leoni Testarov was not so sure that was going to happen. Not this time around. If Remsberg had not made it to the mainland, then the game was most surely over.

If, on the other hand, he had reached Manila and was, even now, preparing for his strike against Aquino, there might still be a chance for success.

Unfortunately, there was no way of contacting Remsberg. His secure base in Manila was known only to himself and Harun. And as Harun was not available, there was no link to guide Testarov to the American mercenary.

So all he could do was sit and wait and wonder.

Testarov watched Serratto fix a drink. The Filipino seemed restless. Testarov allowed that the man had a right to be. This day was an important one in Serratto's life. By the end of it he could very well be the next Filipino President. Or he could be dead. Or on the run.

The thought fascinated Testarov. What would Serratto do if the coup went disastrously wrong? Would he run for his life if exposed? Or would he try to bluff it out? Maybe he would jump on one of his executive jets and flee the country. Put himself in exile on some luxury isle, along with his millions salted away in various banks around the world. Testarov smiled. He might turn out to be another Marcos. Staying out of harm's way, but most probably still plotting his return.

The Filipino crossed the study with his drink and sank into a deep armchair facing Testarov.

"A little early, isn't it?" Testarov asked, indicating the glass in Serratto's hand.

The Filipino smiled. "I think not," he said. "I could not sleep, so I thought it was time to start the day. This could be a new dawn for the Philippines in more ways than one. So I thought I would have a drink to celebrate."

"Prematurely?" Testarov watched the Filipino's face.

"I am not a superstitious man, my friend. I am practical, but I am also vain enough to want to congratulate myself on getting this far. If events prove me wrong, at least I will have had the pleasure of the drink."

"Very practical." Testarov smiled.

"And why are you awake so early?" Serratto inquired of the Russian.

"A great deal on my mind," Testarov replied. "I feel the importance of the day, as well. It did not seem appropriate to linger in bed."

"Still concerned over the loss of the arms cache?" Serratto's tone was keen, his words probing, teasing.

Testarov refused to be baited. "It is a loss," he admitted. "But not devastating enough to cripple us. Or to deter us from our plan of action."

"Good!" Serratto said forcefully. "I hate to hear defeatist talk. We are not dead until they bury us. I for one have no intention of being buried for a long time yet.''

Testarov rose to his feet. ''I must check the men on watch. We must not become too complacent.''

Serratto had returned to the table and was refilling his glass. The Russian stepped out of the study and made his way to the kitchen, where a couple of his Morkrie Dela agents were preparing food and drink.

''Get that up to the prisoners,'' Testarov said. ''Give them a chance to eat it. Then I want the one named Katzenelenbogen readied for travel. The moment I give the word we move him away from this house to that spot along the coast where we rendezvous with the submarine. Understand?''

''Yes, Major,'' one of the agents replied.

''He is no good to us dead,'' Testarov reminded the two KGB thugs. ''His survival is of paramount importance. He must be able to talk when he is delivered to Moscow.''

''What about the other one?''

''I don't care what happens to that one,'' Testarov answered. ''It doesn't look like we'll have time to question him. When the time comes, kill him.''

One of the agents picked up the tray. With his partner following, he left the kitchen and went toward the stairs.

KATZ WOKE EARLY.

He wasn't sure just why, but he felt it had something to do with the fact that this was the day President Aquino was to attend the civic function he had recalled from Hal Brognola's briefing.

If he was right it was also the day Remsberg's Raiders would make their assassination attempt.

The Israeli felt totally impotent. He held vital information that might save Aquino's life and also thwart the proposed coup against the Philippine government. Yet he might as well be on the moon, because there was no way he could get that information to the one group of people capable of doing something about it.

Phoenix Force.

He paced the floor, his mind racing as he devised and, just as quickly, rejected numerous schemes to remove him from captivity. Even if he did escape from this room, there was still the gauntlet of armed guards to go through. That posed another question. The strength of the opposition. For all Katz knew there might be fifty or a hundred men down there. Maybe more. There was no way he could tell. Numbers didn't frighten Katz. But it was the plain, obvious truth, that no matter how good he was, if he was faced by vastly overwhelming odds, his chances of getting out alive were very thin. Dead he was no use to anyone—the information stored in his head would be lost.

His restlessness disturbed Mahmud. The Bajau opened one eye and watched the one-armed Israeli walking up and down the room. He could see that something was worrying the man. Mahmud pushed the blanket off his body and eased out of the armchair where he had spent the night.

Mahmud was still in pain from the beating he had received the day before. The right side of his face was swollen and badly discolored. One of the blows had opened a gash over his cheekbone. Although Katz had done what he could with the scant materials available, the wound was still open and tender. Mahmud's right eye was puffed up and virtually closed. His right hand was giving him considerable pain. When he had examined it, Katz found two fingers broken. With Mahmud's help, he had bound them with a splint made from a piece of wood broken from the inside of a drawer, securing it with strips torn from a bed sheet. A larger section of the sheet had been used to fashion a sling that held Mahmud's hand against his chest.

Trying not to concentrate on the dull throbs of pain emanating from his injuries, Mahmud waited for Katz to turn toward him.

"Did I wake you?" Katz asked when he saw the Bajau.

Mahmud shook his head. "I couldn't sleep. Are you the same?"

"Yes," Katz replied, trying to keep his impatience from souring his words.

"Today is the day those Americans will try to kill the president," Mahmud said. "It worries you not to be able to do anything about it."

"Damn right it does, Mahmud," Katz said forcibly. "It was why we were sent here. To stop these people. And here I am with vital information locked up in a room like—"

"—like an interfering Bajau who should have known better," Mahmud interjected.

Katz had to smile. "Don't be so hard on yourself. You were trying to help."

"Honorable motives don't excuse stupidity," Mahmud remarked.

"That sounds like a slogan out of a fortune cookie." Katz chuckled.

"I think it was," Mahmud said.

"Do you know any that might get us out of here?"

"The only one I can recall said, 'Getting out of a locked room is easy if you have a key.'"

"Is that true?"

"No. I just made it up."

"Pretty accurate though," Katz said.

At that moment a key *was* inserted in the door to the room, then turned, and the door was pushed open. An armed guard stood just outside, his SMG aimed in the direction of the prisoners. A second man appeared, a tray in his hands. He also carried an SMG, the weapon slung from his left shoulder by a strap. He moved into the room, then placed the loaded tray on a small table, bending forward as he did.

Mahmud threw a glance in Katz's direction, then flicked his eyes at the guard bending over the table. The Israeli gave a barely noticeable nod, then glanced at the open door.

In the next few seconds both Katz and Mahmud would gamble with their lives as they attempted to overpower their guards. It was a desperate measure, but one both considered worth taking.

Their bodies stiffened with tension. Each man took a quick breath, preparing to move.

From outside the house came the unmistakable rattle of autofire. The initial burst was followed by another, then more. Within the space of a heartbeat a full rattle of guns sounded.

A firefight had broken out.

There was no time to wonder who had caused it. Or who was involved.

There was only time to act.

Mahmud picked up one of the mugs of hot coffee and threw the coffee into the guard's face. The scalding beverage seared his skin and he cried out in agony, clutching his injured face.

Without hesitating, Mahmud grabbed the guy's SMG, an Ingram. Mahmud slipped his fingers around the grip and the trigger. He pulled the weapon away from the guard, turned the muzzle on him and pulled the trigger.

The guard in the open doorway, whose concentration had been broken by the sound of the distant firefight, jerked his head around at the sound of the blast. He saw his partner, fatally wounded, slip to the floor. Cursing in Russian, the Morkrie Dela heavy lunged forward, his own SMG tracking in on Mahmud.

Katz was more than ready when the second guard moved forward. He drove the sole of his shoe against the heavy door, slamming it against the SMG's barrel, trapping the weapon against the door frame. Before the Russian could recover, Katz grabbed the body of the SMG and yanked it toward himself, stepping aside as the door swung back open under the Russian's weight. Caught off guard by this unexpected move, the Russian stumbled forward, straight into the steel hooks of Katz's prosthesis. Katz slashed the toughened steel into the guard's throat from left to right. Blood bubbled from the deep gouges. The KGB man dropped his weapon, clutching the wounds with both hands, feeling hot fluid pump over his fingers.

Katz retrieved the Russian's discarded SMG, which turned out to be an Ingram, as well. The Israeli commando turned the weapon on its former owner, delivering a short burst that put the Russian down for good.

Glancing over his shoulder, Katz saw that Mahmud had possession of the first guard's weapon. The Bajau had also located a spare magazine for the MAC-10, plus a Walther P-38 pistol, which he pushed into the top of his pants. He freed his injured hand from its sling so he could brace the MAC-10 across his wrist.

A search of the other KGB man turned up two spare mags for the Ingram but no handgun.

"You ready?" Katz asked.

Mahmud nodded. "As much as I'll ever be."

"Let's just hope it's our guys doing all the shooting down there," Katz added. "I guess we'll find that out soon enough."

37

Some twenty minutes earlier, Manning, Encizo and James had breached the perimeter wall of the estate. Dragon Slayer had dropped the trio a half mile from the place, then had swept around the estate in a wide circle that would eventually bring it to the rear of the grounds.

McCarter, still on board the Stony Man helicopter, was to be placed on the roof of the big house so he could attempt to force an entry from above. His intention was to try to locate Katz and Mahmud as the main assault on the base began.

Manning, James and Encizo were to infiltrate the grounds and prepare for a frontal attack. When they were ready Grimaldi would make a low-level sweep over the house, dropping McCarter on the roof. As soon as McCarter was down he would radio a prearranged signal that would launch the attack.

The strategy had been devised during the Force's flight to the estate, after a few hours' sleep at the safe house. On waking they had dressed in black combat suits, consumed numerous cups of hot coffee, and made a final check of their gear.

Apart from their full complement of weapons and grenades, fragmentation and stun, each Force member carried a walkie-talkie. Grimaldi had already warmed up Dragon Slayer. It was still dark when the Force slipped silently from the house and crossed to the waiting helicopter.

Dragon Slayer had eased smoothly into the air, Grimaldi putting the sleek machine on a northerly course. As the flight progressed the Phoenix warriors finalized their plan.

"You sure you want to do this on your own?" Manning had asked.

McCarter glanced up from the Uzi he had been checking; he was carrying the Israeli SMG for Katz.

"Mahmud is my mate," the Briton insisted. "So it's up to me to pull him out of that place."

"You know any one of us would do the same," James insisted.

"I know," McCarter said. "Besides, you did the rooftop routine back at the cannery, and look at the mess you made of that."

James grinned at the tough cockney.

"This could be a tough nut to crack," Manning said. "Let's not forget what that Harun character told David. He believed there might be around twenty-five or more active hardmen in and around the house. There are the Morkrie Dela agents, plus the best of the local Communist cell's goon squad. There may even be a few military personnel backing up this Castillo."

"Has the makings of a bloody good party," McCarter said.

"Trust you to see it that way," Encizo remarked.

"So we get dropped outside the walls," James said. "Make our way in and wait for David to call and say he's on the roof."

Manning nodded. "As soon as we receive that call we go for it."

THE EASTERN SKY was showing light as Phoenix Force slipped silently through the grounds. They had ambushed one patrolling guard, a stocky Filipino armed with the familiar Kalashnikov; they left him bound and gagged beneath a bush.

Now they were in sight of the house. There were a few lights showing. Armed guards could be seen around the house. There were also a number of cars, some of them expensive models, parked in the wide drive.

"Near enough?" Encizo asked. "Or should we get closer?"

"Let's see if we can make it to that big bush," Manning said.

James took a look around. "We won't find anything closer to the house than that," he said.

The three eased up off the ground.

As James, in the lead, moved forward a few yards, stepping around one of the tall palms that dotted the grounds, he came face-to-face with a tall, broad-shouldered Russian.

His Ingram slung over one shoulder, the Morkrie Dela agent zipped up his pants after answering nature's call. He stared at James, momentarily bewildered.

James, who did not want to use his firearm unless absolutely necessary, smashed the M-16 butt into the Soviet's face. The agent staggered back, bleeding. He made a grab for his SMG, but fumbled it. He didn't get a second chance. James lashed out with the M-16 again, clouting the guy across the temple. The Russian grunted, stumbling in a daze. James followed, determined to put his opponent down. He drove the M-16's butt against the base of the man's skull with enough force to crack the bone. The Russian pitched forward, facedown on the grass, and eventually stopped twitching.

"You okay?" Manning asked.

James nodded. "I'm fine. Help me move this big mother out of sight."

They dragged the dead agent into a clump of palms.

"Let's get set," Encizo whispered. "David's going to be calling in any minute."

"You could be right," Manning said as he raised his arm.

The others followed his pointing finger. Materializing out of the predawn shadows, Dragon Slayer, in silent mode, hovered over the roof of the big house for a few seconds, then streaked away across the wide lawns.

McCARTER JUMPED from the open hatch. As he hit the roof he went into a forward roll to absorb the impact.

Above him Dragon Slayer powered away from the house, out across the grounds.

The moment he came out of the roll the Phoenix commando reached for the walkie-talkie clipped to his belt. Keying the transmit button, McCarter delivered his one-word command to his waiting buddies.

"Go!"

The cockney rebel was already moving, aware that time was running out fast. Dragon Slayer's low-level sweep over the house could not have gone unnoticed, and somewhere someone was going to assume that the helicopter had been doing more than just buzzing the place.

McCarter figured that he was liable to have company. So it was in his interests to vacate the roof and penetrate the house quickly.

The Phoenix pro descended the short flight of steps he'd spotted from the air. At the bottom, a door was set into the white-painted wall.

McCarter was just approaching the door when it swung open, disgorging a trio of angry Filipinos who certainly weren't there to welcome the Briton—except perhaps with AK-47 assault rifles.

Agile as always, McCarter dived sideways, landing on his left shoulder, and slipped across the graveled roof to a ventilator shaft.

Bullets snapped viciously around him. McCarter felt splinters strike his combat boots. He curled his legs beneath him and twisted around. Seeing movement to the left, he swung the Ingram's muzzle in that direction.

The blast caught the Filipino hardman in the chest, slapping him off his feet.

The moment he'd fired, McCarter scrambled around to the other side of the ventilator shaft to attack from another angle. His move took the remaining Filipino Communists by surprise.

McCarter, rising to one knee, triggered a long blast at the two remaining enemies, cutting the pair down.

Ejecting the spent magazine, the Phoenix commander slapped in a fresh one. He cocked the MAC-10. On his feet now, he headed for the open roof door. As he neared it he heard a sudden outburst of autofire from the grounds below, and knew that his Phoenix teammates had joined the fray.

WITH MCCARTER'S radioed command the Phoenix trio broke from their place of concealment and made for the house.

They were just feet away from the cluster of parked cars when one of the patrolling guards spotted them. The guy was dressed casually but carried himself like a military man. His responses were swift and deliberate, and if the Phoenix warriors had not been so well trained he might have achieved more than he did.

Without a moment's hesitation the guard opened fire, pumping a steady stream of 7.62 mm fire in the direction of the Stony Man warriors.

The first slugs fell inches short, gouging chunks of grass and earth from the lawn. The Phoenix trio split apart, presenting three separate targets, and took cover by the parked cars.

More slugs came their way, smashing glass and puncturing expensive paneling.

Calvin James disliked being pinned down, especially behind a car that was nothing more than a large bomb. It would take only one misdirected bullet to rupture a fuel tank and cause a searing blast of burning gas. James had seen it happen before and the thought sat uneasily with the Chicago warrior.

He began to crawl along the line of cars, aware that other guards would join the battle momentarily. Reaching the end of the line, he worked around a gleaming Rolls Royce, bringing his M-16 into firing position.

From off to his left an automatic weapon chattered loudly. The radiator grille of the Rolls was chopped apart by the sizzling projectiles that struck next to

James's head. The Phoenix pro flattened himself on the ground, swinging his M-16 toward the gunman.

A chunky balding Morkrie Dela agent in a badly fitting crumpled suit was sprinting across the drive, trying for a closer shot. He was carrying a Heckler and Koch MP-5, and James hoped that the Russian wasn't as proficient with the weapon as Rafael Encizo.

James's M-16 stopped the Soviet in his tracks. The KGB agent's chest blossomed red. He crashed to the ground untidily.

Returning to his original target, James poked the M-16 around the front wheel of the Rolls and expended another stream of slugs. His shots were close enough to distract the guy, and even draw his fire.

Gravel peppered James's face as the guard's slugs whacked the ground inches away.

Then the shooting ceased. Encizo, taking advantage of the guy's apparent distraction, dispatched two slugs, which crashed through his skull.

There was silence for a moment. Manning and Encizo cleared the parked cars and made for the house, with James sprinting from his Rolls and bringing up the rear.

The front doors burst open and armed figures appeared.

Manning and Encizo, opening fire simultaneously, took out half the gunmen in one volley. The wounded fell in agony, all thoughts of resistance gone.

Slightly behind his partners, James heard boots crunching on gravel and turned. More gunmen emerged from an archway farther along the building. His M-16 welcomed the newcomers. One guy went down screaming, vainly trying to stem the blood gushing from his throat. The others drew back, giving James time to free a grenade from his webbing. He slipped the pin, released the lever and tossed it. The enemy scattered, but not far enough. The detonation wiped them away.

As James eliminated the threat before him, a frantic close-quarter firefight erupted between Manning and Encizo and half a dozen wild-eyed hardmen. The latter had just witnessed six of their comrades taken out by the Phoenix warriors, and were determined to avenge them.

With half the group fallen, Manning and Encizo concentrated on downing the remainder.

Manning's SA80 spat out a continuous relay of 5.56 slugs that devoured flesh as fast as he could pull the trigger. The close proximity of the opposition made it difficult to miss. One hardguy was slammed back against the wall of the house. Another communist thug had his throat torn out. A third Filipino agitator died when his was churned to ravaged mush.

Encizo made his contribution by turning his MP-5 on the guy who had suddenly loomed before him, a hulking blond Russian carrying a Franchi SPAS-12 combat shotgun. The black pump-action weapon was trained on Encizo when the Cuban fired his MP-5. The Russian jerked the SPAS-12's trigger in reflex as he died, but the gun had shifted. It voided its charge directly into the lower back of one of the Filipino gunmen. The guy's torso disintegrated under the almost point-blank range. The searing shot tore through flesh, muscle and bone, severing the spine and blasting the kidneys.

Manning keyed his walkie-talkie in the lull that followed. "Jack, you read me?"

Grimaldi's voice crackled over the speaker. "Ready and waiting."

"Bring the lady in. Front of the house. Line of parked cars. I want them taken out. We don't want anyone making a break."

"On my way," Grimaldi replied.

"Should we clear out here?" Manning asked the others. They nodded. "Okay. Let's get inside then."

KATZ HAD BEEN blindfolded when his captors brought him to the room, so he had no idea of the layout of the house. That didn't worry him too much. Whichever way he and Mahmud went, they were liable to encounter opposition. So in that respect one way was as good as another.

With his Bajau companion at his side, Katz moved to the right down a wide corridor with doors leading off both sides. After some twenty feet the corridor opened onto a gallery with a wooden balustrade on one side that overlooked a large living room. That area contained armchairs and coffee tables arranged before a huge open fireplace constructed from natural stone. The wide chimney rose up to vanish through the high beamed roof.

Katz glanced down into the living room. It was deserted. Double doors stood partly open at the far end as if the room had been vacated in a hurry.

From outside the house the gunfire continued. Katz heard the unmistakable crack of a grenade detonating.

"Let's keep moving," Katz said as Mahmud closed up with him.

Together the pair ran through the gallery, barely noticing the display of Spanish armor and weapons that hung from the walls.

At the far side they were surprised by one of Testarov's Morkrie Dela agents. The burly Soviet, armed with an AK-47, lifted his weapon and opened fire.

Katz twisted aside, slamming against the wall with a bone-jarring thump that made his teeth rattle. Three shots zipped through the air, clanging against the armor on the wall.

Before Katz could return fire the Ingram in Mahmud's hands burst into life. A stream of 9 mm slugs pierced the KGB man's torso. The Russian expelled a stunned grunt, falling back, his body afire with pain. Mahmud fired again—this time higher, the burst crashing into the Soviet's broad chest. Hard muscle was not enough to stop the projectiles, and they drove deep into the agent's chest. Katz and Mahmud moved on, not stopping until they reached the far end of the corridor, where it divided.

To the left was a landing at the head of a large staircase, while to the right lay a short passage terminating in a short and narrow flight of stairs. At the top of these stairs was an open door through which the pale dawn sky was visible.

Even as they glanced up the stairs the daylight was blocked by a dark shape.

A man, clad in black, sprang through the door and came down the stairs.

Mahmud began to yell a warning, but Katz held out a silencing hand.

"It's all right," the Israeli said.

Puzzled, Mahmud looked into the face of the intruder.

"And just what are you pair up to?" David McCarter asked, grinning.

"David!" Mahmud greeted his friend enthusiastically.

Katz watched the Briton acknowledge his Bajau friend. Then McCarter turned to the Phoenix Force commander.

"Are you okay?" the tall cockney asked, his keen eyes sweeping over Katz with genuine concern.

"You took your time getting here," Katz stated gruffly, though there was a gleam in his eyes. "In the end we decided we might as well get ourselves out."

McCarter shrugged. "You know what the bloody traffic's like when you're in a hurry. Then we had a few other delays."

Katz nodded. He knew what McCarter meant by delays. The Brit was referring to active combat situations.

"It's still good to see you, David."

"And you, boss."

The gunfire increased down below. Bullets howled, whined off stone and shattered glass.

"Come on, let's shift," McCarter said.

He handed the Uzi he had been carrying to Katz, along with a couple of extra magazines. The Israeli discarded the weapon he was holding and took his own SMG.

"From what we've been able to assess we could be facing twenty-five plus," McCarter stated.

"Let's get to it then," Katz urged. "We don't have time to waste."

Katz's tone made McCarter pause. "You picked up some info?" he asked.

Katz nodded. "I know how the assassination is to be carried out."

"We know who'll be doing it," McCarter said. "Remsberg and Peck. They're hiding out somewhere in Manila. What we couldn't figure was which of the three functions Cory Aquino is attending today will be the targeted one."

"It's the ten o'clock medical center appointment," Katz said.

Before he could elaborate, a group of Morkrie Dela agents pounded up the stairs. The Russians spotted the Phoenix pair and Mahmud before they had a chance to hide.

One of the KGB men rapped out an order.

Two of the Russians dropped behind the stair railing, while the remaining three continued to the head of the stairs, weapons up and firing.

Bullets smacked the wall above the Phoenix warriors, showering them with plaster dust and chippings.

McCarter immediately yanked a grenade from his webbing and pulled the pin. He let the lever go, held the deadly sphere for a count of two, then threw it.

The Morkrie Dela agents separated in an attempt to escape the fragmentation grenade.

The M-67 bounced once when it hit the carpeted floor. It was almost five inches in the air when the six-and-a-half-ounce charge of Composition B detonated. The shrapnel spewed across the landing in all directions.

One of the Soviet agents caught the full blast. The slivers of steel wire tore into his unprotected back and legs, shredding his flesh down to the bone in places. Lifted by the blast, the Morkrie Dela killer slammed into the wall, then slithered loosely to the floor.

The shock wave created by the detonation cata-pulted a second KGB man across the landing. Legs and arms thrashing, he fell down the long flight of stairs. His yell of anguish ceased when he hit bottom and his neck snapped with a dry crack.

Smoke from the grenade created a temporary screen across the landing, and the ever-impulsive McCarter lunged headlong toward the stairs.

Spotting movement by the railings, McCarter aimed his Ingram, sending a stream of 9 mm fire sizzling at the Morkrie Dela agents concealed there. The slugs ham-mered the railings. Splintered wood exploded in all directions. McCarter fired again, shredding more wood.

One Russian gave a pained yell as some slivers pene-trated his chest. He jerked upright, a fatal mistake. The moment his head appeared above the railing McCarter hit it with a burst from his MAC-10. The man was a goner.

Close behind McCarter, Katz glimpsed a survivor from the grenade blast, who had evidently suffered nothing more than a gash across his left cheek. Rising, the guy pawed away the blood running down his face, then remembered the SMG in his hand. He swung the weapon toward McCarter.

At that moment, Katz's Uzi belched out a hail of rounds that quickly found the Soviet's chest. He dropped to the carpeted floor, this time for good.

Defying the bullets winging past, the unstoppable cockney continued to fire short bursts at the railings that offered cover for the remaining Morkrie Dela agent.

The Russian poked the muzzle of his MP-5 through the railing and tried to pick off McCarter. His shots went wild. Realizing his desperate situation, he attempted to remedy it by reaiming his MP-5, but in his haste he caught the front sight against one of the splintered rails, snagging the weapon.

Unemcumbered by any such obstacle, McCarter was free and clear to pick his target. His MAC-10 spit its messengers of death then clicked empty. However, enough 9 mm slugs were expended to terminate the cursing Soviet.

Katz and Mahmud caught up with McCarter as the powerhouse warrior slammed a fresh magazine into the Ingram.

"One day that gung ho style is going to backfire on you," Katz warned the Brit.

McCarter grinned. "You're probably right. But until it does, you have to admit it bloody well does the trick.

Katz had no reply.

As usual the rampaging Briton had tackled the situation with his bull-at-the-gate pace and it had worked. The Israeli could not fault the cockney's results. He just worried about McCarter's life expectancy. But knowing McCarter's luck, Katz decided, he would probably outlive them all and die in bed at a ridiculously old age. Despite the gravity of the situation, Katz found himself grinning at the image of an eighty-year-old McCarter in full combat gear. The picture refused to fade.

"What the hell are *you* smirking about?" McCarter demanded.

Katz shook his head. "David, you really don't want to know."

McCarter glared at him, but failed to intimidate the Israeli. "So don't tell me!" the cockney snapped.

He turned on his heel and started down the stairs.

Katz, still with a faint smile on his face, followed, with Mahmud trailing.

Before they reached the bottom of the stairs, the smile had gone from Katz's face.

38

Leoni Testarov recalled a saying he'd heard years ago. He could not even remember where he'd heard it.

The saying went, "Things are never as black as they are painted."

It was meant to imply that every difficult situation had a positive side to it.

To the KGB man, the maxim seemed totally irrelevant to his present situation.

Testarov always tried to maintain a positive attitude on life, to keep an open mind with respect to altering circumstances. He always believed that it was possible to rescue disastrous situations.

He had done so before, always following the general principle that extreme situations required extreme remedies.

However, the Soviet terror monger saw little chance of finding any remedy to this particular fiasco.

The attack by the elusive group of American specialists, though not unexpected, had nonetheless come as a brutal shock.

Something about the Americans had a demoralizing effect on those who found themselves in opposition. The Americans fought with such determination and closeness that unfavorable odds meant little to them. Once in motion they pushed the fight ever forward, always on the offensive. They struck with deadly force, as true professionals who appeared to act casually and with little regard for personal safety.

Testarov didn't believe that for a single moment. He had studied the KGB file on these men, and throughout their many missions one fact emerged with startling clarity. They valued their lives greatly. Although they took great risks in order to complete a mission, there was never any suggestion of disregard for their lives. These men were simply too good to do that. They were, the Russian admitted with great reluctance, the very best of their kind. As professionals, Testarov admired them. Even respected them. Yet in the same breath he hated them for what they had done to the U.S.S.R.

And he hated the fact that they were here—at his supposedly secure base, striking at the gathered forces and sweeping them aside.

Testarov rechecked his handgun and placed it in its holster. Then he picked up the Uzi 9 mm fitted with an extended magazine. He carried four mags in slim pockets in his leather jacket.

It was time to commence the final act.

The planned coup was destroyed as far as Testarov was concerned. Disappointment was pushed aside by the practicalities of survival. Let Serratto and his minions do what they could to rescue it. Testarov's task now was to spirit away the man called Katzenelenbogen. If nothing else, he wanted to present the man to his superiors in Moscow. It might help to ease the pain of his failure.

Testarov flung open the door of the study. Serratto and Rufio were on the far side of the entrance hall, arguing. Rufio held a Kalashnikov. Serratto turned, pointing to the stairs.

Glancing that way Testarov saw the bodies of two of his Morkrie Dela agents.

Movement at the top of the stairs caught his eye.

Katzenelenbogen, Mahmud and McCarter were coming downstairs. To Testarov, there was something vaguely familiar about the tall man clad in black combat gear who was with the prisoners. It came to him in a flash. He was one of the other members of Katzenelenbogen's group.

Serratto, still arguing with Rufio, snatched the SMG from the ex-secret police official. The Filipino politician stepped forward, firing at the three men on the stairs. A bullet went crashing into the wall above their heads.

Instantly, Katz and McCarter fired, catching Serratto in the chest and throat. The body of the traitorous politician was hurled to the tiled floor. His expensive suit and shirt were stained with blood.

Marcus Rufio produced a heavy automatic pistol from his jacket. He shot once without aiming, then ran toward the front door.

At that moment the door burst open and three more black-garbed figures burst in.

Testarov could hardly believe what he was seeing.

The entire American team. All together in one place.

Rufio skidded to a halt, aware that he was surrounded by enemies who would offer little mercy. There was no way out. The ex-ISAFP man realized he was trapped. If he surrendered he would end up in jail or before a firing squad. There was no way he could fight his way clear.

The man made his decision. He simply jammed the muzzle of the big Colt .45 under his chin and pulled the trigger, blowing his brains across the hall floor.

Testarov drew back into the study, aware that Katz had just spotted him. The KGB man slammed the heavy door and locked it.

The only alternative left now was total flight. To get out before the Americans destroyed everyone in sight.

The KGB man realized he had lost his chance of returning to Moscow with Katzenelenbogen, which made his position precarious now. Returning to Moscow to face the condemnation of his superiors was a form of suicide. It was an accepted fact that failure was frowned on heavily by the gray men of Moscow. They were never very tolerant when operations were less than triumphantly successful. Agents returning as failures often disappeared, some being assigned to dull outposts to reflect on their mistakes, others looking forward to serving out a punishment of many years on the bleak gulag, forgotten and ignored. There were many ways failure was rewarded in the Soviet Union.

Leoni Testarov, who so far had an unblemished record, knew that the collapse of the Philippine operation would be a black mark on his file. Running to the other side of the world would not help to erase it. In fact, trying to escape his responsibilities was the worst thing he could do. Not that he even contemplated the thought. Testarov knew his only course would be to return to Moscow and face up to his failure. He was fully prepared to accept whatever punishment was handed out to him. If he was to die for his failure, then so be it.

It was simply the way the man was made. He took his responsibilities seriously, and considered himself fully accountable and answerable for his mistakes. No matter the reason, he was not going to make excuses or try to blame anyone else. Privately, however, he swore that if he survived, he would make the ones responsible pay some day. But that was for the future. His prime objective now was to survive, to get out of the Philippines while he was still able.

Testarov ran across the room and through a door that led to a den with a bar, a large television set and a video player. This room gave access to a passage that led to the kitchen at the rear of the house. If he could make it that far and get outside, he might be able to reach the Dodge.

Testarov entered the recreation room and came face-to-face with Diego Castillo and Hector DiCenzi, who greeted Testarov calmly. But Castillo's eyes gave him away. He, above any of them, had been expecting a great deal from the coup. Now it was all slipping away.

"Is there nothing we can do?" he asked.

Testarov shook his head.

"Nothing?" DiCenzi whined.

"Except to save yourself," Castillo snapped. "Now get out of my way."

"No!" DiCenzi yelled. "You must protect me! Save me! The others don't matter!"

"Faithful to the last," Castillo muttered. "You are scum."

Testarov lifted the Uzi and fired. DiCenzi slumped to the floor.

"I have a car parked outside," the Russian said. "And a date with a submarine. Diego, you are welcome to join me."

"Only to get away from right here," the Filipino said. "Then I'll take my chances. This is still my homeland. If I survive, there may be another chance. In the meantime, maybe I can continue to serve Moscow and maintain my cover."

"I promise you, if we both survive, there will be other opportunities."

The two moved quickly. They ran along the narrow passage, emerging in the deserted kitchen with its simmering coffee and smells of cooking.

Stepping outside, the pair cut across the gravel area to the white Dodge. Two of Testarov's Morkrie Dela agents were crouched beside the vehicle.

As Testarov and Castillo approached, one of the agents opened the door, climbed behind the wheel, and started the powerful engine. The KGB man and his Filipino associate clambered into the rear. The other man took the front passenger seat.

"Get us away from here," Testarov told the driver. "Head for the coast. The rendezvous point."

Tires spun on the loose gravel as the driver gunned the engine and swung the heavy vehicle around, accelerating as he drove past the house.

Castillo pointed through a window.

"Look!" he exclaimed.

There in the sky, swooping toward the house, was a sleek black helicopter. As it angled lower, a rotary cannon in the nose fired, filling the air with thunder.

Testarov's driver swung the Dodge in a wide loop across the lawn as shells pounded the cars parked near the house.

The black helicopter flashed overhead, made a tight turn, returned for a second run. When the cannon opened up again, continuing its destruction, gasoline spilled from ruptured fuel tanks and exploded in a sudden, violent eruption that sent a huge fireball into the air. Long rippling snakes of blazing fuel arced across the lawn and the front of the house, leaving lengthy black marks. Dull explosions followed one after another as the individual vehicles voided their gas tanks.

Desperately hanging on to the wheel, the driver jammed his foot down on the pedal, sending the Dodge hurtling over the grass. He had to swerve to avoid the tall palms.

"Don't forget, the gates will be closed," Testarov warned.

The driver eased off the pedal, swinging the vehicle back onto the drive that curved toward the gates. Nearing them, he slowed enough for his partner to jump out to open them.

Before he could do so, however, the menacing shape of the black helicopter appeared. It dropped toward the lawn, nose pointed at the Dodge.

39

By the time Katz burst out of the house, the Dodge was already accelerating away. Katz swore forcibly.

Calvin James, who had followed Katz, said, "Dragon Slayer!"

James used his walkie-talkie to contact Grimaldi. Moments later the helicopter swept their way. Katz and James scrambled in through the open hatch and Grimaldi took the combat machine up.

"There's something I've always wanted to say." James grinned.

"What?" asked Grimaldi.

"Follow that car!" James said.

"And don't lose him, Jack," Katz added. "It's Testarov, the KGB man, in that Dodge. I don't intend to let that bastard get away."

"He won't," Grimaldi promised.

Dragon Slayer reached the vehicle near the closed gate. Grimaldi dropped the helicopter toward the ground.

"Open the hatch!" Katz yelled.

The access hatch hissed open.

Katz sprang out, hitting the ground and dropping to a crouch. He felt James drop beside him.

The Dodge's engine suddenly roared as the driver attempted to break away, aware that he wasn't going to get through the closed gates. The rear of the vehicle fishtailed, swinging wildly back and forth. Then the driver appeared to get it under control. He tried crossing the lawn again, probably intending to drive around the house and lose the Dodge in the stands of coconut palms that dotted the plantation.

Katz ran forward, away from the cover of the hovering helicopter. He raised the Uzi and took aim. When he pulled the trigger a stream of 9 mm slugs raked the rear of the car. Holes appeared in the body and both rear tires were punctured.

The Morkrie Dela man who had tried to open the gates turned as the Israeli appeared, raised his Ingram and trained it on Katz. The Russian agent, however, failed to acknowledge the presence of James, who pumped his M-16 effortlessly and drilled the Russian in the gut. Thrown back against the gates, he slumped to the ground.

With the rear tires gone, the driver lost control of the Dodge. It slammed against the trunk of a tall palm. A couple of windows shattered, showering the occupants with glass. The Dodge lurched forward, then the engine coughed and died.

For a few seconds there was silence. Then the driver's door burst open and the wheelman sprang out. Clutching an Ingram MAC-10, he dived headlong into the grass.

Katz ran forward, firing as he moved. Although it was generally not good practice to fire an SMG while in motion—a lot of ammunition could be expended but little else achieved—Katz was not restricted by sweeping rules. The Israeli had achieved total mastery of the weapon from years of constant use. While he seldom made any show of it, he could make the Uzi perform near miracles.

Now that mastery showed. Katz's volley found the driver in middive. He died in midair. Reflexively, his finger curled around the Ingram's trigger. The magazine emptied itself into the earth.

In the short time in which the Phoenix pair had taken out the two Morkrie Dela agents, Testarov and Castillo exited the crippled Dodge.

The KGB man had his Uzi, Castillo his SIG-Sauer P-226. The pair sprinted across the grass, heading for the closest stand of palms and the shrubbery beyond. Eventually they hoped to make it over the wall ringing the estate.

James trotted across to Katz, who was feeding a fresh mag into his Uzi.

The Israeli pointed with the SMG's muzzle. "They're over there," he said.

James nodded. "Yeah, I see 'em."

Without another word the Stony Man warriors took off after the fleeing Russian and his Filipino coconspirator.

THERE WAS no time now for anything but flight.

Total, uninhibited flight.

Now was a time for survival. For the one who was most capable. Most cunning. For the one who wished to stay alive more than any of those around him.

The logistics of planning. The scheming and the preparation. The bribery, cajoling, and the blackmail. All such ethereal matters were cast aside. Useless now.

Here and now, what mattered was pure physical ability—that very thing by which man has tried and tested himself throughout the ages.

Trial by combat. Man against man.

All thoughts of retribution, of facing up to responsibility, of admitting to error, were wiped from Leoni Testarov's mind as he ran through the clustered palms. There was no panic. No real fear. But he did wonder if he was to die within the next few minutes. The idea did not sit lightly on his shoulders. Like most men, he was not prepared for death. Though he accepted the inevitability of dying, his natural reaction was to push the thought to the recesses of his mind.

When a man finds himself facing the possibility of premature death, he naturally rebels. Some fall into a blind panic, race around in circles with the hope of escaping the fateful moment. Others shrink away, losing the will to fight.

Testarov reacted by accepting the possibility of death while realizing that he had an equal chance of survival. The thought of a painful death was enough to spur his fighting instincts.

The Soviet now plunged deeper into the thick undergrowth and prepared himself mentally for the coming fight. Because he knew it was coming. He was not out of danger yet. Unless he was extremely lucky he would not escape without some kind of confrontation. Until that came his main priority was to make for the estate wall and get over it. Perhaps if he could lose his pursuers, he could reach the main highway. Once there he could commandeer a vehicle and try to make it to the rendezvous point up the coast.

As he penetrated deeper into the dense foliage the Russian was thinking that maybe he did have a chance. It would take a great deal of effort on his part. But he had fought the odds most of his life. That was why he had been so successful in his career, until now. Those long years of struggle had created within him a steel core that helped him through the toughest situations.

He wondered briefly how Castillo was faring. The pair had separated once they reached the trees, realizing they stood a better chance if each man went his own way. The decision had been easy to make. Though they both wanted freedom, they had to take different paths. Testarov needed to reach the coast and his submarine, while Castillo had to stay in the country and try to regain his former position. Whether either man succeeded was entirely up to individual effort.

They had parted company with a brief handshake and words of encouragement. At that moment neither knew if he would see the other again.

Testarov's thoughts distracted him enough to miss the tangled roots lying across his path. They caught his left foot and he went sprawling. Winded, he lay momentarily paralyzed, gasping for breath.

Hearing someone moving fast through the foliage, he struggled upright. On his feet, he turned, looking back the way he had come.

And saw the approaching figure.

He recognized the man instantly. It was Yakov Katzenelenbogen.

A half smile formed on Testarov's face.

For a fleeting moment he recalled his ambition of presenting the captured fighter to his masters in Moscow.

The dream died cold; he knew he had no chance of bringing it to fulfillment now. The only worthwhile thing he could do was kill the man.

Testarov saw with some surprise that Katz was still approaching. The Russian was certain the American commando had seen him. Why was he making no attempt to conceal himself? Anger rose briefly in the Russian. He raised his Uzi, pulled the trigger. The blast ripped into a palm trunk near Katz's head.

Katz, stung by flying chips of bark, ducked behind another thick palm. He looked intently ahead, finally seeing Testarov in the thick undergrowth. By Katz's reckoning the stone boundary of the estate was not far off. He figured that the KGB man wanted to get over the wall pretty badly.

"Not if I have anything to do with it," Katz muttered.

He batted aside shoulder-high foliage, ducking to avoid being slashed in the face. Katz hoped to catch up with the Russian soon. He was starting to breathe heavily as his lungs became starved of air. He knew he wasn't as fit as he should be. Despite trying to keep himself robust, the Israeli admitted that he was not as young as he used to be, and that physical exertion was more difficult than it used to be. Not that he would ever allow that to be an excuse for failing to do his job.

Katz spotted movement just ahead and to the left. He paused, searching the undergrowth.

There it was again. It was Testarov.

Katz braced the barrel of his weapon against a palm, aimed, triggered a short burst. He saw Testarov falter, then vanish.

Katz pushed forward, his weapon ready.

When he neared the spot where he had seen Testarov go down, Katz slowed, stopped. He stood still, eyes searching. At first, nothing. Then he saw the spots of bright red marking some of the greenery. The trail led off to the right.

He had hit Testarov.

Katz dropped to a crouch, peering into the shadows near ground level. Looking. Listening. Waiting. Then he heard distant gunfire. He recognized the sound of Calvin James's M-16 as one of the weapons.

A closer sound caught his ear. Nearby, to his right. A soft rustling.

Katz remained still, his body tensed, Uzi at the ready.

The distant gunfire came again.

This time Katz ignored it, concentrating on the sounds close by.

More rustling. Now he heard labored breathing, and wondered for a moment if it was his own.

The gentle rustling erupted into a crash of sound.

Leoni Testarov burst into view no more than twelve feet from where Katz crouched. The Russian's left shoulder glistened with blood and lacerated flesh showed through his torn jacket.

Testarov cradled an Uzi in his hands, pointing the dark muzzle at Katz.

Lurching unsteadily, his face pale and sweaty, Testarov pulled back on the Uzi's trigger.

Katz's weapon was already aimed in Testarov's direction. It burned with the violence of its own rapid fire. As Katz jammed the trigger back he felt something hard and solid strike his left leg. It knocked him to the ground and forced a grunt of pain from his lips.

I'm hit, Katz realized, more in anger than anything else.

He felt a sweeping wave of nausea. Yet Katz refused to give in. He had to locate Testarov. He knew he'd hit the Russian, but he had to make certain.

He twisted to his side, reaching for the Uzi he had dropped. Katz closed his fingers around the weapon, pulling it to him. Struggling against the surge of weakness engulfing him, Katz managed to sit up. The first thing he did once he was upright was to look for Testarov.

But he saw nothing—except the splashes of blood on the ground and dappling the undergrowth where the Russian had appeared.

Leoni Testarov had vanished.

Katz tried to get to his feet, but an explosion of pain forced him to remain still. Glancing down, he could see blood pumping from the wound in his thigh. Katz wondered whether the bone had been damaged.

His thoughts began to drift. Testarov. The fake ambulance. President Aquino. Katz felt himself slipping away, tried to hold on. Somewhere overhead he could hear Dragon Slayer. He hoped they found him soon. Before he passed out. He needed to pass along the information about the ambulance he'd seen leaving the estate and its part in the assassination plot.

Despite everything, Katz realized, Cam Remsberg, isolated in his safe house, would still be planning to make the strike against President Aquino. Phoenix Force had to get to him fast, because time was running out.

THE SECOND SHOT passed close over James's head. Too close. The Phoenix warrior took the most convenient way out and hit the ground.

Just ahead, Diego Castillo swung the P-226 down toward the black commando. He triggered another shot, the bullet whacking the earth inches away.

Tired of being used as a target, James twisted his body in a double roll, then flattened on his stomach, the M-16 at his shoulder. He set the sights on Castillo and sent a short burst in his direction.

The Filipino traitor was pitched forward when the 5.56 mm slugs crashed into his upper body, up through his ribs and into his lungs. He hit the ground hard, spitting blood. By a supreme act of will, he managed to get to his knees, and brought up his pistol, hoping to kill James.

James's M-16 spit three more shots into Castillo, the first in the throat, the second and third rising to shatter the skull. The Filipino crashed onto his back and was still.

James rose, feeling a little shaky. He unclipped his walkie-talkie and keyed the button.

"I'm coming in," he said. "I think it's all over at this end. Going to have a look for Katz first."

40

Black smoke from the gutted remains of the cars rose over the estate into the morning sky.

The Phoenix warriors grouped around Dragon Slayer, which sat on the lawn beside the house.

Calvin James knelt beside Katz, who lay on an improvised stretcher. The Israeli's pants had been slit open around the bullet wound in his thigh. James, his medical kit open at his side, did what he could to stop the flow of blood from the ragged exit hole.

Katz, his face pale from shock, spoke in slow measured sentences.

"The vehicle I saw leave here was an emergency ambulance. The Manila Medical Center Emergency Squad. That was the lettering on the side."

"And the Manila Medical Center is where Aquino will be at ten this morning," Manning said.

Katz nodded. "My guess is that Remsberg and Peck will use it to gain access to the hospital grounds despite the high security. Who will want to stop an ambulance racing to an emergency with all lights flashing?"

"Smart bastards," McCarter acknowledged. "Once they get through the police lines they cruise to a quiet corner, abandon the ambulance and head for their firing point.''

Katz winced as James's gently probing fingers touched a sensitive spot.

"Yakov, let me give you that pain killer," James insisted.

"Not until we're sure all the information has been shared," the Phoenix commander said. "Have you got the license number?"

McCarter nodded. "We've got it. Cal, give him that shot now, no more bloody arguments. If he keeps making a fuss give him a double dose."

The Briton glanced at the silent Mahmud. McCarter knew that the Bajau was feeling guilty because of what he had done, despite his good intentions.

"And if this crazy bugger leaves your side you have my permission to tranquilize him for the next month."

Mahmud hardly dared look at his friend. When he did he saw that McCarter was watching him with a knowing smile on his face.

"You guys get moving," James said. "Time's running out. I'll hang in with Katz until the Air Force teams get here, then ride with him to Clark Field."

"They should touch down within thirty minutes," Grimaldi said, glancing at his watch.

"Then get the hell out of here, you guys," James repeated. "Find those damn mercs and take 'em out before they do any more damage to this troubled country."

McCarter glanced at his watch, shaking his head.

"Time doesn't half fly when you're having fun," he commented dryly.

"Think we'll make it in time?" Encizo asked.

"We'd bloody well better," the Briton growled.

41

"I feel like a goddamn mummy," Milt Peck growled through the bandages covering the left side of his face.

Cam Remsberg glanced at the massive Texan, a grin forming on his taut face.

"You sure as hell don't sound like one," he said.

The mercenary leader and his second-in-command were in the rear of the ambulance as it rolled through Manila en route to the sprawling Manila Medical Center. Both men were dressed in civilian clothing, posing as victims of an auto accident. Peck was laid out on a stretcher, his head swathed in bandages that had been soaked in blood from a chicken. The Filipinos who were acting as driver and assistant of the ambulance wore the white-and-blue uniforms of Medical Center paramedics, and carried all the correct identification.

After leaving the estate, the ambulance had been driven to a secure garage in Manila. There it had been parked until Remsberg and Peck left their safe house and journeyed to the garage to meet the two Filipinos, who belonged to the local Communist cell. In the garage the four had prepared for the trip to the hospital by changing into the appropriate clothing, then had checked their weapons.

The Filipinos were armed with suppressed Ingram MAC-10s. Peck had a Smith & Wesson Model 645 pistol, an Uzi SMG and a Smith & Wesson 37 mm shoulder gas gun with a selection of smoke and CS tear gas cartridges.

Cam Remsberg carried a .357 Desert Eagle in a shoulder rig. He also had an Uzi. But his main weapon was a Walther WA-2000, a high-tech sniper's rifle that featured an unusual design; the rifle was constructed around its most important part, the profiled barrel. Supported by upper and lower arms, the barrel's design ensured that it maintained stability when fired, as the recoil was transmitted to the firer's shoulder in a perfectly straight line. The WA-2000, which had a six-shot magazine, was fitted with a Schmidt & Bender 2.5-to-10x zoom telescopic sight.

Remsberg would be firing at his target from over two hundred yards, from a high elevation, and he wanted the best weapon available, plus the kind of ammunition—.300 Winchester Magnum cartridges—that ensured maximum damage. He would put at least two shots into the target, more if he could.

The Filipino acting as assistant paramedic glanced over his shoulder as the driver spoke, then turned back to Remsberg.

"We'll be there in a few minutes," he reported.

Remsberg nodded. "Here we go," he said to Peck.

The bulky Texan only grunted.

The driver hit the siren and lights, forcing traffic to veer to one side to let them pass.

The driver pushed the vehicle past the morning traffic as they entered the Makati district. The Manila Medical Center lay to the west, near Pasong Tamo Avenue.

It was a fairly new complex, only having come into full operation the previous year. Government funding had helped to finance the construction, and the new wing was the latest addition to the impressive structure.

"Plenty of cops around," the driver said. "Patrol cars all over."

"To be expected," Remsberg said. "Let's just play it the way we set it out."

Swinging into the main approach, the driver was forced to brake at a police checkpoint.

"A cop's coming to check us out," the driver said.

"What you got in there?" the police officer asked when he reached the ambulance. He took the ID the driver handed him.

"Couple guys in a car wreck," the driver said. "If you want to take a look, make it quick. I got one guy in there with bad head injuries. Got to get him straight to surgery or he's dead meat."

The cop peered over the driver's shoulder. He saw one man lying on a stretcher, his head covered in bloody bandages. On the other side of the ambulance another man sat slumped over, his clothing torn and stained.

"Anybody else hurt?" the cop asked, returning the driver's ID.

The driver shook his head. "Hey, you guys look busy today."

The cop shoved his cap to the back of his head. "VIP day," he said. "Okay, move on."

"Thanks," the driver said. He rolled the ambulance along the wide drive, swinging around a curve that hid them from the checkpoint. Instead of taking the right lane, which would have brought them to emergency, the driver took the left lane, and coasted toward the basement parking area.

The entrance to the parking lot was unguarded. Most of the police seemed to be concentrated around the site of the actual ceremony, on the far side of the new wing. The driver took the ambulance down the ramp, into the shadowed basement. He had previously studied a plan of the building, so he knew the layout of the parking area. Following the arrows painted on the floor, he drove across the basement, passing the rows of cars belonging to the hospital staff. He parked in a corner, beside a pair of trucks, and cut the motor.

Remsberg and Peck quickly removed their accident clothing and donned green coveralls that identified them as maintenance men. Their weapons went into long toolbags.

"Good luck," the driver said.

Remsberg nodded. "You just be ready to roll when you hear the war start."

With Peck at his heels, Remsberg made for the bank of elevators a few yards away. The end one was the one they wanted. A notice was pasted across one of the doors, stating that the elevator was not yet in service. Although the official opening was this particular day, the wing would not start to function for another few days. However, though the elevator was signed out of bounds, it *was* operative. All that was required was a master key—which Remsberg had.

He inserted the key into its slot and turned it. The doors slid open. Remsberg and Peck entered the lifting device. Remsberg thumbed the button and closed the door, then keyed the floor-selector button. The elevator began its ascent to the top floor.

The doors opened on a long gleaming corridor. There was a smell of newness everywhere—in the paint, the floor coverings. Even the air, being pumped through silent air-conditioning units, had a clean odor.

Remsberg led the way along the corridor, passing numerous doors until he reached one in particular; it opened to show a medium-size room. This was an administration office, filled with desks, filing cabinets, shelves. There were even a couple of silent, dark computers waiting for the commands that would send the electronic life force racing through them.

Remsberg crossed to the wide windows that looked out over the grounds. From where he stood he was able to look down at the flag-festooned dais that had been constructed in front of the wing's main entrance. Before the speaker's platform were a dozen rows of seats, waiting for the audience that would hear the president declare the new wing open.

Glancing at his watch, Remsberg saw they were on time. They had twenty-two minutes before the ceremony began.

The mercs began setting up. Each man knew his specific tasks. There was no need for words.

Remsberg put a small table beneath the window, took a tripod from his bag and set it up on the table. Removing the WA-2000, he clamped the foresection to the tripod. He clipped in the magazine and fed the first .300 Magnum cartridge into the breech. Taking care not to be seen by any of the cops patrolling near the dais, Remsberg eased open one of the windows just enough to allow the WA-2000's muzzle to protrude. Snugging the weapon to his shoulder, he looked through the tele-

scopic sight and ranged in on the dais. He smiled. This
was going to be an easy shot.

Stepping closer to the window, Remsberg studied the
hospital grounds. Nine floors up, he was able to observe what went on below without being observed himself. There were no other buildings in the complex from
which to see the top floor of the new wing.

Remsberg watched the activity below. Cars were beginning to arrive; the police were directing them to a
designated parking lot nearby. The seats began to fill
up. He noticed that all the police around the dais were
armed with automatic weapons. He glanced at his
watch. More than enough time for what he had suddenly decided to do.

"Milt, I'm just going to have a look around," he
said.

Peck grunted, concentrating on his own task. The
Texan's part in the assassination would come immediately after Remsberg's killing shot. All around the dais,
he would lay down a concentrated barrage of CS and
smoke canisters, in order to create a diversion to cover
their escape.

Crossing the room, Remsberg slipped into the corridor, his Uzi hanging over his shoulder, the Desert Eagle in his right hand.

He made a thorough recon of the floor, covering as
many rooms as he could, trying to satisfy the odd feeling that had come over him. Maybe it was nothing but
premission tension. Allowing his mind to wander and
to dwell on negative thoughts. Whatever lay behind
those thoughts, he found nothing to confirm them. The
floor was deserted. He passed rooms full of equip-

ment. Wards with empty beds. Silent telephones and computers. No reason for any unease.

Yet. . . .

Time was slipping by. Remsberg returned to the office, where Milt Peck stood motionless at the window, observing the arrivals for the ceremony.

"The guys should be in position now," Peck said.

Remsberg glanced at his watch again. Nine minutes left.

Nine minutes before chaos became the order of the day.

42

"This is going to be close," Gary Manning remarked as Dragon Slayer began to lose altitude. They were coming in from the east. This would bring Phoenix Force in at the rear of the hospital complex. From the drop point they would have to infiltrate the place and locate their quarry.

"How long?" Encizo asked.

"Fifteen minutes," Manning said.

"Listen up, guys," Grimaldi called over his shoulder. "Best spot I can see is just to the left. Clear space by those trees at the edge of that construction site. Through the trees and you're on the hospital grounds."

"Okay, Jack," Manning said. "It'll have to do. Take us down."

The combat helicopter dropped swiftly as the Force prepared themselves. The moment the hatch swung open the Stony Man trio went out, jumping the few feet to the ground.

Manning led the way into the trees. They moved with as much speed as they could, emerging on open ground. A low wall marked the boundary of the hospital grounds.

Pausing briefly, the Phoenix warriors made swift plans.

"That'll be the new wing," Encizo said, pointing out the freshly constructed block jutting out from the main building.

"If the opening ceremony is taking place at ground level," McCarter suggested, "our assassin is going to be looking for a high point. Somewhere that will give him a clear field of fire without exposing his position."

"I'd go for somewhere in the building," Manning said. "And an ideal place would be in the new wing itself. Overlooking the ceremony. Empty building. No one about."

"It's our only shot," McCarter said. "Let's go for it."

"We can't just walk into an empty building," Encizo pointed out. "The place is probably locked up with cops guarding it."

"He's got a point," Manning said.

"I know that," McCarter snapped. "On the other hand, if our mercenary friends did choose it as their spot, how did they get in?"

Manning shrugged. "I don't know. Maybe they took the bloody elevator."

"Oh, sure," McCarter said. "And I suppose they... Dammit, Gary, you could be right."

"About what?" the Canadian asked.

"You clot, the elevator," McCarter raved. "Most big buildings like these have basement parking lots for the employees. And they have elevators to take those employees to the various floors. All our chums would have to do is drive into the basement park, leave the ambulance and ride the elevator up to their chosen floor."

"What have we got to lose?" Manning asked.

They crossed the wall. In a series of short runs, covering each other all the way, the Phoenix warriors reached the sprawling hospital building. Crouched at the base of the building, they took a moment to decide their next move.

"The basement entrance is probably at the front," McCarter said.

"We might find a service door along the side somewhere," Encizo suggested.

They turned the corner and made their way along the other wall. Manning suddenly raised a hand. Just ahead, a short fight of steps led down to a door set in the lower wall. A sign above it identified it as a service door for use by maintenance personnel only.

The door was locked—or rather, by all odds it should have been locked. Instead it had been propped open just a crack. Evidently a workman of some kind had jammed a piece of wood into the door. Manning pulled it open and the Force entered.

The wide, low-ceilinged basement stretched out before them. Regularly spaced, thick supportive pillars stood in shadows thrown by the strip lighting embedded in the ceiling. To their right, daylight streamed from the top of the ramp that allowed access to and exit from the basement.

Apart from a few rows of cars, the Force could see nothing of interest.

Impatience broke McCarter's immobility. He moved deeper into the basement, slipping from pillar to pillar. Manning and Encizo followed.

McCarter, pressed against the face of one pillar, gestured to Manning and Encizo to join him.

"Elevators," the cockney stated, pointing to the bank of steel doors.

The trio remained still while they studied the area. It was Encizo who saw someone pacing near two parked maintenance vehicles. He led the way along a row of pillars until they could observe the guy more clearly.

Now they could also see an ambulance parked beside the two trucks.

"That's our baby," McCarter said, reading the license plate; the number tallied with the one Katz had given them.

The Phoenix pros readied their weapons, which had all been fitted with suppressors on the flight in. Manning and Encizo, aware that they would be working in tight situations, chose Uzis. McCarter retained his MAC-10. Now the former SAS man slipped his Ingram from his shoulder.

At a signal from Manning the three split up. McCarter and Encizo swung wide of the area, then drew in to approach from the rear. If they had been free with their time they could have reached their target without being noticed or heard, but each of the Stony Man warriors could almost hear the seconds ticking closer to the ten o'clock deadline.

The pacing Filipino had not been terribly alert, but he suddenly caught a whisper of sound off to his left. He spun in that direction, weapon rising. He opened his mouth to warn his accomplice, but nothing escaped his lips.

Realizing that the guy was about to discover his partners, Encizo, who was approaching the Filipino from behind, launched himself across the final few feet. He hit the guy hard in the lower back, pushing him forward. The thug smashed his face into the side of the parked truck, leaving a smear of thick blood from his crushed nose. Hurt but not out, the Filipino turned to face his attacker. He swung an angry fist at Encizo; the Cuban ducked. Encizo rammed the Uzi into the guy's groin, pulled back and slashed the weapon up to connect with his jaw. There was a meaty crack and the guy flopped to the basement floor.

During this confrontation, the second Communist thug, sitting behind the wheel of the ambulance realized something had gone wrong and grabbed the suppressed SMG on the seat beside him.

Reaching for the door handle, he froze.

A figure clad in combat gear was aiming a suppressed Uzi at him through the glass.

"Leave the gun," Gary Manning ordered. "Get out and keep your hands where I can see them."

The driver did as he was told. He was suddenly confronted by a second man dressed like the first. This one, equipped with an Ingram, pushed him against the side of the ambulance and frisked him quickly and expertly.

"Turn around," Manning demanded.

The driver obeyed. He had no choice.

"I'm going to ask a couple of questions," Manning said. "If you want to stay alive you'd better give me the right answers."

The driver began to sweat. His fear increased when a third man appeared. This one had the driver's partner with him. The Filipino's hands were secured behind his back, and he had a bloody face.

"Where are Remsberg and Peck? What floor?"

The driver stared at them. The question had caught him totally unprepared. Not only had these people been able to find them, they also knew the names of the American assassins.

McCarter stepped up to the driver. He placed the cold muzzle of the Ingram against the man's cheek.

"Like the man said—make it the right answer, chum, or else I'll blow your bleedin' brains all over this ambulance."

The driver had never considered himself a hero, let alone a martyr, and the threat of imminent death chilled him to the bone.

"They're on the ninth floor, at the far end of the wing," he blurted out.

McCarter gave him what the driver might have called a wolf's grin, ordered him to put his hands behind his back and secured his wrists with plastic cuffs.

"Dump them in the back," Manning said.

The Filipino Communists were bundled into the rear of the ambulance and the door slammed shut on them.

McCarter went straight to the elevators. He saw that the notice pasted on one of the doors had been crumpled. He thumbed the button. Seconds later the elevator whined as it started down the shaft.

As a precaution the Phoenix commandos stood to one side of the doors. The elevator reached bottom. The doors slid open to show an empty car.

The Phoenix trio stepped inside. Encizo touched the ninth floor button, the doors slid shut and the contrivance started to rise.

McCarter watched the numbers flash on the indicator.

"I don't usually go all the way on the first date," he mumbled softly to no one in particular.

The elevator came to a stop. The doors opened and the Force stepped out.

The corridor lay before them, empty and silent.

Manning pointed to the left. His partners nodded in silent agreement. That direction would lead them to the extreme limits of the new wing.

From now on everything would transpire in silence. Any word, no matter how quietly spoken, might carry to the enemy. Such a warning might even trigger the assassination attempt prematurely.

Manning checked his watch. It was two minutes to ten. He signaled this to McCarter and Encizo.

Progress along the corridor was slow.

Manning led the way, checking doors, while McCarter covered him; the Briton watched for things Manning could not see while he was checking the rooms. Encizo brought up the rear to make certain no one attacked from behind.

With a minute to go Manning held up his hand and signaled a halt. He pointed to the last door. It stood slightly ajar. Every other door along the corridor had been firmly closed.

Manning didn't need to use words. Both McCarter and Encizo realized the implication.

They eased up to the door.

From inside the room came the faintest murmurs. The rustle of clothing. A faint metallic chink.

Manning crouched, his Uzi aimed at the door. Encizo adopted a similar position, only standing upright. It was left to McCarter to make the initial play. He did it in his usual style.

With a quick nod to Manning and Encizo, the Brit raised his foot and planted it against the door. He shoved it wide open, then went in low and fast, breaking to the right to leave the field clear for his partners.

It was all set out before them—like a posed tableau.

Two men. Tables set in front of the windows. One holding a hi-tech scoped rifle on a tripod. The other a tear-gas gun with a supply of canisters.

For a split second the men were motionless, too stunned to react.

Then the scene came to life.

Cam Remsberg turned from the window, dropping the WA-2000 to grab the Uzi that lay on the table.

McCarter fired before the merc had curled his fingers around the weapon. A stream of slugs hissed from his MAC-10, chunking into Remsberg's torso with stunning force. The merc leader was slammed back against the wall, his arms flapping loosely. Pulverized by the gun's messengers of death, he slithered along the wall, leaving a bloody trail as he crashed to the floor. He slammed down hard, his left arm flailing wildly. It was the last part of him to die.

Milt Peck also grabbed his Uzi and was bringing it to bear on McCarter when Manning and Encizo opened up. Twin bursts enveloped the Texan. Manning's shots blasted into Peck's stomach, while Encizo's took him in the chest. Peck let out a startled yell as he was thrown across the office by the force of the slugs. He attempted to regain his balance, ignoring the wounds, and half raised his Uzi. Manning fired again, further puncturing Peck's doomed chest. The renegade merc hit the edge of a desk before landing on the floor in a writhing, bloody heap.

McCarter crossed directly to the window and looked discreetly at the scene below.

The rows of seats were filled now. The dais held its quota of officials.

And mounting the steps to take her place before the microphones was the diminutive yet striking figure of the Philippines's First Lady. The president who had stepped in and defeated the man responsible for her husband's assassination. Winning a presidential election against overwhelming odds, ignoring repeated threats of violence from the opposition, Cory Aquino had nobly struggled to maintain democracy on the islands. Her years in office had not been easy, but the lady was proving to be an able leader. Gains were slow but positive, and given the chance, she would eventually give back to the people what the previous regime had taken away.

At least she was still alive and able to continue, McCarter thought. He turned from the window, giving Manning and Encizo the thumbs-up.

"Let's get these bodies out of here," Manning said.

The Canadian, with McCarter's help, draped Milt Peck's limp form over his shoulders. The Briton carried Cam Remsberg. Encizo dumped the weapons back in the tool bags.

The Phoenix warriors rode the elevator back to the basement. They placed the dead men in the rear of the ambulance. Encizo freed the driver from his riot cuffs, then took his uniform.

Settling behind the wheel, Encizo started the engine. "You guys set?" he asked.

"Roll this thing out of here," McCarter said.

Encizo drove smoothly from the basement and out along the curving drive. There was a patrol car parked near the end of the exit road, but the cop on duty waved them through with barely a glance. The ambulance rolled away from the hospital and out along the highway.

Manning unclipped the walkie-talkie on his belt and keyed the button. "Ground to Dragon Slayer. You there?"

"Hearing you," Grimaldi replied.

"We're heading for the safe house. Meet us there. Over and out."

"Home, James, and don't spare the ruddy horses," McCarter said to Encizo.

EPILOGUE

Clark Field

"How's Katz?" Hal Brognola asked over the secure line.

"Fine," Manning reported. "He's starting to get grouchy, so he must be getting better."

"What's the medical version?"

"The doctor says he was lucky. The bullet missed the bone and didn't do too much tissue damage. He's going to have a stiff leg for a while, but plenty of exercise will put that right."

"Katz may have to sit out a couple of missions," Brognola said. "In the meantime, tell him and the rest of the guys thanks. You did a good job. That comes direct from the Man. Also a similar request from a certain lady over there."

"I hope she never finds out just how close we came to not making it in time."

"The thing is, you did," Brognola reminded the Canadian.

"It got a little messy at times," Manning admitted.

"Bound to when you have to play with no rules,"

"Katz was a little annoyed that he didn't stop the Russian."

"Testarov?" Brognola pondered for a moment. "As far as we know, his body hasn't turned up yet. He could still be in the Philippines somewhere. Hiding out. Or dead in a ditch. Main thing is, the KGB involvement was wiped out. It may give them something to think about if they want to try anything like that again."

"Hell, we can't be there every time," Manning said.

"No? You've just shattered one of my illusions." Brognola chuckled. "I thought you guys were invincible."

"Almost, but not quite," Manning said.

"The tidying up should be complete in a day or two," Brognola said. "The Filipino administration has been kicking some ass over this. It seems that when the kick-off for the coup didn't materialize, a lot of people became upset. With all the principals taken out they had no one to coordinate the overall plan and it just fell apart."

"Any mention of U.S. involvement?" Manning asked.

"Not a word," Brognola said. "The Air Force people body-bagged the dead mercs on the island and took the live ones into custody. They'll all be shipped back to the U.S. along with Remsberg and Peck. There isn't anyone around to finger them."

"What about the Filipinos who were involved?"

"Arrangements are being made to hand them over to people President Aquino sends in. What happens to them is up to the locals.

"Soon as you guys are ready the Air Force will fly you home," Brognola said. "When you get back we'll have a full debriefing."

"WHEN DO YOU think you'll come back?" Mahmud asked.

McCarter shrugged. "You know my business, chum. Here today and gone tomorrow."

The Bajau, still showing the marks of his contact with the Morkrie Dela agents, watched his British friend open another can of chilled Coke.

"Are you still angry with me?" he ventured.

"I bloody well ought to be," McCarter said.

"David, I am sorry. I realize it was foolish and could have placed you all in danger. What else can I say?"

"Nothing, you idiot," McCarter said. "Just don't do it again."

"At least that is hopeful," Mahmud said. "It sounds as if you might be coming back after all."

"I wouldn't be surprised," McCarter said. "You seem to get into as many scrapes as I do."

"AND DID YOU find out how Santos managed to listen in on the ambassador's calls?" Katz asked Jack Milligan.

The security man smiled. "Simple," he said. "He knew where and when I did my sweeps. Just waited until I'd completed my checks, then slipped in his bugs, recorded his information and took the damn stuff home with him each evening. Christ, it was so damn obvious. He was there under everyone's nose and we couldn't even see it."

"It's the commonplace that tends to get overlooked," Katz said. "The man you see every day. So ordinary and mundane, you just don't connect him with anything underhanded."

"But I should have," Milligan said. "It's my damn job to spot those things."

"Don't be too hard on yourself, Jack. I've made a few errors in my time. Security can be tough to manage. It's hard to keep it up day after day. When things seem quiet and routine, that's when concentration slips.

"On the other hand, you gave us a lot of help with other things. If it hadn't been for you, we might not have found that island or pinpointed the arms cache."

"I have to admit it's been a busy few days," Milligan said. "You guys know how to keep the pot boiling."

After a few more words with Katz, Milligan left to rejoin the others.

Alone in his bed in the base hospital, Katz found himself reliving that hectic firefight when he and James had pursued Castillo and Testarov.

The Russian's disappearance had been nagging Katz ever since, but he knew there wasn't much he could do about it. There was no way to check for Testarov's body. The reports coming in suggested that the Soviet had either hidden himself away or had died somewhere in the remote countryside. At any rate, none of the reports mentioned further investigations. It seemed that Leoni Testarov had been written off.

Nevertheless, Katz couldn't simply abandon the problem. He knew that during that final confrontation he had hit Testarov with a number of bullets. But obviously not enough damage had been done to stop the Russian permanently.

So where was Major Leoni Testarov of the KGB?

Dead?

Alive?

And if he *was* alive, what was he thinking?

SOMEWHERE BENEATH the South China Sea was the Lenin, a Soviet Navy nuclear submarine, on course for Cam Ranh Bay, Vietnam.

"Sit down, Vassily," the captain said.

The younger man—the submarine's doctor—sank gratefully onto the padded bench, resting his arms on the table.

"Will our patient live until we reach Cam Ranh Bay?" the captain asked.

Vassily Orchuk smiled. "He will live much longer than that," he said.

The captain raised an inquiring eye. "I am surprised. He was barely alive when the landing party brought him on board."

"I must admit that when I saw him I didn't expect him to survive for more than an hour or so. But the man has a strong will to live."

The captain poured two shot glasses of vodka and pushed one across to Vassily Orchuk. The doctor picked it up.

"What do you think happened back there on the Philippines?" he asked suddenly. "Only this man, Testarov, has survived. He did some wild talking before the anesthetic wore off. He was mumbling about everyone being dead. All his men gone. The operation going sour. Something about American specialists."

The captain gave Orchuk a warning glance.

"Take my advice, Vassily, and do not ask too much. Especially about the KGB and their schemes. They are a law unto themselves. Stay out of it. Let Testarov handle his own affairs. He'll need all his strength for when he gets back to Moscow. I have a feeling he'll have a lot of explaining to do. He may have survived the Philippines, but he could have even a harder time when he gets home."

Vassily Orchuk downed his vodka, keeping his thoughts to himself. He was remembering the condition of Leoni Testarov when the KGB man had come on board.

Testarov had lost a great deal of blood. When Vassily operated on him, *seven* bullets had been removed from Testarov's body.

Even then, during the surgery, the young doctor had been surprised at the way Testarov's condition had remained stable. The man seemed to be fighting even while he was unconscious.

There *was* something keeping Leoni Testarov alive. A deep-rooted force that defied physical injury and burned with a need to continue.

That something, Vassily realized, would ensure Testarov's survival. It would sustain him through his return to Moscow and the hard time he would face at the hands of his Kremlin overlords. He would undoubtedly come through the physical and mental strain.

And his inner strength would sustain him beyond his Moscow trial, carrying him along the private road that only he could see, toward whatever destiny he had chosen.

Leoni Testarov had a mission in life—Vassily Orchuk was convinced. It would dominate his existence. It would fill every waking hour, and the KGB man would not rest until he completed that mission—or died in the attempt.

From Europe to Africa, the Executioner stalks his elusive enemy—a
cartel of ruthless men who might prove too powerful to defeat.

DON PENDLETON's

MACK BOLAN

Moving Target

One of America's most powerful corporations is reaping huge
profits by dealing in arms with anyone who can pay the price.
Dogged by assassins, Mack Bolan follows his only lead fast and
hard—and becomes caught up in a power struggle that might be
his last.

Nile Barrabas's most daring mission is about to begin . . .

THE BARRABAS BLITZ

JACK HILD

An explosive situation is turned over to a crack
commando squad led by Nile Barrabas when a
fanatical organization jeopardizes the NATO alliance
by fueling public unrest and implicating the United
States and Russia in a series of chemical spills.

Mack Bolan's

by Dick Stivers

Action writhes in the reader's own streets
as Able Team's Carl ''Ironman'' Lyons,
Pol Blancanales and Gadgets Schwarz
make triple trouble in blazing war. Join
Dick Stivers's Able Team as it returns to
the United States to become the country's
finest tactical neutralization squad in an
era of urban terror and unbridled crime.

"Able Team will go anywhere, do anything,
in order to complete their mission. Plenty
of action! Recommended!"
—*West Coast Review of Books*

Able Team titles are available
wherever paperbacks are sold.

AT-1